To: Colleen,

With best wishes

Jeanne Cherry

5/18/2012

❧ ❧ ❧

These were dangerous times. The rumbling of war in Germany was on everybody's mind. The Bolsheviks were rampant, forcing Communism on the people of Russia. Those who defied them were murdered or deported to Siberia—a death sentence in a land of harsh living conditions, a land of ice and snow and vast forests, a land far east of the sun.

❧ ❧ ❧

Chapter One

His cheeks were red; lips pressed tightly together were chapped and turning blue from the bitter cold wind. Wisps of wet, blonde hair escaped from the rough handmade cap, forming small icicles on his forehead that melted against his skin like teardrops. Intense cornflower blue eyes full of despair squinted through snow-covered eyelashes, searching for the winding road buried under a foot of newly fallen snow.

Pine trees, tall and majestic with branches covered in snow and ice, were hanging low with long icicles that reached out like fingers against the passing sled; like sentries shielding the occupants from the howling wind and blowing drifts.

Sasha was perched on the small front seat of the sled. His muscular arms and body, used to hard labor, strained as he pulled on the reins, guiding the tired mare in the right direction of the once visible dirt road. Wild-eyed with fear, the mare whinnied and puffs of steam blew through her nose. Desperately, she shook her head to rid the snow off its long mane, which blinded her vision. Her hooves slid on the ice buried under a foot of newly fallen snow causing her to stumble, threatening to overturn the precious cargo in its hold.

"Whoa! *Szarna...Pomaludku.* Whoa! *Szarna...*Easy now..." In a raspy hoarse voice barely audible to the mare's ears, Sasha tried to soothe the skittish mare.

Huddled in the back of the sled was his wife Anya. Gripping the sides with frozen and numb fingers, she tried to shield herself from the falling snow. Blankets wet, rough, and threadbare offered little protection from the open heavens, emptying its cargo onto their world.

Agonizing moans muffled by the wind reached Sasha. Anya moaned again. This time, long, deep, guttural. Each bump of the sled was like a knife stabbing her back causing a new contraction, each one stronger and

1

more intense than the last. Her deep blue eyes brimming with tears were full of terror, and gasping with dry lips she prayed, "*Hospudzi Pomarzy Nam.... Hospudzi Pa Miluj Nas.... God help us.... God love us. Let this child be born safely.*" Anya took another deep breath. She closed her eyes before the next contraction ripped through her body.

*I must find shelter soon...or we will perish...Hospudzi...Hospudzi ...Pomarzy name...God...Oh, God...Help us...I have to find a way out of this whiteness...*Sasha's thoughts echoed his wife's plea. He was lost and desperate. Panic set in, quickening his heartbeat as if two steel forceps were squeezing the breath out of him. Striving to fight fear with reality, Sasha began to recall the events of the past few weeks.

Terrifying images so clearly in his mind kept him awake. Trying to sleep was useless. The visions of his cousin, Father Kosciusko, a Polish priest and two other priests, crawling on the ground where the Communist soldiers castrated them and left them for dead, plagued Sasha's mind. His cousin's face was bruised and bloody beyond recognition. His frail body, with arms and legs flung in bizarre twists, looked like a fallen scarecrow in an evil garden.

Carefully, he had picked them off the ground one by one and placed them on the wagon with several sacks of potatoes and other farm supplies. After a harrowing ride through the woods and backroads, dodging the soldiers and the Partisans, he crossed the Polish border and reached the designated meeting place in a Catholic church, a sanctuary for priests hiding from the Communists.

Gasping for breath Sasha sat up in bed, his pulse was beating rapidly in his throat. He felt clammy and cold sweat enveloped him. For an instant, there was only terror of a remembered dream. He closed his eyes and opened them again forcing the visions out of sight, and gratefully they faded from his mind. Fully awake and before first light, with trembling hand he pushed the blonde hair from his brow and breathing deeply he forced his heart to be still.

Anya stirred beside him. Feeling the movement, he turned to look at his wife. He grinned at her as she was rubbing the sleep from her eyes, peeking at him from under long lashes with one eye open.

However, the eyes that met hers were distressed and concerned. She reached up and tenderly touched his cheek, eager to dispel the anxiety, which clung to him like a shroud. "I love you Sasha." She whispered with huskiness of sleep in her voice. Her words were like magic; the terror fled from his beloved face for the moment. He gazed at her with longing. Her pale skin was rosy, creating a rosy glow to her cheeks. Long, chestnut color hair spilled over on the pillow, framing her beautiful face. It always made Sasha want to bury his face in its softness. He ran his fingers through the silky strands, but was soon lost in troubling thoughts.

His body next to her was tense and restless. Sensing his dark mood return, she caressed his unshaven cheek with fingertips and kissed him lightly on his lips, then snuggled closer, enjoying the warmth of his body. Sasha stroked her hair, inhaling deeply the aroma of lavender she used to wash it and to bathe in. Placing his hand on her abdomen, he felt little butterfly flutters against his palm, as if the baby inside was trying to communicate, moving restlessly, trying to get free of the womb it held captive. The time was close. Sasha was worried.

Anya's back was aching. The labor was getting stronger and a wave of pain swept over her. As the wave crested, she swallowed rapidly, repeatedly until it subsided into the uneasy knot in her stomach. She moved out of her husband's embrace and slipped from the bed slowly, leaving the covers onto the cold, bare wood floor.

The room was drafty. The early February mornings were brutal with strong winds and snowstorms. She could feel the freezing air coming in through the cracks of the log wall onto her bare feet and arms. She quickly wrapped herself in an old bathrobe, pushed her long hair back from her face and, shivering, stood still listening to the wind howling wildly outside.

Glancing toward the window, she marveled at the beautiful patterns of snowflakes that created the illusion of a lace curtain. The beauty of it fascinated her. She reached for his hand, calloused and rough, but strong. She lifted it to her face and gently brushed her lips over it.

3

"Come here, my love, and look at this wonder of nature."

Sasha yawned, stretched his tired body and reluctantly got out of the warm bed. Shivering, he slipped his feet into worn sheepskin slippers, wrapped himself in the blanket and followed her to the window.

"Sasha, look at the beauty of this. It is almost like hand-woven lace." She touched the window with her fingertips, tracing the creation of a snowflake, marveling at it.

"How is it that nature creates such innocent wonder and man creates such hate and destruction?" She lifted her head and looked sadly into his blue eyes. "Why, Sasha? Why can't we live in peace?"

Sasha sighed and touched her cool, smooth forehead with his lips. He thought for a moment, stared at the snowflakes on the window. "It is a fair question, Anya. Man's greed for power and money has always created wars and suffering. We are slaves to the government that looks down on us as if we are nothing but a pile of ants that they can step on without a thought. The government preaches equality. Ha!" He almost laughed. "They don't want us to think, love, have memories of our loved ones, or simply enjoy the fruits of our labor."

He hesitated chewing on his bottom lip, then shook his head as if in disbelief. "However, the most disturbing fact is that we can't have free will. Our entire life is controlled by the government."

Shuddering, Anya leaned slightly closer to him, with a whispered plea to hold her tight. She was scared. Turning slightly, he faced her solemnly. "Stalin equals Hitler. They are both butchers of the worst kind. Their hunger for control of every human being is voracious." He reached for her hand and held it tight. "And, they will not rest until every man, woman and child are bent to their will. And those who resist face a terrible fate. Siberia's snows are red with innocent people's blood."

A tremor passed through Anya. "Sasha, while you were gone, more men and women with their children were deported." Her eyes clouded over with tears. She sighed deeply. "Several of our friends were arrested in the middle of the night last Thursday."

She shivered as images flooded her mind. "They were herded like cattle

4

out of their beds, piled into the wagons and taken to the waiting trains in Toloczyn. I recall a man who bravely dared to ask why they were being arrested. He was old and had no fear of asking. But when the Communist soldier put a gun to his head, the man crumbled to the floor. The soldier laughed, kicked him in the stomach and yelled that he was lucky to be too old to work, or he would be joining the rest of the traitors." Anya hesitated for a moment. Her cold fingers touched Sasha's cheek. Gulping down the tears threatening to spill from her eyes, she whispered, "The soldiers questioned several of the men in the village. They are looking for you." Her tears flowed freely now. "I was afraid they would come for us. Our neighbor, Luba, offered to hide us. There is a secret door in her back storage room that leads to a deep, dug-out basement." She shivered remembering the dampness and darkness of the dugout. "We stayed hidden there while the soldiers were in town."

Sasha reached for Anya's hand and held it tightly. "Anya," he said after a moment, "why did you not tell me this the minute I came back?"

She turned her head away from him, "I did not want to worry you. There is word that someone has reported you."

Sasha knew what that meant. Who would have talked, he wondered? The underground activists were very careful. Their activity, smuggling the priests and those in hiding from the Communists, was secretive and well hidden.

He held Anya closer and wrapped the blanket around her.

"Sasha, whoever it was must have talked out of fear. They are threatening to take the women and children if they do not find you."

Shaking slightly, she pulled herself out of her husband's embrace and began pacing the floor frantically. "All of us could be deported to Siberia. I begged you not to go! What will happen to us now? You have risked our lives for your cousin who may be dead by now." Slowly she turned to Sasha. Her eyes blazing with terror, she blinked her tears away and desperately gestured with her hand, pointing to an unseen distance. "I cannot bear the thought of our children being dragged off to Siberia," she cried.

Anya's words were like poison arrows piercing his heart. He knew the consequences of rescuing his cousin. Watching his Anya, so distraught and afraid, was more than he could bear. He reached for her, but she walked away from him.

The early morning light crept slowly in through the frosted windows, creating sinister shadows on Anya's tear-stained face. With a deep moan, she stumbled to the bed and sat heavily on it, gasping. A sharp pain attacked her insides. The pains of labor were prominent. Sasha recognized the signs. He quickly crossed the floor and sat on the bed beside her, enveloping her in his strong arms.

His heart skipped a beat. Anya was right. He did endanger the family. Now he wondered how long he could stay in hiding.

With their sixth child on the way, it would be difficult to stay out of sight for too long. He stroked her hair trying to calm her, but the fear within him was like a storm churning a warning of danger close by.

"Anya, I am so sorry for endangering all of us, but I could not let them take Stas, not without trying to rescue him. He was my childhood pal. I promised my aunt I'd watch out for him. And yes, he may be dead by now, but at least I tried."

He kissed the top of her head reassuringly. "I promise you that nothing will happen to us." Yet, deep inside him, Sasha knew that his promise was empty. He pulled her closer. "I could not bear if anything happened to you and the children. God will protect us. He has, up to now."

With her face buried in his chest, she said quietly, "I am sorry, Sasha." A little smile formed on her lips. She reached up and with trembling fingers, touched his cheek lightly. "One of the reasons I love you so much is because I know how soft your heart is."

Another dull pain in her back made her twist uncomfortably. Glancing toward the window, she noticed the dark sky full of heavy clouds. "The weather looks very threatening. It may snow very soon." She grimaced with another pain.

Sasha watched her closely. "Anya, if the baby decides to come today, we will have to take the risk and drive into town." Scratching his head, he

6

tried to think. "The only midwife in our village was deported last week and there is no one else who can help with the birth."

Anya nodded. "I wish there was a way to get word to my mother. She has delivered many children and is as good as any midwife."

"I know," Sasha agreed, "but your mother is snowbound and too far away. I can't leave you and the children alone." He paused. "I can't think of anyone we can send to get her." His face was thoughtful, his brow furrowed. "I will make preparations for the journey to the hospital in Toloczyn. It will be dangerous in many ways however I can't let you have the baby without some medical help." Brushing her forehead with his dry lips, he looked towards the window for signs of snow. "We will have to take our chances."

Alarmed, Anya gasped, "Sasha, what about the children? Who will stay with them? Nicolaj is only ten years old!" she cried. "Yes, he is capable, but in this storm he will be scared. We cannot leave him alone with the girls!"

Frustration gripped Sasha as he paced the floor faster. He did not know what to do. He sat hunched on the bed holding his hands together as though in prayer. "Anya, we have only one choice. I will have to ask Luba to help Nicolaj."

Anya's eyes lit up. She nodded in approval. Luba was a very kind woman. She had lost two children of her own in childbirth and after her husband was deported to Siberia, Luba and Anya became good friends, depending on each other for moral support and helping each other when in need.

"Sasha, get the children ready now!" Another pain in her back made her gasp. "Sasha!" she paused to catch her breath. Panic filled her eyes. "Bring the children to Luba's now!"

They had been on the road for several hours. Anya would not last much longer. The hospital in Toloczyn was another fifteen miles away; too far now at the rate they were traveling.

The swirling night clouds closed in on them like a dark cavern; the visibility was getting worse. Sasha kept looking back at Anya, tears freezing on his handsome face, helpless to do more than he was doing.

"*Hospudzi, Hospudzi,* God, please let me find some shelter! Help me find some warmth for Anya. Help me find a house soon," Sasha prayed aloud.

Anya's moans grew louder as the contractions increased, gripping Sasha with fear in his very heart. The wind and snow were at its worst. Anya's agonizing cries cut through the wind. "Sasha, I can't hold on any longer. The baby is coming! Oh! God, I cannot stop it!"

Sasha strained his eyes as snowflakes blinded his vision. Nothing was in sight, nothing that could give them shelter.

What can I do? he thought. *God, help me!*

He pushed on, coaxing the weary horse to keep moving. It seemed an eternity before he came upon a winter-covered tree with wide branches extending like a huge umbrella. A sigh of relief escaped his lips. "This tree will give us shelter," he said to himself. He urged his horse underneath the tree's branches so heavy with snow they hanged low as if welcoming, embracing its guests. He pulled on the reins. The horse stopped, snorted, blowing wisps of steam from its nostrils, shaking its powerful head with gratitude.

His heart pounding in his chest, Sasha jumped from the seat and slipped on the ice as he ran to the back of the sled. He pulled himself up, and crawling in, he embraced his laboring wife, pulling her onto his lap and cradling her head in his arms, kissing her tears away.

"Anya must not give up!" He looked towards the heavens. "God, give her strength to survive."

Breathing heavily, Anya's contractions came faster and stronger, making her twist and turn as she tried to find a comfortable spot that would give her some relief. She gripped Sasha's hands, squeezing them as if in a vise. Her fingernails pierced his skin forming little rivulets of blood. Her pale face contorted with pain. As the moon gleamed again from behind the clouds, Sasha saw her frozen tears shining like diamonds on her long eyelashes. Her body shivered violently.

Far East
Of The Sun

ಜ ಜ ಜಜ ಜ ಜ

Janina Stankiewicz Chung

reed edwards company

For information regarding permission, please write to: Permissions Department, The Reed Edwards Company, P.O. Box 562, Wilbraham, MA 01095-0562

First Printing September, 2008
10 9 8 7 6 5 4 3 2 1

Printed in The United States of America

Cover Art: David Jarratt

Published by:
The Reed Edwards Company
P.O. Box 562
Wilbraham, MA 01095-0562

Stankiewicz Chung, Janina.
    Far east of the sun / Janina Stankiewicz Chung. –1st ed.
            p.   cm.
    LCCN 2007926951
    ISBN 978-0-9795347-1-3

    1. Fiction. 2. Russian heritage--Fiction. 3. World War II --Fiction.   I. Title.

ISBN: 978-0-9795347-1-3
Library of Congress Catalog Number: 2007926951

My deepest thanks…

To my son Jesse Moreno and his wife Dianne, whose help came my way when I needed it the most.

Special thanks and love to my dear daughter Katherine Bonatakis. She has held the family strings tightly in her loving hands throughout the years.

To my dear friend Karen Krasinski, who took the time from her very busy work schedule to spend late hours helping me put the first pages I scribbled into context.

To my brilliant editor, Rita Schiano, who believed in me and helped me with details and the broad contours. I thank her for her support and encouragement.

To Bill Lemke for his help in contacting my editor. Bill encouraged me and rooted for me all the way.

And to those very special people who offered their friendship and support—especially Rosemary Halpin, Beth Alicea, the girls at the Ox, and Chris Peck.

And my deepest love and thanks go to my loving family: My dearest sons, Joseph and Donald whom I adore, my beloved grandchildren and great-grandchildren; and to my beloved sisters and brothers. Thank you all for your love and support

Sasha moved her to a corner of the sled and covered her with dry blankets he had in his satchel. She was still shivering. Desperate to keep her warm, he covered her body with his own, shielding her from the cold.

"I love you, my dearest wife, I love you!" he whispered, his breath caressing her face.

Anya felt the warmth of his body; the warmth of his love comforted her for a moment. She closed her eyes briefly, and then another wave of contractions consumed her.

The time was close. The child would be born in wilderness.

The falling snow was relentless, as if the sky had opened up emptying itself of huge flakes, covering everything in winter whiteness. Sasha and Anya huddled in the corner of the sled under the safe haven of the colossal tree branches. He tried his best to protect her from the cold and wind consuming them.

"Anya," he urged her, "You must hold on until the storm subsides. I will try to find a house." *A safe house,* he thought. These were dangerous times and one had to be careful to whom one talked to or associated with. "Please rest for a while, and then we will go on." Anya nodded weakly and tried to smile for him. But, the smile froze on her face as yet another contraction sliced through her body like a butcher's knife.

Sasha kissed her cold brow and held her closer to him, feeling the tremors from the contractions. They were coming stronger and faster. He looked out at the heavy snowfall and knew the chance of them going on any time soon was very unrealistic.

I must not panic, he told himself. *I must protect my Anya the best way I can.* In spite of the frigid air, Sasha began to sweat from the anguish he was feeling. *I cannot lose them! Dear God in Heaven, I cannot lose them! Matushka Swiecaja Pomarzy Minie, Holy Mary Mother of God, please help me!* He prayed over and over.

Anya dozed for a moment as the warmth of his body covered her, comforting her. Then another contraction consumed her and she screamed with a horrifying wail. "Sasha! No! My water broke. I feel the baby coming...." She moaned again.

Sasha quickly moved Anya to the middle of the sled and placing the blankets beneath her he felt a warm wetness flow from under her. He glanced at her undergarments; they were wet and soiled with blood. Gently he removed them from her body and covering her nakedness with another blanket, he could see that the child was on its way.

In the bitter cold, my child takes its first breath.

The ferocity of the wind subsided as if the knowledge of the coming event made it have pity on the mother and child. Sasha said a quiet prayer of thanks and continued to hold his Anya while she struggled with the birth.

She was getting weaker. "Sasha," she whispered, "I love you, my Sasha. I have always loved you and always will." She grasped his hand. "Please, take care of the children the best way you can." Blinking the tears from her eyes, she pleaded, "Hide them, Sasha, and you hide with them." She moved slightly to ward off the pain. "All of you must be careful and stay in hiding." Weakness overcame her and she closed her eyes.

She felt warm tears raining on her cheek from Sasha's eyes, and one teardrop found its way to her lips; she savored its salty taste as if it was the nectar of the most beautiful flower. *I must be strong and survive this*, she thought in her pain-torn mind. *I can't leave Sasha and the children.* She struggled to visualize the children in her mind. A faint little smile formed on her lips at the memory of them.

Nicolaj, her first born son, with blonde hair so much like his father's and deep blue eyes so much like her own, this handsome child with high cheek bones, strong chin and an infectious smile that reflected mischief in his dancing eyes. Nicolaj had a gift of gab and at ten years old, he was tall and very mature, taking on the responsibility of caring for the other siblings without aforethought.

His sister Marina, age seven, was a beauty. Her thick, chestnut hair was like her own; long and silky worn in thick long braids. Merry blue eyes with a touch of a slant were exotic looking and beautiful. Her dimpled smile touched Nicolaj's young heart and made him fiercely protective of her. Marina adored her brother. She was his helpmate and never too far away from him.

10

Little Katrina, fair-haired like Sasha, was a pretty child, with high cheekbones and rosy plump cheeks. Quiet and serious, she loved to stay close to her mother.

They are good children, Anya was thinking in her pain-torn mind. *I must survive this birth. I cannot lose another child.*

To ease the pain, she continued to concentrate on her children. Her mind went back to that very sad day when her young son learned, at much too young an age, the meaning of grief.

"Nicolaj, please do not cry, my child. Your little sister is an angel in heaven now." Anya tried to comfort her young son, distraught by the loss of his baby sister. "Come with me and see your *Dziedushka* and *Babushka*."

She led her son to the family room. His grandparents and family were already there. The room once bright and warm now was dark and gloomy. Gathered family took on the somber tone of the day. Hushed voices and serene sobs of the women hovered in the air.

Anya noticed her husband, standing stoically dressed in black. The sun streamed in through the tall windows as if trying to dry the tears on his cheeks. She stood next to him and held his hand tenderly as they mourned the loss of their second-born child. Stasia was born a blue baby. And although she lived just a few days, her sweet cherubic face framed with blonde hair would be a lasting memory.

Nicolaj, at two years of age, did not understand where heaven was or what an angel could be. He was crying because the people he loved most were sad. Even at so young an age, he felt the sadness of his parents and of his *Dziedushka* and *Babushka*. Nicolaj wiped his tears and pushed his blonde hair from his forehead. He looked up at his parents, gently tugging at his mother's skirt.

Anya looked at her son. "Nicolaj, you must be tired, my child." She gently stroked his hair. "Come here, let me hold you."

Nicolaj raised his arms to his mother. She picked him up and held him close to her heart, nuzzling his neck, as if some premonition warned her that some day she might lose this handsome, fair-haired child of her heart.

Her mind cleared. She shook the memory of her children and she felt the labor intensify. Yes, she has known much heartache, and now another child is ready to enter the world under the most devastating circumstances.

Another contraction rippled through her. She was getting weaker as the pain took control of her body. Anya closed her eyes and tried to concentrate on the pain. *No. I must survive. My children, my Sasha need me.*

With all the strength left in her, Anya pushed to release the child from her womb and into the cold world. She held onto Sasha's hands and pushed until the pain blinded her eyes. Sasha held her, terrified. Their child was coming through and he did not know what to do. Then with another push, their baby girl entered the frigid cradle of humanity protesting and screaming at the unfairness of it all.

Sasha's face went pale at the sight of the small child. Beads of perspiration broke out on his upper lip as he picked up the wriggling little body. Gently, he cleaned the baby the best he could, kissed her wrinkled little forehead, then wrapped her in Anya's shawl and placed her on her mother's stomach. She was so tiny; too small to survive.

What am I to do now? Sasha thought.

He glanced at Anya. She appeared to be resting; her breathing was shallow her eyes were closed and exhaustion was visible on her face. He leaned and whispered to her, "Anya my darling, we have a baby girl. She is very tiny, but with God's help she may survive." Anya nodded her head weakly and reached for the baby. She touched it and placed her cold hand on top of it. Sasha covered them tightly and jumped off the sled. He looked out from under the branches of the tree and smiled breathing a sigh of relief. The heavy snow receded to a gentle sprinkle of snowflakes. Now he could go and look for some shelter.

He went back to the sled. Anya seemed to be sleeping. *Good.* And he grinned at the sound of his baby's little cries. *Like a meowing kitten,* he thought. *Thank you, God. Give them strength.*

He jumped up onto the seat of the sled and snapped the reins, urging the protesting horse to go on. Small snowflakes were still falling gently, and

Sasha could see the moon shining through the clouds, illuminating the barely visible road. The horse struggled through the deep snow, pulling the sled with a sense of urgency.

There! Is it a mirage? Sasha squinted his eyes trying to see what he thought might be a light flickering in the distance. He urged the horse to go faster towards it. The horse whinnied and protested, but quickened its step. The light became clearer, closer. Cautiously, Sasha approached the log cabin. In some places, drifts of snow accumulated as high as the roof. Thin spirals of smoke rose from the chimney and through the kitchen window he could see signs of movement. The aroma of food cooking reached his nostrils and his stomach groveled loudly, begging for nourishment.

"God...Oh, God...Let this be a safe house where we can find shelter," he prayed in a whisper. "And let there be food for Anya."

A barking dog announced the approaching strangers. Sasha held his breath. "God," he prayed again, "let the people inside this cabin be friendly and not political."

Suddenly, the heavy door creaked open slowly, revealing a beam of light. Through a crack in the doorway Sasha could see an elderly man and woman peering at him cautiously. He let out a sigh of relief; they seemed to be friendly enough. At least he did not see any weapons in the man's hands.

"Whoa! Stop now, Sharna!" Sharna gratefully obliged. She shook her head and pawed the snow with her front hoof as if saying "Thank you." Sasha jumped from the sled, stumbling on the slippery road as he ran to the door to greet the old couple.

"Do not be afraid! I am not here to harm you. I am not armed!" He raised his hands up above his head as if in surrender. "My wife just gave birth on the sled and may be bleeding to death! Please help us!" Sasha pleaded. The heavy snow was covering him quickly and the frigid air was making his teeth chatter. Puffs of air escaped his lips creating smoke circles around his mouth. Weak with fatigue he fell to his knees begging.

One never knew who to trust the man thought. He carefully looked at Sasha, noting his appearance. Sasha's meager clothes were not hiding any weapons. The wet cap on his head was askew giving him a comical look, which made the old man grin, and Sasha's genuine plea for help seemed sincere. Sympathy sprang into Ivan's eyes as he looked at his wife.

"Karina, they need help." The old man yelled to his wife.

Karina wiped her wrinkled face with her apron and looked straight into Sasha's eyes. The anguish and despair she saw was real. "Ivan! I know they need help. Don't tell me what to do!" Ivan looked at Sasha, lifted his hands to heaven in a gesture of resignation. The elderly couple quickly donned their coats and hurried outside.

Karina peered into the sled. Horror reflected in her old eyes when she saw Anya, motionless with the baby swaddled in an old blanket on her stomach. Bright, red blood was everywhere, freezing quickly as it flowed. Karina made a sign of a cross on her breast, "*Hospudzi... Oh, Hospudzi*," she prayed. Then, as if God heard her prayer, she heard a gurgling little noise from the baby.

"Ivan! Get into the sled and help to get this woman into the house!" Ivan sprang into motion with an agility of a young man and quickly was inside the sled beside Anya. Sasha followed him and the two men gently lifted Anya with the baby, the umbilical cord still attached to the mother. Anya moaned and opened her eyes.

"Sasha," her voice was very weak.

"It is all right, my love. We are safe now."

Sasha carried Anya while Karina held the baby. The snowflakes began to fall heavily again, covering Anya and the child in the old woman's arms. As they were entering the cabin, Anya screamed, "Sasha! Stop! Please, No!" She gasped for breath. "Please stop. I feel as if another baby is coming!"

Thinking that the pain and stress of the childbirth had made her delirious, Sasha kept on walking. Anya screamed again. "Sasha, please! Put me down!"

He guided her back onto her feet and held her in his arms, holding her close to his heart. She was wet and cold, her hair was sticking to her face and her lips were blue and trembling. Anya looked into his blue eyes and drew strength from the love shining there like a warm fire.

14

Then it came again and this time Sasha felt the contractions wracking her body. Anya screamed, grabbing his arms and shoulders with a strength that came from deep within. With disbelief in her eyes, her body contracted once more and pushed another child onto winter's white blanket.

Astonished, the old man quickly grabbed the newborn girl. She was quickly turning blue from the wind assaulting her and protesting loudly, she began to wave her little arms in the frigid air as if protecting herself from the falling snow. She was quite tiny, no more than three pounds it seemed, but was feisty and ready to fight the world, wailing with all her might.

They hurriedly brought Anya and the babies into the house and settled them on the couple's bed. The elderly woman took charge. She gathered linens and blankets, ordered Ivan to boil some water on the huge brick fireplace that served as a stove. Then she found a sharp knife and with Sasha's help, cut the umbilical cords of the two girls freeing them from their mother. The babies wailed loudly, but warm blankets and Marina's soothing voice calmed them. She handed the girls to Sasha; he cradled them with huge tears in his eyes. Gently, he hummed a song softly. Snuggling into his warmth, their little eyes closed, they went to sleep.

Karina tenderly removed Anya's blood-soaked clothes and bathed her with the warm water. Anya sighed with relief and looked gratefully at this stranger who so unquestioningly opened her home. As if reading her thoughts, the old woman wiped the tears from Anya's eyes. "I'm Karina. Do not be frightened. You are safe now. You will be all right." A warm smile spread on Karina's aged face. Under a colorful, flowered 'babushka' scarf strands of gray hair fell loosely around her face. Slightly slant eyes set deep twinkled at her. Anya relaxed, feeling secure and safe.

"I am Anya," she whispered.

Karina untangled Anya's hair, wiped it dry with a towel, letting it spill onto the clean linen. She clothed Anya in her own warm nightgown, and maternally tucked the blankets around her. "Ivan, get some vodka for Anya. It will warm her insides."

Ivan rushed to the kitchen for a bottle of homemade vodka, poured a shot glass full and gave it to his wife. Karina gently lifted Anya's head and

15

poured a little of the fiery liquid between her parched lips, causing her to sputter and swallow. She instantly felt the warmth flow inside her body.

Gratefully, she closed her eyes and whispered, "Sasha, the babies…. Are they all right?"

With tears flooding his blue eyes, Sasha lifted her cold hand and held it to his face. "Yes, my dearest. We have two baby girls; one is blonde and the other dark-haired, just like you."

Anya smiled faintly, squeezing his hand in response. "Please, let me hold them."

Karina hurriedly bathed them in warm water as they wailed loudly, then swaddled them in clean linen and placed them in Anya's weak arms. She cradled her daughters, burying her face in their softness, inhaling the aroma that only newborn babies have. Hungrily they sucked on their little fists until they found their mother's milk.

"What shall we name them?"

Sasha smiled at this perfect picture of mother and her babies. Then he laughed, "Anya, we thought of one name, not two! I think the dark-haired baby should be named Alexandra as we planned, and the blonde little one? Well…let me think." He turned to Karina. "What do you think? What name shall we give her? After all you will be the Godmother." Karina gasped at Sasha's words. She was touched. Sasha turned to Anya. "Do you not agree?" Anya smiled and nodded her head in approval. "Yes, I would like that."

Karina thought for a moment. "The little one looks to me like she should have a very poetic name. We should name her Janushka."

Anya and Sasha smiled, nodding their approval. She held her squirming daughters to her breasts where they snuggled into the warmth of their mother. Anya soon dozed off to dreams of the past years.

16

Chapter Two
1928

She ran barefoot through green fields and meadows breathlessly chasing a dozen white geese she was minding. The geese were happily waddling, honking with their feathers flying, enjoying the chase. Summer in Zarowna, Anya's family home, was in full bloom. The tall, green grass caressed her ankles, making way for her running feet. Daisies and bluebells with patches of buttercups swayed gaily with the rhythm of the light wind. Fragrance of the flowers filled the air. Butterflies and bees zigzagged in the sky, dizzy drunk with the pleasure of the summer day. A wild rabbit darted from under a bush, hopping along looking for its mate. Birds sang cheerfully while gathering food for their young, who waited patiently in their nests; their little beaks open in anticipation.

The sun high in the cloudless blue sky smiled down on Anya and sent its rays to warm her beautiful face. Anya's bone structure was delicate, striking, rather than exquisite, the kind that would last on into later years. Her skin was flawless, with an outdoor cast of tawny and her body in a summer dress was slender, yet well rounded. The golden highlights of her chestnut hair framed her blue eyes—large, direct, and clear, with lashes so long and wispy that her eyes looked dreamy and full of secrets.

There was something very fresh and challenging about her, but there was warmth and wholesomeness, too. She bore herself with grace, energy, and pride. Anya was the talk of the village. Eligible suitors called with gifts and promises, asking for her hand, but Anya's heart belonged to Sasha.

As she picked daisies to make a crown for her head, she paused and listened, hoping to hear his voice singing the song he wrote for her. Oh, how he could sing! His rich baritone voice vibrated through her very heart. Anya looked at the daisy she held in her delicate hand, its yellow heart, its petals as white as snow, brought a smile to her delicate lips. Slowly, she

17

started playing the game. "He loves me. He loves me not. He loves me. He loves me not." She held her breath as the petals fell to the ground. As she plucked the last petal, a sigh escaped turning her lips into secret smile.

"*On mnie miluje*! He loves me! Oh, I know how he loves me!"

Anya twirled and turned and danced as light as a butterfly with the joy of young love. *Next month I will be eighteen. Will he ask my mother for my hand?* Anya wondered. Then, as if a cloud passed across the sun, the smile left Anya's lips. If only her Papa was still here. How she miss him.

Four years had passed since her father died at the young age of forty-three. An officer of the Czar, he had suffered massive injuries during the First World War.

His image flooded her memory. Oh, how handsome he was–so tall and lean with a muscular body from riding horses. How proud he looked in his uniform. He wore a saber on his hip; his chest was full of valor medals. Anya's Papa was something to behold. He would have approved of Sasha, she knew in her heart.

Anya studied the blue sky and tried to picture him in heaven smiling down on her, his arms outstretched waiting for her to run to him as she did when she was a little girl. It had been a thrill to see him ride up on his white stallion. He sat tall, an accomplished equestrian with a smile that broke many hearts. Yet, he had eyes only for her mama. She remembered how he would lift her up onto his magnificent stallion, how she would snuggle up to him, inhaling his masculine scent.

More memories flooded her mind, but with a sorrow etched deep in her heart. A tear found its way down her cheek. She sighed and wiped it away. Then, as if he knew that she needed him, Anya heard his voice singing in the distance.

She lifted her head to listen. *Yes, it is my Sasha.*

She quickly put the daisy crown upon her head. With her hair flowing around her shoulders, she looked like a fairy princess.

He must not see me crying. She wiped the tears away, put a smile on her face and ran to meet him.

Chapter Three

Breakfast was a very happy and rowdy occasion in the Petrosewicz household. The seven brothers awoke each morning by the sun rising over the lush green fields and meadows and peeking into the windows as if happily saying, "Good morning!"

Roosters stretched their necks as they crowed; the chickens noisily ran around, busily pecking at grain left over from the last feeding. Cows were mooing, restless, waiting to be relieved of the heavy load of milk, while other farm animals seemed anxious to be, off to pasture or to start a workday in the fields.

Mornings were a happy time for the women. They rose early with the sunrise and were busy cooking on the cavernous brick fireplace, the width of the entire kitchen. Pots hung from an iron bar, along side of the smoked shanks of ham and slabs of bacon. The activity was almost frantic, as they chatted and sang their favorite songs while waiting for the men and the children to come down for their morning meal. Beautiful oak tables laden with thick slices of smoked bacon, cured ham, smoked sausages, and fresh eggs surrounded the large dining room. Fried potatoes with salt pork and onions were steaming in a big bowl. Aroma from freshly baked bread reached the bedrooms upstairs assaulting their senses and their empty stomachs.

A handsome bunch they were. Tall and lean, with sun-bronzed faces, sun-bleached hair and strong muscular arms used to hard labor. The quick smiles on their faces and the laughter in their eyes made the girls hearts quicken and their eyelashes flutter with flirtation and the promise of young love.

They hurried with their toiletries, put on their homemade work clothes and ran down the stairs, pushing and shoving each other as they did when they were little boys. There was much jovial laughter as they took two steps at a time, trying to beat one another to the table. However, they could never beat Sasha. Somehow, he always managed to be the first at the table, with a big grin on his handsome face, challenging his siblings to beat him at everything they did.

Yes, Sasha, with his devil-may-care attitude, his swagger, a song on his lips and a smile that never left his face was full of dreams and adventures in his heart. However, today was different. Today, he hurried through breakfast, swallowing big gulps of milk, chewing his food quickly, and thinking only of his Anya waiting for him in the meadow with her geese. Oh, the sight of his beautiful Anya made his world bright, as though the sun shone only for him. He longed to be near her, to see her bright smile, her blue eyes so full of mystery and promise. Her chestnut-colored, hair, the way it cascaded down to her waist, made him long to run his fingers through it.

Yes, today would be different, for today he would ask her to be his wife. Sasha was twenty-eight, ready to settle down and start a family. He yearned for children of his own and his Anya would give him strong sons.

As he hurriedly tended to his chores, he thought only of his Anya and of the lifetime they would spend together. When his work was finished, Sasha sped down to the river to wash and refresh, then rushed back to the house to put on clean clothes. He checked his face in the mirror. Yes, he needed to shave. Afterwards, he combed his blonde hair and looked at his reflection once again. Staring back at him was a face with a huge grin and twinkling cornflower blue eyes. He winked at the reflection and grinned wider as he anticipated holding his Anya in his arms. A vision of her appeared in his mind, running to him with her long hair free of braids flowing in the wind, her face flushed and lips open waiting to be kissed. With the vision in his mind, Sasha hurried down the stairs and out the door he ran to meet his destiny.

Chapter Four

Breathless, she scurried through the fields of wheat and potatoes, ignoring the scratches on her legs and arms from the brush filled with berries. Any other day she would have stopped to pick some of the juicy morsels, but nothing in the world mattered now, only the man she was anxious to see. She strained her ears to hear his voice. In the small clearing she saw him strolling along, singing, his Russian Wolfhound, Misha, happily running beside him, its tongue hanging from exertion and the heat of the day.

The sound of Anya's feet on the grass made Misha lift his head; his nose took in the air sniffing the familiar scent of her. Misha bolted toward her, ears flapping in the air, tongue hanging from the side of its mouth, and tail wagging wildly. Greeting her with adoring eyes, Misha sat at her feet and begged for an affectionate pat on his huge head. Anya laughed gaily, and scratched behind his ear lovingly. She looked up. Sasha was standing before her smiling.

Anya was a vision of loveliness and with the crown of daisies on her head, she appeared like a bride already. He held his breath and opened his arms to her. "*Hadzi maja miluja.* Come here my love."

She poised as if a butterfly perched on a branch and then flew into Sasha's wonderfully strong arms that held so much love and tenderness. How safe and secure she felt held by him. Her Sasha would love her and take care of her for the rest of her life. She knew it in her heart. She snuggled into him, placed her head on his strong shoulder, inhaling his manly scent – a scent distinct, familiar. She thought of her father.

Sasha held her closely, her young body pressing innocently against his sent ripples of pleasure throughout his body. He kissed her brow and her closed eyelids. Stroking her silky hair, he lowered his mouth to her luscious open lips waiting for him. How innocent was her kiss. Sasha smiled and thought that his Anya would soon know the passion that was flowing

21

through her veins when he made her his wife. He would be gentle with her, wake her young body with tenderness.

Anya flushed, her body responding to something she knew nothing about. Sasha's arms held her tightly around her waist, his mouth on hers made her want more, but she did not know exactly what *more* was. She slowly moved away from his embrace and with wide blue eyes full of trusting innocence, gazed at him. She saw a gentle smile on his loving face, and knew her Sasha was ready to ask her for her hand.

"Anya," he whispered breathless, "I would like to see your mother this evening."

"Why, Sasha?" she asked softly, her face blushing.

"I have something very important to ask her."

"What are you going to ask her, Sasha?" she asked coyly.

Sasha picked a daisy and took her right hand in his. With trembling fingers, he twisted the stem around her finger and with volumes of meaning looked deeply into her eyes. Anya's face lit up with joy. She drew a deep breath, unsure of what to say. "You are always welcome in our house, Sasha. My mother will be pleased to see you." She then added quickly, "However, beware of my brothers! They will be questioning your motives for this visit," She giggled gaily. Sasha laughed heartily, slapping her bottom playfully.

She smiled again and threw her arms around Sasha's neck. He picked her up—she was as light as a feather—and twirled her around, her long hair swaying around them both.

Sasha's heart swelled with happiness as he envisioned a bright future ahead of them. He showered her face with light fluttery kisses lingering slightly on her luscious lips. Gently he put her down and placed her hand in his and sang gaily as they headed for the Czarapin house.

Chapter Five

They walked hand-in-hand through lush green meadows ablaze with thousands of bright yellow enormous dandelions and countless other flowers. The daisies swayed gently in the wind, covering the fields like a white carpet for the soon-to-be bride and groom.

The valley stream flowing swiftly alongside of the meadow was inviting. Tall birch trees graced the meadow, their branches full with leaves provided cool shadow from the burning sun. It was a favorite spot for Sasha and Anya to stop and enjoy the serenity of the brook. They ran quickly following a path leading toward it, jumped in and splashed their faces with cool, clear water, then filled their cupped hands and drank thirstily.

Misha followed them in, lapping up the water with his tongue and frolicking like a puppy. He spotted a fish and tried to catch it; however, the fish was too fast for him.

Geese waddled behind them, honking and trudging along. Then, at the sight of the water, ran in fast as they could their strong wings splashing, diving in and out, as they swam, washing and grooming themselves with their beaks.

Sasha and Anya sat on the cool, green grass laughing at Misha and the geese's antics. They rested for a short time, enjoying the sun shining upon their faces and the closeness of one another. Sasha gazed upon Anya's loveliness longingly. She looked up into his face with dreamy eyes that melted his heart. "What are you thinking, Sasha?" she asked.

He looked deep into her blue eyes. "I am thinking of how happy you make me. When I am with you, Anya, I feel complete." She snuggled closer to him feeling the strength of his strong arms around her. Holding her close, he hummed the folk song she loved most. Anya was special. Watching her in the sunlight, long curly lashes soft against the flush of her cheek, Sasha felt a glow of possessive pride. Yes, Anya was special. He sensed a realm of possibilities within her, strength within that could endure life's greatest

23

challenges and hardships. He said a silent prayer that her mother would give them her blessing so they could marry soon.

Hugging her to him and kissing her tender lips, Sasha was determined to make Anya his own. Excitedly, they jumped up. Anya giggled and yelled at Sasha, "I bet you cannot catch me!" She ran laughing with Sasha coming up fast behind her. He grabbed her around the waist, lifted her high in the air, and twirled her around until she begged, "Sasha, please stop! I am getting dizzy!" He put her down kissing her flushed cheek and taking her hand in his own they walked slowly towards the house, their destiny. Each of them lost within their own, deep thoughts.

In the distance, they saw the winding dirt road lined with weeping willows, its low branches creating an archway leading to the red brick, two-story house built by Anya's grandfather. It was a lovely house in the middle of a meadow designed to shelter many generations with spacious rooms and wide, tall windows to give light and cheer to each room. A circular driveway in front of the house welcomed many a traveler. There were two round, white pillars on the front porch holding up the second floor veranda. The porch was wide and covered the length of the house. Climbing rose bushes stretched their branches like fingertips grasping the rails, creating a wall of roses of many colors.

The gardens surrounding the house were magnificent, tended lovingly by Anya's mother and grandmother. Beds of flowers were blooming in wild profusion, the shrubbery trimmed and elegant as if waiting for an important occasion to happen.

To the back of the house on the right side were the stables and barns. The cattle now in pasture grazed on the bountiful grass while the young calves ran happily alongside their mothers. There were dozens of chickens and proprietary roosters walking around guarding their territories as well as their hens. Huge fields of wheat and barley swayed in the wind, forming ocean-like waves extended as far as the eye could see. It was a remarkable sight and Sasha held his breath at the beauty of it.

They were nearing the house now and both were nervous and apprehensive. Anya could not stop blushing and was as jumpy as a young filly. After all, this may be a very important day in her life! She may be betrothed today and be the envy of all the girls in the village!

The yard was buzzing with activity. The field hands and Anya's brothers were returning from a day of hard work, all sun-bronzed and exhausted from the heat. She noticed her brothers laughing heartily as they dismounted from their horses. No doubt, Antos, the rascal of the family, must have told them something about his escapades with the girls, she thought.

The brothers spotted Anya and Sasha coming towards the house holding hands, each paused and looked at Anya protectively. Were Anya and Sasha alone all afternoon? There would be many questions asked!

Sasha sensed the tension and Anya's sudden discomfort. "Are you very nervous?" he whispered.

"Yes. Worse than having a tooth pulled," she admitted and tightly gripped his hand.

Walking over to the brothers, he waved to them in greeting. Shaking their hands he nervously shouted, *"Kak pazywajicie?* How are you?" He turned to Antos. "How are all your girlfriends, Antos? Are they still chasing you?"

Antos shook his head, his hazel-green eyes twinkled with merriment and his mouth twitched with laughter. "Yes, Sasha, they are still chasing me. However, you know that I am not the marrying kind. I will leave that to you and my brothers."

The attempt at humor worked, the brothers relaxed. Michal, Nicolaj and Ambroz laughed with amusement. Antos had good looks and a charming grin. Every young girl fluttered her eyes at him as he strolled through the streets of the village. However, Antos did not intend to settle down yet. His sights were set on Engineering School in Moscow.

Antos studied Sasha and Anya, closely. Their flushed faces and twinkling eyes told the story. Love was in the air and he could not be happier for Sasha.

Sasha noticed the close observation and grinning, quickly said, "We spent the afternoon walking in the woods and talking."

The brothers chuckled and said nothing. They watched Sasha's discomfort with glee, waiting for an explanation.

Sasha's face turned beet red, his mouth went dry as he tried to utter the words.

"Anya and I will have something to tell you after dinner."

The brothers hooted at Sasha's announcement, looking at each other knowingly. Sasha was going to ask their little sister to marry him. They smiled at Sasha, pleased.

Sasha's kind heart was well known. Children followed him, listened raptly while he sang to them, laughed loudly as he played games and teased them. Sasha's high spirit and "take charge" attitude made him well liked by all. Yes, Sasha will be welcomed into the family.

Anya's mother, Rozalia, appeared in the doorway. She was a small woman with piercing hazel eyes that seemed to see all. Yet, there was also softness in her eyes that conveyed the sorrow and heartbreak she had endured since the loss of her husband, Michal.

The resemblance between daughter and mother was striking. Rozalia's lips were full and set in a manner that showed strength, authority and determination. Rozalia held her head high and proud, commanding respect from all.

She looked at Anya and Sasha with a secret smile on her lips and motioned for them to approach her.

"Sasha, it is good to see you. Will you stay and have dinner with us?"

Sasha glanced at Anya who was still blushing profusely. "I will be honored to dine with you. I bring you greetings from my family with best wishes for your health."

Rozalia nodded her head in acknowledgement. "I will have to visit them one of these days, and buy some of that wonderful honey from your father." She chuckled. "Your mother tells me that he spends more time with the bees than her. However, she does not mind. He is happy when he walks through the orchards. It is quite a sight to see, with the bees swarming around him."

"Yes," Sasha said. "My father loves his bees and my mother is very

26

tolerant of the time he spends with them." Sasha was perspiring under the scrutiny of the entire family. He wiped his brow and pushed his blond hair back into place. Rozalia sensed Sasha's discomfort. "How is your mother feeling? Last time I saw her she was suffering with arthritis in her legs and hands." Rozalia rubbed her hands as if trying to feel her pain.

"Thank you for asking," Sasha said. "She does suffer a great deal but manages to get around."

The aroma of savory food wafted out from the house. "Your sisters have been busy all day preparing freshly made sausages," Rozalia smiled affectionately, "and I am sure that the two of you could use a little nourishment." Sasha licked his lips hungrily almost tasting the sizzling sausage. Rozalia laughed. "Let us go in and join the rest of the family."

Sasha's stomach was growling. He looked at Anya. "Are you as hungry as I am?"

She giggled, touching her empty stomach. "I could eat a horse right now."

Antos, who was walking behind them, heard her comment and grinning, ran over to his horse, grabbing the reins and pulling the horse aside. "Anya, you are not touching my horse!" he hollered at her. The brothers laughed hysterically, pushing one another through the door as they did when they were little boys.

A tender smile appeared on Rozalia's face as she stood with hands on her hips watching her frolicking brood. She shook her head from side to side, scolding them playfully. "Boys, you are still rascals!"

Antos grabbed his mother by the waist and twirled her around until she was dizzy.

"Antos," she laughed, "put me down! You are making me dizzy." He twirled her around one more time then put her down, kissed her on her forehead and followed his brothers inside the house.

Anya's two sisters, Juzia and Marina, heard the commotion as they were busy setting the dinner table. Rowdily, the brothers tumbled into the spacious dining room, shoving and pushing each other trying to get to the chairs first.

Juzia and Marina watched their brothers' antics with amusement. "Are they ever going to grow up?" Juzia asked laughing.

Then, they saw Anya and Sasha entering the room behind the brothers. Anya's eyes were sparkling, yet darting nervously. Juzia nudged Marina, "Look, Marina, Anya is as nervous as a young filly."

Marina nodded grinning at Juzia. "Yes, I think our Anya and Sasha have been alone too long today. Something is brewing in their hearts."

"Anya, shall we set another setting for dinner?" Juzia asked grinning.

Another rush of color stained Anya's cheeks. "Yes, Juzia, Sasha is joining us for dinner," she stuttered nervously.

Juzia placed the last dinner plate on the table, looked at her jittery sister and smiled. "I will get another setting." She walked over to the credenza, took another setting and placed it next to Anya. "I am sure you will want Sasha to sit next to you. Am I right?" she teased. Juzia was a year older and from the time they were little girls, she teased and tormented Anya relentlessly.

Sasha sat next to Anya, glanced at her with a reassuring look and touched her hand squeezing it lightly. He smiled lovingly at her, urging her to relax. The brothers jovially took their seats at the table laden with hot steaming food. Anya's mother and sisters joined them. Rozalia sat at the head of the table as was the custom and everyone bowed their head as she said Grace. *"Spasiba Hospudzi.* Bless our visitor, Sasha, and bless this house and all those who reside in it. And thank you for this bountiful food we are about to partake in. Amen."

Bowls filled with potatoes and crispy fried salt pork, sautéed onions in butter, oven dark bread, smoked slices of ham and sausages, baked chicken and fresh vegetables from the garden passed from hand to hand. The aromas wafting through the air made everyone eager to eat.

A bottle of vodka appeared and in traditional Russian custom, the brothers filled their shot glasses and toasted, *"Na zdarowie."*

"Sasha, what brings you here?" Antos asked, grinning at his brothers with a conspiratorial wink. The brothers chuckled while filling their plates with food.

They were teasing Sasha, and he knew it. "Well," he stuttered. "There wasn't much work on the farm." Shrugging his shoulders, he continued. "So, I decided to visit my neighbors." Perspiration was dripping from his brow. He took out his handkerchief and wiped his face before turning to Rozalia, "May I have a word with you after dinner?"

Rozalia nodded. "Yes, Sasha, but let us enjoy our food first and then we can go into the library and have some of the berry juice I have made."

However, Anya's brothers would not let Sasha off the hook that easy. With a huge grin, Antos continued to tease Sasha. "Hey, Sasha, whatever it is you want to discuss with mother, you can discuss amongst all of us. We are as one in this family, right? No secrets." He looked at his brothers. They all nodded their heads in agreement, choking on their food with laughter. "Come on, Sasha, we know what you want to ask. Go on...get down on your knees and ask our little sister for her hand."

Not believing her ears, Anya looked aghast at her brothers. She glanced at her mother and sisters for support, but they all were staring at Sasha, sitting still as a statue in his chair. Anya grabbed his hand under the table and squeezed it. He turned and looked at her. Her blue eyes were pools of water and her cheeks were beet red. He rose slowly from his chair and pushing it aside, he knelt in front of her. Taking her by her shoulders, he turned her to face him.

Anya trembled like a leaf. She had waited for this moment and now Sasha was going to ask her for hand in marriage. Her mind was whirling; she felt dizzy. She inhaled small gulps of air. A gasp escaped her lips as she looked up to see her family watching them. She could see the approval in their eyes. A warm glow spread through her entire body. She turned to Sasha. His eyes were soft and loving; a tender smile spread across his face.

"Anya," he whispered, "will you be my wife?"

The threatening pool of tears now spilled from her eyes as she gently took his face into her hands, and whispered back. "Yes, Sasha, I will be your wife."

The brothers cheered loudly, laughing and talking at the same time. Anya looked up at her mother with a nervous smile on her lips. Her mother stood up and walked over to her daughter. "Anya, today you have promised your hand to Sasha. I want to be the first to congratulate you." She took Anya's burning face into her hands and kissed her flushed cheek gently, then hugged Sasha warmly.

"Your engagement is now official." She turned to her family. "And now, let us celebrate!"

Chapter Six

A crown of white roses and daises with a touch of baby's breath adorned Anya's glorious hair styled in thick braids and pinned around her head. Juzia, her maid of honor, trembled holding their grandmother's floor-length lace.

She proudly pinned the veil to the crown of flowers on Anya's head. A vision of loveliness stared back at them in the mirror. Anya's deep blue piercing eyes so much like her father's stared back at her without apprehension or fear. It was her wedding day. Today she will take her Sasha as her husband and make him a good wife and a good mother to the children they hoped to have. This she vowed to herself.

The white satin bridal dress with a scooped neckline, elbow length sleeves with lace spilling to her wrists and fitted bodice, fashioned lovingly by their mother, flowed gently to the floor enhancing her slender body. With trembling hands she gently smoothed the folds of the gown and touched the veil framing her lovely face. *I am a bride today.* She looked at Juzia, outfitted in a light green dress, flowers in her dark blonde hair, eyes sparkling with excitement and anticipation of merriment and dancing.

"Anya, you are a beautiful bride," said Juzia. She hugged Anya tightly and kissed her flushed cheek. "I wish you a wonderful life full of laughter and happiness." Anya was special to her, as younger sisters often are.

Complimenting her lovely light blue eyes, Marina, tall and slender, wore a dark blue skirt with a fitted lace, powder blue long sleeved blouse.

She loved Anya and was very happy for her. Filled with emotion, Marina took Anya's hands and held them to her heart. "Sasha is a lucky man today. Be good to him and he will take care of you all your life," she said tearfully.

Anya knew that. Yet, she felt a tug at her heart knowing that as of today she will no longer be a part of this loving household. She will live with

31

Sasha's family, with his six brothers and two sisters. She briefly felt a pang of panic.

The door opened and Anya's mother walked in looking lovely in her yellow satin dress, her hair pulled back in an elegant chignon, her hazel eyes sparkling with excitement. She looked at her daughter and blinked away the tears that were threatening to spill. "You remind me of how I looked on my wedding day. If only your father was here to give you away." Anya was Michal's favorite daughter, with her strong will and spirit. *It will sustain her always*, he would say.

"Anya, you are loved by us all. We wish you joy and happiness with Sasha. And may God bless you always."

It was time to go and meet the groom.

The wedding party and many guests that came from far away to celebrate the well-known and respected families joining in matrimonial union were waiting. The church was vibrating with anticipation of the bride walking down the aisle.

Sasha was fidgety in his new suit. He tugged at the sleeves of his white linen shirt and straightened his tie. His blonde hair was combed back neatly, his face clean-shaven. His blue eyes were on the door through which his Anya would soon step. He nervously stepped from one foot to the next as if in a dance. Anya's brothers watched him with amusement.

Sasha's mother and father stood next to him. His mother, Aniuta, was tall with high cheekbones and light blue eyes with long eyelashes that created an illusion of dreamy eyes. Her light brown hair braided and pinned around the crown of her head. She was an attractive woman, intelligent and well read. She had full control of her large family and ruled them with authority.

Beside her stood Alexander, Sasha's father, a handsome man with a sun-bronzed face and a twinkle of laughter in his blue eyes. He was always full of humor, ready to dance or sing with the rest of his sons. He watched his son, a slight smile on his face and whispered to his wife, "Look at him! He is as nervous as a little boy!"

Soft organ music rose above them, announcing the bride. The door opened and the vision that would sustain Sasha all his life appeared in the doorway. His breath caught in his throat at the sight of her, her loveliness assaulting his senses. His bride came closer, a slight smile on her lips and a light in her eyes that shone with pure love.

"My Anya..." he whispered.

Chapter Seven

Anya stood in the middle of the room dressed in her traveling clothes. The pleated brown skirt and cream-colored blouse with lace spilling from the neckline, complimented her slim figure. A small hat with four colorful feathers was perched over her smooth brow. She glanced at her right hand. Her wedding band was gold and shiny. Twisting it around her finger, her eyes registered each item in the room, all the things she had known since childhood. *All this will be here tomorrow. I will be gone.* She walked over to the window and pushed the curtain back. The trees and gardens were in full bloom. Her eyes became misty. She smiled wistfully, pushed a stray strand of hair from her forehead and looked around at her belongings packed and ready to be loaded onto the carriage waiting to take her to her new home. Her childhood was over. Next time she returned to visit, she would be a wife and possibly a mother. Her heart was beating like a drum. She felt dizzy with emotion swirling inside her.

The wedding ceremony, the dinner and dancing were over. They had danced well into the early morning hours and Sasha and his brothers would not let her rest for a moment as she gaily floated from one to the other, laughing and enjoying the merriment. Oh, it was a glorious day! The guests lingered on and departed slowly. Sasha's family bid their farewells at sunrise, hurrying home to start preparing for festivities, as was the custom, to welcome the new Mrs. Petrosewicz. It would be another day of dancing and merriment.

Now, her wedding gown and veil were stored away with the memories. It was time to say goodbye to those she loved with all her heart. She walked slowly down the stairs, looking at the portraits of many relatives and family hanging on the wall. However, the one portrait she looked at the longest was that of her father—dressed in his officer's uniform with gold stripes on his shoulders, several medals of valor on his chest, the saber sword at his waist. He was an impressive figure, exuding power and elegance. His mustache, the envy of many young men, tickled her when he kissed her cheek. She loved the feel of it, and right now, she would have loved to run into his arms and tell him proudly that she is now a married woman.

Anya looked into his eyes, so much resembling her own, and whispered, "*Ja cibie miluju, Papa*." She turned to say goodbye to the rest of the family and felt Sasha standing behind her. He took her into his arms and gently held her, allowing her to grieve in silence. She felt the strength of his arms and knew that whatever future trials she would face, this man would sustain her. She was safe and loved.

"Anya, it is time for us to go, my darling. It will be dark soon. We must hurry," Sasha said.

"Yes, my love, I am anxious to be alone with you. Let us say our goodbyes."

Her mother walked towards her and hugged her intensely. "God bless you, my child. I wish you much happiness."

Anya replied, "*Spasiba, Mama*." She kissed her mother's cheek and then said goodbye to Juzia, Marina, and her brothers.

Antos picked her up and twirled her around, making light of a sad situation. "Little sister, we love you and will be here for you. Sasha, you are taking a very spirited filly. Be happy!" He hooted with laughter and put her down, offering her hand to Sasha.

Anya blushed again and playfully slapped Antos on his cheek. "Antos, you have always been a rascal!"

They settled in the carriage and with one last look at her girlhood home and her family, they were off on life's journey as Mr. and Mrs. Petrosewicz.

The apple orchards on both sides of the road were in full bloom. The white flowers covered the trees like a bridal veil welcoming the newlyweds. Anya was in awe. Each tree was heavy with apple blossoms. She could see swarms of honeybees drawing the sweet nectar from the flowers; the buzzing was like a song of their own. It was a marvelous sight. Nature was at its finest.

Sasha pulled on the reins to slow the white Arabian stallion prancing with pride. It seemed to say "Thanks" as he came to a stop in front of an apple orchard in its full bloom He took her hand and let her down from the carriage. She stood still for a moment unable to discern the buzzing of what seemed to be a thousand bees. "Do you see all these orchards and all this land? This wonderland belongs to my family, and now it is yours." He pointed to the beehives. "The buzzing that you hear is what my father treasures most—his honeybees."

He took her hand in his. "Come, Anya." She pulled back hesitating. He smiled encouragingly. "Do not be afraid. The bees will not hurt you."

The sight that greeted her was incredible. She could not believe her eyes. Rows of beehives on wooden legs were scattered in the meadow as far as the eye could see. "There are at least a hundred beehives!"

"Sasha, this is truly a factory of bee workers. Oh! I must see all of them and the inside of the hives. Do you think your father will be kind enough to show it to me?"

"My father will be very happy to show you his treasured bees and how he takes care of them. He takes pride in showing off his treasures."

He tightened the grip on her hand as she danced around him with anticipation of new adventure, trying to keep her still. "Anya, stay still or you will disturb the bees. They are very skittish and spook very easily and sometimes they will fly in swarms and attack. The sting can be very painful. If you are allergic to the sting, you can get very sick. Stay still for now." He laughed at her excitement and held her arms with both hands to keep her quiet. "Now, observe them at work."

"How did your father start this? It must have taken years to build all these hives. How did he do it?"

"When Father was just a boy, a bee landed on his arm, stinging him. He swatted the bee, killing it. He picked up the dead bee and carefully examined it, taking notice of every little detail. He was fascinated. How could this little creature both produce honey and sting so bad? He wanted to know more.

"Their neighbor, Bubenko, had several beehives on his farm. Father

36

asked if he could help him care for the bees. Bubenko was very impressed and invited my father to come by anytime. From then on, my father spent all his spare time tending to the beehives, watching and learning.

"And this," Sasha pointed proudly to the hives, "is the result. Each day, he watches his bees at work. He mourns for every hive that perishes in the harsh winters. The bees know him and buzz around him in swarms as he tends the hives." Sasha's chest puffed with pride. "And he has never been stung! They seem to know that he loves them! Anyone else, including my mother and me, has to wear protective netting and clothes to go near them. And so, here we are at a most productive honey farm in all of Russia."

"What does your father do with all that honey? Does he sell it? "

"Yes, he sells it and also gives it away to needy families. Father has a saying '*Jak ja maju-ja daju.* If I have it, I will share it.' He believes that honey is God's own food and has many healing benefits. He talks to the bees, nurtures them as if they were his children. People come from far distances to buy father's honey."

"My mother uses honey in mixing her healing herbs," Anya said.

They stood hand-in-hand fascinated by the very organized swarms of bee workers flying toward the fields of wild flowers. Each swarm had a purpose and knew exactly what to do.

"Now that I see how hard they work and the benefits of the honey we enjoy, I will never kill another bee again, or think of it as a pest. I feel so awful when I think of how many I have swatted from fear." Tears sprang into Anya's blue eyes. "Sasha, I am so sorry I hurt them!"

Sasha hugged her to him and kissed her forehead. "Anya, I know what you mean. Many people kill the bees from fear. It is only because they don't understand them." He reached down and wiped her eyes lovingly, then kissed her sweet lips.

After a short walk, Sasha said, "We better get going. My family left shortly after the festivities and must be anxiously waiting for us. We do not want to worry them."

They walked back to the waiting carriage. The horse eyed them gratefully, stomping his foot and shaking his head, as if eager to get back to the safety of his stable and some grain to eat. Sasha helped Anya into the carriage, hopped up onto the seat beside her and with a tug on the reins, the horse sprang into a trot on the familiar dirt road.

The main road led to a driveway that crossed a small wooden bridge over a running brook with water clear and cool. If one looked closely enough, one could see fish swimming around happily, chasing after food by jumping out to catch an insect. It was a very serene spot, where one would want to stop, remove shoes, and stretch out on the thick, green grass.

The Petrosewicz house was situated a short distance beyond the brook. It was a lovely place full of character. Two stories high and built with weathered brick which cast a soft rose color; the facade interspersed with wide white shuttered windows. The hipped roof had faded long ago to a quiet green with three straight chimneys rising from it. The focal point of the house was a wide, wooden porch that gave the illusion of a white skirt around the entire house that opened out from all four sides.

An acre of well-tended lawns and flowerbeds surrounded the house. The apple orchards were to the right of the house stretching everywhere with apple blossoms covering the trees. The slight wind fanned the scent of flowers for miles around.

The beehives were on the other side of the orchard. It was a magnificent sight. The house and the mountains, the orchard, and beehives stood in peaceful coexistence, neither detracting from the others beauty.

As Anya and Sasha crossed the bridge, they could see much activity on the porch and on the grounds. They could hear beautiful music; violins and balalaikas were in tune with each other playing Russian folk songs. The brothers had begun the festivities for the newlyweds. Neighbors from other villages gathered with their children running and playing hopscotch in the yard.

"I am so hungry, Sasha. We have not eaten since this morning."

Sasha pulled on the reins to slow the horse as they entered the yard. "I am very hungry, too. But I am also hungry to hold you in my arms, Anya." He looked into her eyes and his burning gaze made her shiver. Anya blushed profusely and leaned over to kiss his starving lips.

"I want to be in your arms also, Sasha. I am glad we have this gathering of family and friends, but I can't wait to be alone with you." Sasha sucked in his breath with excitement and anticipation and pulled Anya to him, kissing her tender lips. Their playful exchange of kisses made them breathless and lightheaded. They laughed as only lovers do on their way to the wonder of love and discovery of each other.

Dusk descended on the merriment of the wedding party. The neighbors departed with many good wishes for the bride and groom. Sasha's family retired to their rooms leaving the newlyweds alone. Anya stood in the foyer of the big house waiting for Sasha to join her and go up to their wedding chamber. She was nervous, yet she could not wait to be with Sasha, alone at last.

He came out of the kitchen and, grinning, lifted her into his arms. She was light as a feather. He nuzzled her neck, kissing it lightly as he carried her up the flight of stairs without catching his breath. Clinging to him, giggling, biting his ear, she teased him relentlessly.

"Anya, stop it or I will put you down right here and make love to you on the stairs right now!" he teased.

She giggled louder and showered his face with light little kisses all over. He stopped in front of the bedchamber, opened the door and carried her in. Lit candles throughout the bedroom cast trembling shadows on cream-colored walls. Sasha held Anya in his arms looking at the spacious bed. A goose down comforter covered it and numerous puffy pillows were scattered by the bed-board. Sasha sucked in his breath at the sight of Anya's bridal nightgown placed on the side of the bed. He put her down slowly and wrapped his arm around her waist, relishing the closeness of her. "Look at the lovely nightdress, Anya." he whispered. She turned and gasped. It was a lovely vision of the finest silk and French lace, sewn lovingly by her mother.

Feeling his nearness and his warm breath on her creamy shoulders and slender neck, she faced him. He saw the longing in her eyes. Anya stood frozen to the ground, waiting for the heat of the passion to melt her, waiting for this man to make her his own.

*I am Sasha's wife now. I will cherish and love him always. Hospudzi....
Please help me to be a good wife,* she prayed.

She reached up and caressed his face lovingly feeling the wetness of a
tear slowly making its way down his cheek. "Sasha, why are there tears in
your eyes? Are you unhappy?"

Taking her hand in his he tenderly brushed his lips against it. "Anya,
the tears are from happiness. Finally, you are mine, my wife. I love you and
I will always take care of you."

He smiled at her, touched her cheek with his hand. *Such a soft cheek,*
he thought. She leaned toward him, a sensual, feminine, instinctive
movement. He felt the desire rising in him.

"I love you," she said softly. Holding her face in his hands, he kissed
her eyes with fluttery little kisses. Marveling at the new intense feelings
running through her body like a wild burning fire, she moved closer to him
wanting more.

"Sasha," she whispered, "I want to wear my bridal nightgown for you.
"Sasha exhaled a long sigh of desire.

Slowly he undressed her letting his hands run over her body feeling the
silkiness of her skin against his fingers. He unpinned her hair it fell heavily
in golden waves down to her waist. Sasha reached for the gown and handed
it to her. She shivered as she put it on letting it flow over her skin, feeling
its silky coolness. Anxious, nervous, and tingling with anticipation of the
unknown, the bride turned to her groom and untied his cravat. With
trembling fingers, she undid the buttons on his shirt and holding her breath,
she shyly touched the blonde hair covering his chest. Gently, Sasha took her
hand in his and holding her close, led her to the bed. He kissed her mouth
softly, tasting the sweetness of her lips as she trembled and opened her
mouth to him. She reached up and twined her arms around his neck pressing
her young body into his. He slowly slid the straps off her shoulders, letting
the gown fall around her feet, like a bridal veil. She lifted her eyes, no more
the shy violet, but rather a rose unfurling itself in the warmth of his love and
looking deep into his passion-filled eyes, she melted into him.

On a fine morning in early May just as dawn was breaking, Sasha's son fought his way into this world. Hearing the cry of the baby, Sasha stopped his caged pacing and listened for sounds from Anya. Having not heard any, he moved towards the closed bedroom door. The door opened and his mother-in-law appeared. "You have a son and they are both fine." Wiping her hands on a towel, she pushed her hair off her face.

Sasha's throat constricted with emotion. After eleven hours of waiting, fatigue and relief set his muscles trembling. On very uncertain feet, he started through the door past his mother-in-law, and then abruptly stopped. "Can I see them now?"

"You may go in, Sasha. Anya and your son are waiting for you." He released her abruptly and hurriedly stumbled into the bedroom, bumping into Juzia and Marina, who had come to help deliver the baby.

"Juzia," Marina said, "I think that Sasha is the only father in this world."

"You are right, Marina. It does appear that way, does it not?"

Laughing, they joined their mother on her way downstairs to announce the good news to the rest of the family.

Sasha stopped short by the bed. He held his breath and his eyes opened wide. A tender smile formed on his lips at the sight that greeted him. Anya's long hair covered the entire pillow framing her lovely face, creating an illusion of the Madonna and her child. Looking up at Sasha with tired eyes, she held out her hand to him. He knelt beside the bed. "Anya, my darling wife, you gave me a son!" he whispered. "Let me look at him." She gently uncovered the baby. Sasha glimpsed a shadow of blonde hair sparsely covering his perfectly formed little head. One eye opened as if taking his first peek at his father. Sasha's heart filled with emotion. He touched his smooth cheek.

"Shall we name him Nicolaj, as planned?" he asked.

"Yes, Nicolaj is a strong name," she answered, weak with exhaustion. Anya closed her eyes, happiness filling her entire being. She thought back to the day she arrived at the Petrosewicz household as a bride. Adjusting to a new way of life was difficult for her. The house was always bustling with activity. Cooking, cleaning, and washing for the seven brothers and the rest of the family was a never-ending chore. Each day was tiring for Anya, but the nights filled her with happiness snuggling in Sasha's arms.

Yet, there were times when Sasha's frequent hunting trips kept him away for several days and Anya grew lonely. She missed her family. Aniuta was a very kind and loving woman, but her arthritis kept her in bed reading her beloved books most days. To fill her lonely moments, Anya ventured out to the beehives. Her father-in-law welcomed her visits and they became good friends. She never tired of watching the bees at work or helping with gathering the honey.

One day when Sasha was away, Alexander noticed the sadness in her eyes. "Anya," he patted her arm paternally. "Do not look so sad. Sasha will be back soon."

She wiped a tear away from her cheek. "I do miss him, Papa, and I worry that he may get hurt out there in the woods."

Alexander laughed lightly and patted her cheek. "Anya, Sasha has been hunting since he was four years old. His grandfather taught him well. He knows the woods and knows how to use his rifle." He smiled tenderly at her. "Sasha is a free spirit. He needs the freedom of the forest. I think that once you start a family, he will slow down and stay home more often."

Anya blushed at the mention of starting a family. She already suspected she was with child.

With memories flooding her mind, Anya sighed deeply. Tightening her hold on her baby fell into deep sleep.

The next few years were full of love, joy, and sorrow. Nicolaj charmed everyone and became a focal point in everyone's life in the Petrosewicz household. As he grew older, he spent time with his grandfather in his beloved orchards and beehives. Nicolaj was not very fond of bees. The buzzing and flying about scared him, so Grandfather talked to them in a soft voice. The bees seemed to listen as they buzzed around very close to Nicolaj's face, as if responding to his loving words.

Anya joined them at times on their walks and she, too, communicated

42

with the bees. She laughed when they landed on her arm or face without harming her. Anya loved the bees as much as Grandfather did.

Oh, those were good years. Life seemed so rich and easy with family gatherings, weddings, and the birth of children. Most evenings after a hard day's work in the fields, Sasha and his brothers gathered on the porch for the daily merriment. The brothers played their balalaikas and violins, while Sasha sang Russian folk songs. Village neighbors joined the festivities, singing and dancing, eating and drinking vodka straight from the still. Women sat next to their men, knitting scarves, hats and mittens for the children, while the men enjoyed their talk of crops, the weather, and politics.

And then the wheel of fate turned.

Chapter Eight

These were dangerous times. The rumbling of war in Germany was on everybody's mind. The Bolsheviks were rampant, forcing Communism on the people of Russia. Those who defied them were murdered or deported to Siberia—a death sentence in a land of harsh living conditions, a land of ice and snow and vast forests, a land far east of the sun.

All personal beliefs were silenced. Seized property was burned to the ground or occupied by the Bolsheviks. Possessions with meaning were destroyed. Priests and other religious clerics went into hiding, performing the religious rites in secret. Those who were caught were castrated and deported to Siberia, or were murdered. Churches were robbed and burned leaving gaping skeletons of the once majestic structures. The village people were ordered to watch the atrocities performed by the Bolsheviks as they raped and mutilated the Catholic nuns. Anyone caught protesting met the same fate. No one was safe. Landowners, *Kulaki,* went into hiding and when caught, were deported to a monstrous death in Siberia.

It was a clear night. The moon's half face illuminated several horse riders galloping towards the village of Razna, located some thirty miles from Minsk. Razna was home to Sasha's sisters, Irena and Martina, their wealthy husbands Fedor and Mihal, and their children. Fedor owned a very large pig farm and had vast land holdings; Michal owned cattle and horses with numerous acres of much needed wheat. Thus, their fate was sealed as a *Kulak.*

Irena and Fedor were asleep after a hard day working in the fields and tending to the animals. The faint sound of galloping horse's hooves in the distance seemed to Fedor to be a dream. He closed his eyes and turned over embracing his wife, cuddling his face into her neck. He loved her dearly.

Half asleep, his mind went back to the day he asked Irena's father for her hand. How nervous and apprehensive he was to face a man who may

44

not look at the match kindly. Fedor was tall and handsome. His hair was light brown, but in the summer sun it became almost blonde. He was some twenty years older than Irena, a bachelor in his late-thirties who had waited for the right woman to come into his life.

When he met Irena at a church dance he could not erase the vision of her loveliness from his mind. She was only seventeen years old and a very spirited beauty. She danced by him with her golden hair cascading down her back, mesmerizing him with her lovely smile.

When the dance finished, he walked over to her. "Irena, may I have a word with you?" Fedor asked.

"What is it that you want to ask me?" She smiled with a mischievous look in her eyes.

Her direct look into his eyes made him feel like a schoolboy. "Irena," he stammered, "you are the prettiest girl here. You captured my heart from the moment I saw you. I would like to court you."

Leaning against the wall, Irena giggled. Glancing downward she answered, "I would like that very much, Fedor. But you must ask my father for his permission."

From that day on, she was his sunlight.

They married without objection from any of the family members. After all, Fedor was a wealthy man, a good man. Irena gave him five children– two daughters and three healthy sons.

Fedor's dreams shifted to the sound of horses' hooves. They seemed to be closer. He woke with alarm, realizing that it was not a dream. He listened. They were near.

"Irena," Fedor called to his wife, shaking her gently. "Get up, Irena. I hear horses coming this way. I fear that it may be the Bolsheviks. Go and wake the children! Get them to the shelter we built in the woods. Go now." Fedor urged her. "I will run to Mihal's house and warn them to do the same. Hurry, Irena!" He embraced her and kissed her quickly, tasting the tears flowing from her eyes. "If anything happens to me, take the children to your father's house."

She clung to him not wanting to let go. Gently he pushed her away and disappeared into the night. She would remember that last kiss for the rest of her life.

Dressing quickly, Irena's hands shook as she tried to button her shirt. Distraught, she ran to the children's rooms to wake them. They protested loudly, rubbing the sleep from their eyes. "Hurry, children we must run to the shelter and hide there. Follow me, hurry!"

Mihal's house was a half mile away located near the woods away from the main road. At breakneck pace, Fedor ran across the field of high grass and heavy bushes keeping out of sight. Out of breath, frantically he knocked on the door of Mihal's house. "Wake up and open the door!" Fedor kept banging until Michal appeared in the doorway.

"Fedor, what is wrong? Why are you waking us up at this hour of the night? Are Irena and the children all right?"

Fedor pushed Michal inside the house. "Michal, I think the Bolsheviks are on their way here. They must be at my house by now. I told Irena to get the children to the shelter in the woods. Hurry Michal! Get Martina and the children to the shelter with Irena. We don't have a minute to waste."

Michal stood six-feet tall with a powerful built. Hearing the news of approaching Bolsheviks, his knees felt very weak. He knew what could happen to the landowners who resisted the Bolshevik regime. Someone must have reported them of their underground activity.

In a split second his mind went back to the time of his youth, to when as a very young boy of sixteen making passes at young Martina. He knew then that she would belong to him. How lovely she looked as his bride as she floated in his arms in her wedding finery the day they married. Their eyes were only for each other. Martina gave him four strong sons. *How am I to protect them from the Bolsheviks now?*" he wondered. Michal shook his head to clear his mind of the past and ran to wake Martina and the boys.

Martina was sitting up in bed with hair flowing down her back in wild curls as Michal stumbled into their bedroom. "Martina, hurry, you must dress quickly and get the children up." Martina jumped out of the bed.

"Michal, what is happening? What is wrong?" Michal pulled her to him embraced her and kissed her lips quickly.

46

"You don't have a minute to spare! Run to the shelter to join Irena." He gently held her and looked deeply into her eyes. "The Bolsheviks are here! Hurry! I will try to stall them. Run out the back door and into the woods. Hurry, my darling." With a last kiss on her forehead he let her go and ran outside.

Martina quietly gathered the protesting children and slipped out the back door. Running quickly, she pushed on through the trees onto the path leading to the shelter. And after what seemed an eternity, they reached the ravine and Martina saw Irena waiting for them urging them to hurry inside.

Fedor sprinted back to his house and found it empty. As he stepped outside to join his family in the shelter, the first Bolshevik soldier galloped into the yard. The soldier spotted him and fired a shot in his direction. The bullet hit him in the right leg above the knee. Fedor fell and hit his head on the doorstep. In an instant, his world turned into darkness.

Irena and Martina heard the gunshots. The frightened children huddled closer. Irena took Martina's shaking hand and whispered, "I am so worried for our husbands. They should have joined us by now." She looked into Martina's stricken hazel eyes clouding with tears and squeezed her hand. "Martina, we must be strong and wait to see what happens. They may be on their way to join us now. Please, do not cry. It will upset the children. Oh, I wish we knew what was happening!"

Irena prayed as she paced. *If anything happens to my Fedor, I will have no will to live! Hospudzi! God! Please let Fedor and Michal escape safely!*

"Martina, I would like to go to the edge of the clearing. From there I can see the house very clearly. I will be very careful and stay close to the trees. The Bolsheviks will not see me in the ravine."

Martina objected, but Irena was adamant. "I have to know if Fedor and Michal are safe. I have to go."

Martina made the sign of the cross over her chest. "Irena, you must be very careful and don't linger there too long. Stay to the edge of the ravine. Go now and hurry back!"

Irena sneaked outside through the opening in the ground covered by branches and moss. Very quietly, she crept to the edge of the forest, spotted the ravine and jumped in it covering her head with leaves. Peeking out, to her horror she saw flames engulfing the entire house illuminating the driveway as if it was daylight. Irena could see the soldiers running around with torches waving them and yelling obscenities at Fedor. They grabbed him and dragged him into the wagon. His limp, lifeless body covered with blood appeared to be dead.

She covered her mouth with her hand and stifled a scream and the urge to run to him, to see if he was still alive. She fell to her knees moaning, feeling his pain and collapsed on the wet ground burying her head in the musty smelling grass. She lay there weeping and praying to a God that seemed to have forgotten all of them.

Creaking of the wagon wheels pulling away caused Irena to look up. With swollen eyes, she watched in horror as the soldiers, jubilant with the nights work, rode away with her beloved husband. Irena crouched in the ravine until the soldiers were out of sight. With a heavy heart and flowing tears blinding her vision, she crept from the ravine and slowly made it back to the shelter.

When Martina saw Irena's face, she knew that the worst has happened. "Irena, what happened? What did you see? Did Fedor escape?"

Irena collapsed into Martina's arms sobbing uncontrollably. "They took Fedor away in the wagon. I don't know if he was alive. They burned the house. Nothing is left. What are we to do?"

Michal, armed with a hunting rifle, perched in the window watching the driveway. He knew that the soldiers would be on their way to his house by now. The first soldier on his black stallion appeared around the bend in the driveway. Michal aimed his rifle and waited. Three other soldiers with a horse-drawn wagon came into view. Michal froze. In the darkness he was barely able to distinguish a man with hands and feet tied to the wagon. Was it Fedor? Michal sat transfixed on the windowsill wondering what to do. If it was Fedor, then he knew he must try to somehow rescue him.

"Michal Romanowicz, come out and give up. We know you are there.

All the women and the children must come out also! Give yourself up! There is no escape. If you do not, then we will shoot your friend, Fedor. He is in the wagon. Do you hear me?"

Michal's heart filled with hatred for these brutal men. He could not shoot without risking Fedor's life. He sat for another moment willing his body to stop trembling, and then made the decision to give up and plead for Fedor's life.

He stepped out the door with hands raised high. "Please let Fedor go! I will go with you and do as you say."

The soldier glared menacingly at Michal. "Get the women, *Kulak*, bring them out and get them into the wagons. All of you are going to your new luxurious homes in the Siberian wilderness where you can build an ice castle and pretend you are the royalty!" He sneered at Michal and laughing, pointed to Fedor. "See this *Kulak* here? He thinks he is the Prince of Russia, with all his land and big house. The Prince is on his way to wonderland. And so are you, my friend. Now get the women!" he shouted at Michal, waving his rifle impatiently.

"The women and the children are not here, they are visiting their parents. Take me! I will come with you!" Michal shouted. The soldier got off his horse ran to the porch where Michal was standing. Making a lewd gesture, the soldier shouted at Michal, "*Yob Twaju mac!* Son of a bitch! You will come with me dead or alive!"

He pushed Michal causing him to stumble, and with the butt of his rifle hit him on the head. Michal fell back, his head exploding with bright light, and then darkness.

In the early morning Irena and Martina with their children walked back to the burned remains of what were their homes only a day before. Devastated, they picked through the burned and charred rubble trying to salvage anything with meaning.

There was no sign of Fedor or Michal. Irena stood in the middle of what once was her house and raised her hands to Heaven. "Hospudzi, Hospudzi! Why have you forsaken us?"

Broken and weary they gathered their whimpering children together. "Hush, children, don't cry. We will go to *Dziedushka's* house." Irena with purple lines of weariness under her eyes tried to reassure them. "Now, let us look for some transportation. Martina, go in the woods and look for a horse or a cow that might have survived. I will look in the barn for a wagon. Children, you stay right here. Do not whine now. You must help us."

They approached the Petrosewicz house late in the evening. Sasha, alert as always, was first to run outside when he heard the wagon rumbling on the gravel in the driveway. He knew of the Bolsheviks raiding, burning, and deporting people to Siberia. Fear gripped his heart. However, the sight that greeted him was unexpected and it made him stumble back.

Martina and the children were huddled together on a charred wagon they salvaged from the burned barn. Seated on the small seat in front of the wagon was Irena. Haggard and disheveled, with hair hanging from under her babushka over a tear-stained face, she held the reins of a tired horse, which had escaped during the raid into the woods. Her eyes once bright and merry, now stared into nothing. He quickly ran down the steps of the porch.

"What has happened? Where are Fedor and Michal?"

"Sasha," Irena cried, "The Bolsheviks came and took Fedor and Michal away! They burned our homes! Everything is gone. Oh, Sasha, they will be coming this way before long! What are we to do?"

Sasha helped the distraught and scared children off the wagon. They quickly ran to the house as their grandparents were coming out to see what caused the commotion. They stopped short at the sight that greeted them. Their grandchildren's faces were tear-stained and dirty with soot. Irena and Martina were limping behind them, sobbing and holding on to Sasha. Anya and Sasha's brothers appeared in the doorway. Shock and fear took hold of them and all asked questions at the same time.

"Come in the house, everybody," Alexander called anxiously. "Irena and Martina and the children must be tired and hungry. Let them eat and rest. We will talk tomorrow and decide on what to do."

The thundering of numerous horses' hooves approaching the Petrosewicz house at a fast pace was heard breaking the serenity of the moonlit night. Sasha awoke with a start. In an instant, he was alert. He heard his father and brothers running down the hallway and sensed the panic and urgency in their voices and movements. The Bolsheviks had made their way to Byolarussia and now they were on Petrosewicz property.

Anya was awake now, too. Sasha glanced at her and saw panic in her eyes. Her hair disheveled from sleep hung around her shoulders, her face was pale, her hands clenched tightly together.

"Sasha, what is happening? Who could be coming here at this time of the night?" The fear made her voice quiver and her limbs turned to liquid.

"I don't know, Anya. God only knows why anyone would be riding at this hour. But I don't think that they are friendly visitors." He quickly got out of bed and in the dark stumbled, trying to locate his clothes. "I will go and see who it is." He found his pants and pulled them on. "Anya, hurry and go to the children, as they will be frightened," Sasha whispered with urgency in his voice.

Anya jumped out of the bed, pushed her hair back of her head tied into a knot and dressed in a hurry, then ran to the children's rooms. The children were sleeping. She sat next to them on their bed and waited for the rest of the women to gather.

Sasha ran from the bedroom and nearly collided with his father and brothers.

"It must be the Bolsheviks," Sasha's father said in a breathless and quivering voice. "Be ready to fight for our lives."

The brothers looked at each other with frightful understanding and ran to arm themselves with hunting rifles and handguns. Sasha, rifle in hand and his faithful dog Misha beside him, went to the window and gingerly pushed the curtain aside to get a glimpse of the riders.

The moon was high and full, illuminating the sky with silver rays reaching down to embrace the earth. In the shadows, Sasha saw the silhouette of the riders: at least fifty men all armed. The moon shed light on their uniforms. They were Bolsheviks. He broke out in a cold sweat. Fear gripped his heart, knowing that their life of prosperity, peace and tranquility was over.

The shouting and gunshots came closer. To the right side of their house, he saw smoke coming from the beehives. "No! No! Not my father's beloved bees!" he cried.

Smoke and flames erupted from the orchards as their beautiful fruit trees were set ablaze. He glanced towards the barns and his heart froze. The traumatic clucking of the chickens and agonizing squealing of the pigs flashed vivid images of the butchering taking place. The horses escaped into the night. He could hear the slaughtering of their beloved milking cows. Fire quickly transformed the barns into crematoriums. Tears ran down Sasha's face as a wild urge to kill ran through him.

He grabbed Misha, who was baring its teeth and growling, ready to protect its master. Together they snaked through their home away from the windows, making their way to the back door and onto the porch. Sasha fell to his stomach and quietly moved to the railing with Misha beside him. He could hear his father and brothers doing the same. Soon they were beside him. Quietly they huddled together and made their plans to protect their families. But, before they could execute their plans, Bolsheviks surrounded the house. They were heavily armed and ready to kill and rape the women both young and old. There was no way out for the Petrosewicz men; they would have to lay down their arms.

The officer of the regiment pulled his horse to a stop in front of the porch. He was a big man with a scarred face and a big nose that had been broken a few times. A long mustache covered his thin lips; his mouth seemed a constant smirk. Sasha held on to Misha. A sick feeling filled his stomach.

"Seize their weapons," the officer ordered.

Sasha looked at his father and brothers. They knew they did not have a chance of overpowering these men. Slowly and carefully, they laid down their rifles and guns, put their hands up, and stepped off the porch.

"What do you want?" Sasha's father asked. "Why are you destroying everything?"

The officer looked down at him from his huge stallion and spit in his face. "You rich pig! All *Kulak* are enemies of the Communist regime and must pay for resistance."

Sasha's father looked up at the soldier and pleaded. "Take whatever you want, but don't destroy what is left."

"We will destroy whatever we want. Who the hell are you to tell me what to do?" With those words he aimed his gun and fired, killing Sasha's younger brother, Josef. He then aimed the gun at the father. "You will do as you are told or the next bullet will go through your head."

Sasha ran to his brother and cradled his head in his arms, sobbing. Josef, so full of life only a moment ago was still, his beautiful eyes staring forever into nothingness.

The women and whimpering children gathered in the family room heard the shot resound from the porch. They froze with fear. Nicolaj gripped his mother's arms, his eyes wide-open and questioning sensing danger.

"Be quiet, Nicolaj, don't move!" Anya warned him.

Nicolaj nodded and took hold of Marina's hand protectively. The smoke from the burning beehives and the orchards filtered in through the windows. It stung his eyes. The cries of the animals cut through his young senses with a searing pain. His young heart filled with an emotion he did not quite understand. He had only known love and comfort, a quiet life full of music and song. Now strange men, shooting and yelling strange words were shattering it. He knew, too, that his father and *Dziedushka* were out there with his uncles trying to protect them. He wanted to run outside and be with them. After all, he was a man too.

He put his small arm around his mother, comforting her. "It will be all right, *Mamushka*, you will see. Papa will make things right." His small hand was stroking his mother's hair. "He always knows how to make things right."

He looked at her face now grim with worry and tried to make her smile. She put her arm lovingly around him this boy of hers, so sensitive and loving, and kissed his brow tenderly.

Another gunshot sounded. The door flung open with a loud *bang.* A huge officer appeared, holding a gun. "Get out! Everybody, get out!"

Anya grabbed Nicolaj's hand and held onto him tightly. She motioned for the women to follow and slowly they made their way onto the porch lit with the soldier's torches. Anya gasped and stumbled at the sight of Sasha crouching on the floor holding Josef's body. Next to him was his father. Bitter tears were streaming down his face, as he held his other young son.

Anya and Sasha's mother screamed at the sight and ran to the dead men held so tenderly by their loved ones. The officer motioned for the soldiers to hold the two women. They grabbed Anya and Aniuta, twisting their arms painfully behind their backs.

"I'll shoot all your sons if you move again, you sluts!" the officer threatened.

"Please let me hold my sons," Aniuta pleaded. "*Please!* I will do as you say. Just let me hold them for the last time!"

"Please let me hold my sons," he mimicked. "Here," he gestured with his hand at his groin, "hold this!" The soldiers laughed and called out obscenities at the women pointing and gesturing vulgarity.

Alexander's face became red with rage. Hatred for these evil men grabbed him by the throat. For a moment, he had difficulty breathing. He grabbed the soldier's leg with strength he did not know he possessed and brought the soldier down. Desperately, he tried to resist the urge to hit out, to smash that gloating face until it could speak no more.

With the speed of lightning, Sasha and his three brothers sprang into action. Sasha grabbed the officer and with the butt of his gun smashed him on the head. The soldier fell backwards against the porch railing and lay still. Misha snarled and bared his teeth, then pounced on the officer's chest, ready to go for his throat. The officer groaned and opened his eyes. Misha glared at him growling and snarling, showing great teeth ready to strike. Sasha quickly shouted an order, "Stop, Misha!"

Misha reluctantly obeyed the command, moved off the officer and ran into the night as one of the soldiers fired at him. The bullet barely missed its target, lodging into a tree.

The brothers went for the other two soldiers, knocking them senseless to the ground. Aniuta ran to her deceased sons. She cradled their bodies in her arms, sobbing and kissing their eyes shut for the final time.

The commotion attracted the other soldiers who swarmed the porch, surrounding the family with no escape. They grabbed the men, pushed them into the corner of the porch and tied their hands and feet. Mercilessly, they took turns punching and kicking them in the head and ribs. Then they gathered the women and children to the middle of the porch, pushing them, leering, yelling, "Now, you bitches will pay for this!"

Anya, sobbing and terrified, held on to Nicolaj and Marina as she moved with the women. She glanced at Sasha, tied up and bleeding from his head, and mouthed, "I love you."

Sasha looked at her tenderly and with bloodied lips mouthed back, "I love you, too."

The officer, his eyes filled with hatred and contempt, slapped Sasha's face hard, leaving an ugly handprint on his cheek. He then pointed to Sasha's two sisters.

"Get these two bitches and their children to the wagons! We know who you are! You thought that you escaped, you filthy Kulaki? We have your husbands. They are on their way to Siberia now. And that is where you are going." The sisters fell to their knees begging and screaming with agony, "Please! Please let the children stay!"

The officer spat on the ground and snarled. "Let the older ones stay, but the little ones go with you."

Two young soldiers pushed and shoved the bewildered women with their children, as they held on to their mothers crying. Sasha's mother and father watched their daughters and grandchildren herded with horror in their eyes. Blinded by their tears the sisters held out their arms to them. "Please," Irena begged, "let us hold them for the last time. Please!"

One burly soldier with an injured leg slowly limped over to Irena and slapped her hard on her face. "You bitch! You have no 'voice,' woman. You are no more than that pig in the pig pen!" He slapped her again and limped away.

55

Irena held her hand to her face. *I will not cry. I will not cry ever again!*

She gathered her two younger children and with her head held high, she walked to the wagon and helped the children in. Martina followed her with her young son, climbed in, and sat next to Irena. Irena reached for Martina's hands and held them tightly for comfort. They were on their way to Siberia and they would not see their loving family again.

Chapter Nine

Muddy tracks of the soldiers, wagons, left imprints on the hearts of the remaining family. Irena, Martina, and the children were gone from their lives, possibly forever. Gloom and despair fell on the household like a dark curtain.

Sitting by the window, his lifeless face a mask of grief, Alexander was looking out at the destruction. His eyes took in the charred remains of the beehives. No longer did he smile at the sight of a bee buzzing in the yard searching the bloom of the flower in the apple tree. The trees were barren now. Their branches were sticking out like angry fingers reaching out to heaven in despair. Large black crows, with wings spread wide cruised around the slaughtered animals, swooping down to pull a piece of freshly decaying meat then settle down on the branch to feast. Neighbors and family members with somber faces, stood in the yard huddling in small groups, talking in hushed voices, recounting the horrible events.

Coughing from the stench of the decomposing flesh, Alexander nodded his head and whispered to himself. "Yes, it is the end of a life we have known."

The sound of soft footsteps behind him startled him. Soft arms went around his neck. Aniuta bent her head to her husband's, stroking his hair. He leaned back against her and touched his cheek to hers. Then reached up and gently stroked her face. His gentle fingers traced warm tears flowing from her eyes as her quiet sobs of sorrow echoed through the silent house.

"What are we to do now?" Aniuta asked softy.

Without saying a word, he held her face tightly between his hands, for long agonizing minutes.

"I don't know what to do next, Aniuta." Pulling her to him, he sat her on his knees. Gently he pushed her hair off her forehead and said softly. "The Bolsheviks did a good job of destruction here." Coughing, he paused.

"I don't think they will be back. Their evil deed is accomplished. But amazingly, they spared the house." He looked around as if to make sure that he was right. "We have shelter, but no means of survival without our livestock and crops. What is salvaged will barely feed the family through the winter." Aniuta nodded in agreement.

"What are we to do? We cannot put them out!" she cried. "Sasha and Anya have small children. Where will they go?" He felt her despair.

"No," Alexander said. "We can't put them out. We will have to take care of each other the best we can and somehow, with God's help, we will survive until next spring. God will provide."

Two wooden caskets on the pallbearers' shoulders were heavy as lead. They moved slowly, their faces grim and eyes staring ahead as if in a trance. The newly dug grave was beckoning to them; the smell of the black fresh earth surrounding the gaping wide hole, assaulted their nostrils.

Behind them, Alexander, bent with grief was holding his wife by her arm. Step by tortured step they kept moving, their family and neighbors, following in quiet grief.

Choking on his tears, Alexander whispered to Aniuta. "This is like walking towards the Cavalry, to put my sons on the cross." Sobbing, Aniuta hung on to her husband.

"How are we to bear this?" she cried. "My sons, my sons," she moaned. She would never laugh with them or scold them again. They were gone. She shivered with cold. Her blood turned to icy water running through her veins. She was cold. Flashes before her eyes of her boys, lying face down on the porch, their lifeless bodies twisted in bizarre forms. Blood, blood was everywhere.

Someone was lifting her up from the ground, murmuring her name. Alexander wrapped a cloak around her, and kneeling beside her and rubbing her cold hands. "Aniuta," his voice broke through her foggy mind.

She put her hand to his face. Her rock, her steadfast husband, was crying. "Trust in God, Aniuta. He will give us the strength. You must believe that," he whispered.

They laid their sons to rest in a family plot up on a hill overlooking the now burned apple orchard. "One day this orchard will bloom again, but their eyes will not see the glory of it." Alexander whispered. He stood by Aniuta as she knelt in the black dirt to touch the caskets, as if to feel her sons' faces through the wood one last time.

They gathered for dinner of meager rations of salvaged chicken, potatoes, turnip, and carrots. Alexander looked around the table at his remaining family. His face was sallow and his hair seemed to have become gray almost overnight. Sadly, he eyed the food. "Let us say grace," he whispered hoarsely. "Dear God in Heaven, thank you for sparing this house and bless all remaining in it. Open the heaven gates and welcome our two sons. They were good men. Dear God, take care of them. Amen."

Everyone was solemn and quiet, busy with his or her own thoughts. "Papa," Sasha said breaking the silence. "I talked to a man from Zaruwna. He said that Anya and I could find work in *Kolhozy*. They will provide us with a small cabin. There is school for the children and the village where Anya's mother lives is only five miles away." He glanced around the table as if looking for approval. "We can't impose on you, Papa."

Alexander lifted his head with a thoughtful look in his eyes. "Sasha, stay here through the winter. If we are careful in rationing the food, we will have enough to survive and when spring comes, we will talk about it again."

Sasha and Anya readily agreed. They were not anxious to be under a Communist regime.

It was early spring. Sasha could smell it in the air as he enjoyed his long walk home from his job at *Kolhozy*—the Workers Control Compound organized and controlled by the Communist Party. The compound encompassed several acres of pastures on which the seized cattle and other animals grazed. Huge food processing and storage buildings loomed behind the compound where Sasha worked with many of his neighbors from nearby farms and villages. It was backbreaking, pulling feed and grain from full wagons stacked to the limit.

He enjoyed the walk the four miles to and from work through fields of grazing cattle, sheep, and horses. It was a serene time, with false peace and quiet. He knew that it was false because at any moment, it could be shattered with horse riders from the Partisan party or soldiers from the Communist regime.

The upheaval of the war had created many factions: The Communist regime, the German Nazis, and now the Partisans—rebels who worked behind the enemy lines to weaken the opponent's hold on their homeland. The Partisans also supported the military operations of their allies. They performed reconnaissance and sabotage, disturbing enemy movements as much as possible. Partisans did not belong to the regular army, but operated under a military force. Some were renegades, escapees from German prison camps, refugees from the German and Stalin terror. Criminals took advantage of the war and used the Partisans as cover, butchered the men and raped the women with glee. Destruction was their raging force. Sasha was careful not to attract the attention of either party.

At the compound, Sasha's easy manner was contagious from the start. The soldiers liked him and befriended him. Before long, they made him a supervisor of the storage building. On several occasions, they invited him to sing with them during a break in the day, and at times, they gave him extra portions of bacon and flour to take home to his family.

Sasha thought of his Anya, by now home from her job. She and the children would be setting the dining table and waiting for Papa to come home. Oh, how he looked forward to time with his children. *Papa is home!* They would cheer, jumping into his arms with such joy on their little faces, waiting for him to sing to them. Every evening his pretty Marina sat on his lap, looking up at him with her dimpled smile and silky chestnut hair in two long braids that flowed down her back. She was a little beauty who melted his heart. Katrina, blonde, chubby, with blue eyes and pudgy cheeks, would crawl over, pulling herself up onto his other knee. Nicolaj, always sat on the floor beside him begging, *Papa, please sing for us!* Sasha ruffled his hair, so much like his own, as he laughed and sang their favorite Russian folk songs.

"Oj nie wiecier wiedku klonic, ni sasno bushka zwinic.

Oj gary, gary maja luczyna, da garu z taboju ja. "

The children listened attentively, memorizing the lyrics and music, enthralled with their father's singing. Nicolaj and Marina would join in, humming and singing along with him. It was a happy time for them. They managed to enjoy the little they had.

With the Party having destroyed their livestock, they were dependent on rations. Food and milk were scarce, yet each night Anya lovingly prepared their meager dinner. There would be no milk for the children this week. The rations dispensed by the Party had run out and it would be another week before they were able to get more. However, God would provide, as He always did. Sasha had strong faith in Him.

He was nearing home. The setting sun cast bright orange shadows along Sasha's path. His step was light and he was lost in the beauty of the sunset. He did not hear the footsteps behind him. Three Partisans overpowered him so quickly he did not have a chance to fight them off. He struggled fruitlessly as one held him in a chokehold while the other men tied Sasha's arms behind his back with a rough, heavy rope.

Sasha struggled to catch his breath. "Who are you? What do you want with me?" he croaked, his windpipe almost closed off.

"You know who we are;" a familiar voice answered him. "You have been avoiding us too long. It is time you joined our Party."

Sasha recognized the voice of his boyhood friend. "Ambroz?" Sasha could barely whisper. His mind was foggy from lack of oxygen. He had heard rumors of Ambroz' activities with the Partisans, but he did not want to believe it.

"Is it you, Ambroz? What are you doing?" Sasha croaked again. The arm choking him did not let up. "I am your friend. Why are you doing this to me?"

Ambroz did not reply, but came from around the back and stood in front of Sasha, a sneer on his round, scarred face. He was not tall, but had a wiry body and muscular shoulders. His red hair was long and unkempt. With hands on his hips, he laughed cruelly, seemingly enjoying Sasha's fear.

61

"You are coming with us, my friend. We heard that you are a Communist sympathizer! That makes you a traitor and not a friend of mine!" bellowed Ambroz.

Sasha looked sadly at his friend. "Ambroz, we grew up together. How can you do this?" He tried to free his hands, but the Partisan punched him in the stomach. Sasha doubled over, trickles of blood formed on his lips. "You know me, Ambroz, I am not a traitor. I don't take sides. I prefer freedom."

Ambroz sneered, slapped Sasha's face and barked to the other two men, "Take this bastard away! He is nothing to me!"

Sasha panicked as they roughly pushed him through the bushes. He struggled with the rope binding his hands, thinking of Anya and their children at home, waiting for him, worried and frightened. Abductions like this had become all too commonplace. Many women were left waiting for their husbands or sons, who were never to return. Now his Anya, four months pregnant, would be one of them. *How will she survive if I cannot get free?* Sasha kept trying to free his hands, but the rope was too tight, cutting off the circulation and causing numbness. Then, in the shadows of dusk, he saw the horse-drawn wagon guarded by five more armed and dangerous Partisans. They were too many to fight.

They dragged him onto the wagon. Lying face down, the dirty straw strewn over the flooring stuck to his face, the smell making his hungry stomach sick.

Dusk was approaching; the sun touching the horizon in a glorious orange plume as the heavy wagon made its way slowly through the woods. The wheels creaked in protest as the path, rutted and with huge roots like gnarly fingers, made the journey difficult. The rocking and jostling of the wagon caused Sasha to bump his head repeatedly on the floor. He did not know where they were taking him. Each time he lifted his head to look, a Partisan's boot found its mark in his ribs. Through squinted eyes, he watched them, seated around him with rifles pointed at his head, a bottle of vodka passing back and forth. They jeered and laughed at Sasha, spitting at him, kicking him for no reason other than to satisfy their own sadistic pleasure.

It was getting dark now; the horses were snorting and heaving from exertion. Finally, the creaking wagon wheels stopped. They had arrived at their destination. The Partisans jumped out of the wagon, dragging Sasha with them, making him stumble and fall. Hooting with laughter they lifted him up, but his knees buckled under him. Pulling him to his feet, they led Sasha to a dark log cabin.

Ambroz knocked repeatedly on the door until an old man answered it cautiously. Recognizing Ambroz, a toothless grin broke on his prune-like face.

"Come in. Come in."

In the dimly lit entrance, Sasha observed stairs leading to a second floor. The dining room was to his right. The kitchen and living area was to the left. He made a mental note of the layout. It was difficult to distinguish if anyone was there due to the poor lighting, but Sasha could hear voices and a commotion coming through the door.

Ambroz grabbed Sasha by the shoulders and pushed him into the living room where a sinister-looking man was waiting. He was tall, well built, with muscular arms and a heavyset body. Brushed back from his forehead was his light brown hair. Dark circles under his eyes revealed lack of sleep and his skin was sallow from lack of outdoor light. Sasha scanned his uniform. No decorations of great distinction. Sasha wondered just how strong was this Partisan Army.

Ambroz saluted the man, despite the commonness of his uniform. "This man is a traitor. He refuses to join us. I will leave him to your judgment. Do with him as you want." Ambroz saluted, turned on his heel, and left.

Sasha waited, his hands still tied behind his back. The officer stared at him, his eyes searching Sasha's face with a hint of recognition. He motioned for Sasha to follow him into the adjacent room. Closing the door behind them, he turned to Sasha.

"I know who you are." He stared into his eyes. "Your father and I were friends. He was a good man who died, unfortunately, before his time. If he were here with us, I know he would make you see things as they are." With his hands clasped behind him, he paced the floor in front of Sasha. "We have to fight the Communists from taking everything we worked for. Don't you see that?"

Sasha stared at the man. A glimpse of his father and Mr. Michalewicz in the memory of Sasha's mind showed him two good friends. Sadness overcame him. "Mr. Michalewicz, I remember you now. My father spoke very highly of you." Sasha looked directly into his eyes. "When you visited, you brought us candy." A sad smile appeared on his lips. "How are your wife, Jadzia, and your family?"

Mr. Michalewicz was annoyed. He did not want to remember his friends or his past life. "My family is well," he replied gruffly.

"My father had much respect for you. So in his memory, tell me now, are you the head of the Party?"

"Yes, I am in charge. We have been working against many odds to free our people from the Communist regime. I need more men. Men like you."

Sasha shook his head. "Mr. Michalewicz, I can't do that. I don't think that our small groups can fight the huge Communist regime. What you are striving for is to no avail. I have a family and I want to go home to them. I want to protect and care for them as best I can and in my own way."

Mr. Michalewicz looked sadly at Sasha. "I'm sorry, Sasha. I can't let you go. If you don't want to fight with us, then you will stay here and work until we don't need you anymore. I am doing this out of respect to your father. Otherwise, you would be killed for refusing."

Sasha thought for a moment, "I don't have much choice, do I?"

"No, my friend, you don't. You will be guarded closely. I want you to understand that. So, please be careful. Do not try anything foolish and do not try to escape. I will do my best to protect you from the rest of the men."

"I understand, and I will do my best to stay alive," Sasha answered gravely.

The two men looked at each other and knew they would survive whatever comes their way. However, Sasha also knew his words were empty. He knew he would escape.

For four interminable months, Sasha looked for any opportunity to escape. It troubled his mind and his heart the anguish his family was suffering not knowing if he was dead or alive. He wondered, too, just how much longer the Partisans would tolerate his resistance to join their party. He figured his willingness to labor hard with the jobs they put before him had kept him alive these months. As if reading his thoughts, Ambroz came in, slamming the door behind him.

His old friend paced before him, his face red with anger. "Sasha, we brought you here four months ago. Our patience is running out and so is your time." He moved close to Sasha's face. Smelling his bad breath, Sasha backed away slightly. "You have the choice, right now, of joining us or face the consequences of being a traitor." His sneer revealed rotten teeth.

Sasha, gaunt and pale, looked at his old friend. "Ambroz, what you are doing is to no avail. The Communists will not prevail. You and the rest of the party will be deported to Siberia. I will not join your party."

"Oh? So you know our fate?" Ambroz shouted. "Think about your own." He paced, agitated. "You are the one who does not have much choice. Your wife is expecting soon. Do you not want to get home to her?"

The reminder of Anya saddened Sasha. Ambroz, noticing the sadness in his eyes, played his hand.

"I saw her, walking to work the other day. She certainly is a beauty, your wife. Even with her swollen stomach. Yes, quite a beauty!" He smacked his drooling lips, jeering. "All the men talk about her, how they would love to have a chance with her."

Sasha's face reddened with anger. He wanted to grab this swine around his neck and choke him until he no longer could breathe. He held his arms at his side, willing his hands to stay still.

"Oh, do not worry, my friend. I am sure she is a loyal woman. I am sure she will not even give a second glance at anyone. Although, raising a family by alone is difficult. I am sure she is managing. However, with a new baby coming soon, how will she provide for her family?" Ambroz smiled cruelly.

"No, no, I'm sure she will stay loyal to you. All those men, all their offers to take care of her and her children, your children keep her safe, ease her loneliness." He paused for full effect. "Yes, you are a lucky man, Sasha, to have a woman like Anya."

Sasha did trust his Anya. He knew without a doubt her love for him was forever. He felt sorry for his old friend. He was so desperate, so willing to employ any means for his beliefs, even when it meant betraying an old friend. "Ambroz, our way of life is gone forever. Why don't you see that? It will never be the same." Regret and sorrow reflected in Sasha's eyes. "We must accept those facts and survive the best way that we can."

Sasha's calmness agitated Ambroz. "*Job Tajo mac,* Sasha! You son of a bitch. You are wrong!" he yelled. "We will fight. We will win and you will pay for refusing!" With that statement, Ambroz pushed Sasha out of his way and stomped out of the cabin.

The small, log cabin was deep in the forest, surrounded by tall pine trees and heavy brush. It had a dirt floor and bars across the one window facing the wooded area. He did not know exactly where he was or how far he was from Sorojevsko, but overhearing conversation from some of the men, he had a sense of where he may be. He knew by the faint, soothing sounds of flowing water that a river was not too distant.

Deep in thought, he stood in the middle of the poorly lit room. An oil lamp on a wooden table illuminated the bed, its sagging mattress home for many bed bugs that came out at night to feed on his flesh. He made his plan: he would escape. He would follow the river and find his way home.

Sasha walked to the window and opened it quietly. He listened. No one was nearby. He walked over to the wall and retrieved the knife he had hidden between the logs and, as he did each night, started to chip away at the cement holding the bar. With each scratching noise he stopped to listen, worrying that someone might hear him. Grabbing the steel bar, he began to shake and pull on it. His eyes widened with surprise and joy; there was movement! Elated, hope took root in his heart.

I will get out of here. I must, before Anya has the baby.

"Nicolaj, I have to go to work now," Anya said to her son. "Please take care of your sisters." She pushed the hair off Nicolaj's forehead thinking how lucky she was to have this boy help with the girls and all the chores. At eight years of age, he took the responsibility as the man of the house. "You are my big helper, you know. Thank you, my darling son."

Anya looked at her son tenderly and kissed his cheek. Her own face, once with rosy cheeks, was white and pinched. She was no longer smiling. She was tired and haggard, her expression sad and grim. The once sparkling blue eyes had lost their glitter when the Partisans captured her Sasha. Her chestnut hair, still long and beautiful, braided and wound tightly around her head, a remembrance of lost youth. With dry, rough hands, she tied her shawl around her neck, and slipped into her threadbare coat, sagging on her thin body despite being heavy with her fifth child. Anya gathered her protesting and clinging children into her arms, kissed them goodbye and gently caressed their pretty, little faces, promising to be back soon.

She stepped out into the cold bitter winter and bent her head against the wind, which swept down on her. Dead leaves scurried past her, brown and brittle, catching and chattering in the doorways. The wind brought with it the sharp scent of plowed fields. She began the four-mile walk to the *Kolhozy* where she worked cooking breakfast for the many soldiers and workers. Her feet slid on the frozen ground with patches of ice strewn around like squares in a quilt. The cold penetrated her worn out shoes, her toes aching and numb. Pushing her work scarred bare hands deep into her coat pockets to keep warm Anya hurried down the treacherous and ice-covered road.

Every morning she thought about Sasha as she made her way to the *Kolhozy*. However, today felt different. She felt consumed by her loneliness. A tear found its way onto her wind-burned cheek, freezing into a crystal.

"Where is my Sasha now?" she cried out.

There had been no news of him. She did not know if he was dead or alive. With so many men disappearing, the belief was that they were in labor camps. She wanted to believe it was so.

She remembered the night the Bolsheviks stormed in and destroyed the lives of the Petrosewicz family. In her mind's eye, she could still see the officer standing on the porch, so huge and menacing, blood dripping from his head from Sasha's blow, red rivulets flowing between his fingers. She could still see the sneer on his scarred face as he stepped over Sasha's dead brothers.

"If any of you cause any resistance you will face the same fate!" He warned. "Let this be a lesson to those who do not obey the Communist rule."

She remembered crying as she watched Sasha's two sisters and their small children being taken away to meet their fate in Siberia. Their terrified faces crying out in silent desperation.

Anya recalled seeing Sasha's father walking through the burned orchards and his beloved beehives that next morning. His face twisted in pain, tears falling heavily down his cheeks. Sobbing, he fell to his knees and raised his hands to heaven. "*Hospudzi, Hospudzi!...Paczumuty zabyl nas.* Why have you forsaken us?"

She remembered how Aniuta rushed to her husband and knelt on the ground beside him, her arms wrapped around him, tenderly rocking him back and forth until his tears subsided. "What kind of monsters are these people to do such evil?" he asked his wife.

Aniuta gently took him by the arm and helped him to his feet. "People do strange things for greed and power. We will survive this somehow."

Three months later Sasha's father died in his sleep. Anya believed he had truly died of a broken heart. He joined his two sons on the hill overlooking the orchard.

Aniuta and Anya became the strength of the household. Their family began to grow once again. Katrina was born a pretty baby girl with blonde hair and blue eyes, full cheeks and a chubby little body. Nicolaj fell in love with the tiny cherub and Marina was in awe of her. Like her brother, the new baby made her feel very grown up and protective. Now *she* was the older sister.

Spring had arrived and with the new baby and very little food to go around, Sasha and Anya desperately tried to find a way to survive. Weary and discouraged Sasha sat at the kitchen table facing Anya. His face was

68

gaunt and worry lines around his eyes were prominent. He wiped the sweat off his face.

"Anya, it is time to go and find work at the *Kolhozy*." Sasha announced quietly. Anya's face showed concern. She held her hands tightly, however, hope of seeing her mother again sprang into her heart and a thin smile appeared on her lips. "Oh, Sasha, we will stop at my mother's house and rest there until you find work." She grabbed his hands with urgency.

"We don't want to impose on her, Anya." Sasha said gently. "We should go straight to the *Kolhozy* compound."

Stricken, Anya pleaded, "Please, Sasha, I have not seen my mother in two years. Please, she won't mind. We will not be a burden to her." Tears welled up in her blue eyes as she pleaded.

Sasha hugged her tightly. "Anya, I can't bear to see more tears in your eyes. I think we have cried a river already. We will go to your mother's."

They made their way slowly, the old horse struggled to pull the wagon laden with their meager belongings. Nicolaj, Marina, and Katrina huddled together in the corner of the wagon bouncing off the wall each time the wheels went over a rut in the road. They were hungry and thirsty; the sparse dry bread they ate for lunch did not satisfy them.

After a long harrowing day and night of travel, the sight that greeted them made them gasp with despair. The willow trees that graced the driveway were no longer there. No doubt the soldiers used them for firewood. Only stumps remained with gaps between like an old woman's rotten teeth. The once majestic house was now in need of repair. Sections of the house were scorched; roof shingles hung loosely in numerous places. Several windows had broken glass; jagged pieces remained in the frames creating a sinister look to the house. The soldiers and their horses had trampled gardens that were previously so lovingly cared for by Anya's mother. The shrub trees were neglected and dry. There was little life left of the greenery and flowers.

Anya and Sasha walked slowly, remembering their day of engagement and the beauty of this home with all the glory of family life and love.

Lost in her memories, Anya was nearing the *Kolhozy*. In the distance, she could see the soldiers with rifles on their shoulders patrolling the grounds. Shortly after they arrived at Rozalia's home, Sasha found a cabin in Surnaya, a village near the commune where they now lived. Their lives were destroyed; everyone was reduced to working in a slave capacity for the Communist Party. It was about survival now. Russians were people with innate strength, people who were proud and honest, not afraid of hard work. They worked their own land, milked their own cows, and raised their own cattle, benefited from the fruits of their own labor. Now, everything went to the Communist community. It was a concept difficult to accept.

Anya entered the compound. The soldiers stared at her. She was a beauty despite being heavy with a child. Pointing at her stomach, they made rude remarks about her pregnancy. Keeping her head down, she noticed a tall soldier walk toward her. She kept walking, ignoring him. He came besides her almost touching her. She sidestepped him, but he took her arm. Stiffening she looked up at him. Laughing brown eyes looked down at her. "Don't worry. I am not going to hurt you." He squeezed her arm reassuringly. "I will walk with you so the soldiers will leave you alone." Anya was grateful, but not totally convinced that this soldier meant no harm. "*Spasiba tovarysz,*" the soldier gave her a warm smile. "I have a sister, she is pregnant also. I would not want anyone to make fun of her." Anya quickened her step as she continued walking with him by her side until she reached the building where she cooked for the soldiers.

She entered the gloomy building feeling the warmth from the kitchen, took off her shawl and her coat, and walked over to the stove where the fire was crackling. Stretching her frozen hands above the stove to warm them, Anya stared into the flames wondering where Sasha may be. Her eyes clouded over with helpless, silent tears slid unbidden and unchecked. With cold fingers, she wiped one shining tear away and put her hand back over the stove.

Sasha, where are you? I need you my darling. The baby will be here soon. Come home. She missed him desperately and prayed to God that he was still alive.

FAR EAST OF THE SUN

With a dull knife, Sasha continued chipping away at the cement in the window. The progress was slow and he was anxious and worried about Anya. "She must be close to giving birth," he thought. Tonight he would make his move. He sat on the sagging bed and waited for the lights to go out in the cabins of the compound. When all went dark, he blew out his oil lamp and felt his way to the window. Now, with a pounding heart and adrenaline racing through his veins, Sasha gave the loosened bar one more tug. It moved. He tugged at it again with all his strength left in him. It did not move this time. He was perspiring profusely. He wiped his brow and took another deep breath. "Come on, you son of a bitch! I have been chipping at you for a month. Come on now. Loosen up!" The bar kept its hold. He banged on it with his fist, then grabbed the one chair and flung it against the bar and walked away in frustration.

A crumbling noise stopped him. He looked back and hooted with joy. The bar was hanging loose from the window. He grabbed the bar and moved it to the side. Breathing heavily, he pushed himself through it, dropping onto the wet, cool grass.

The darkness was like a heavy coverlet with the moon asleep behind the clouds. Sasha's tired eyes tried to distinguish which way to go. He crouched along the wall, stepping carefully on the dry leaves while keeping his focus on the sleeping guard. He stopped within a few feet from the guard and looked around cautiously. Not seeing any other guards, Sasha took a deep breath and like a panther leaped at the guard, grabbing him by the throat, choking him with all his strength. The guard went limp. Sasha grabbed the rifle and ran quickly for the woods. In the darkness he stumbled and fell, scratches from the brush stung his legs and arms. Sasha sat on the green moss beside a huge tree trunk, catching his breath and listening.

"Etu starnu! Etu starnu! Znalez jeho. Find him."

The guards were in pursuit. Sasha jumped up and ran in a direction he prayed would lead him to the river, pushing through low branches, tripping over tree stumps scattered along the path. A faint, distant sound stopped him. The river was near. Sasha headed in the direction of the rippling sound until he came upon the bank of the river. Stopping for a second, he focused his hearing on other sounds in the night, listening for the guards' voices. All was quiet. Had they give up the chase?

He was not sure which direction to follow so he decided to head for the downhill path of the river. He inhaled the fresh air deeply as he walked, breathing in the smell of freedom. He hummed softly one of his folk songs, one his children and his Anya loved him to sing. The possibility of seeing his family again gave him strength. He walked and walked until exhaustion overtook his spirit. Feeling secure, Sasha settled on the soft moss carpet of a huge birch tree. He covered himself with dry leaves and settled into an attentive sleep.

The birds chirping happily as they welcomed the new day woke Sasha with a start. He shielded his eyes from the sun's brightness and looked around cautiously for any sign of the Partisans. All was quiet. Sasha stood, stretching his body stiff from the damp night air.

Crack!

Sasha dove to the ground; his ears perked.

Crack! Crack!

Whoever it was, they were near. Staying close to the ground, he noticed that the birds had not fled their branches, had not sensed a danger to them. Sasha lifted his head slowly. *There!* Lowering his head, he waited for the figure to appear. Then he saw the wide eyes watching him. It was a deer, its ears standing up, listening for any danger, ready to flee. Sasha stood up slowly. "Hello, my friend. I will not harm you." As if understanding Sasha's words, the deer lowered its ears and began to nibble the leaves of a nearby bush.

Sasha began his walk toward home. The bend of the river was familiar to him and he knew he was near. In the distance, he could hear a dog barking and voices of children playing. Sasha began running. Soon he was upon the familiar buildings of the village.

He made his way carefully past the *Kolhozy* hoping to see Anya at work. He walked slowly, the anticipation of seeing her quickened his heartbeat. With his eyes downcast and darting in all directions, he avoided inquisitive stares. He did not see her and yet he could not risk asking

72

anyone where she could be. Disappointed and worried that Anya may have given birth already, or that something might have happened to his family, Sasha quickened his pace. His heart pounded harder and faster with every step. Had his family been deported to Siberia? How would he know? He passed several people he knew, but was afraid to engage them in conversation for fear they may report him. He was nearing his house now. His eyes misted at the sight of it. He noted that the grass and the weeds were taking over the yard. He did not see any activity. The children were not outside playing as was normal. Alarmed, he ran toward the house.

Misha, very old now and lying in the yard, was alerted by the sound of running footsteps. Trotting to the edge of the yard, the dog sniffed the air, taking in the familiar scent of its master. Misha bounded towards Sasha with the spryness of a pup, whining and barking. Sasha stopped and knelt down to pet his faithful dog.

"Misha, my old friend, I am so glad to see you!" He stroked his head noting that Misha's legs were not too steady. He was getting old. He hugged him with fond memories crowding his mind. Misha, as if sensing Sasha's wistfulness, lapped his face, his tail wagging joyfully.

"Misha, you are still the greatest protector of the family."

Misha barked excitedly, and on wobbly legs bounded for the house as if to show Sasha the good job he had done.

Sasha opened the door and slowly entered the house. Anya's mother came out from the bedroom having heard the dog barking. She screamed in fright. The raggedy man with long hair and unshaved beard standing in front, she did not know. She tried to slam the bedroom door on him.

"Rozalia, it is I, Sasha." He pushed his hair aside from his face and smiled at her.

She gasped, "Sasha? Is it really you?"

He nodded, smiling. "Where is Anya?" he asked anxiously. "I did not see the children in the yard. Is anything wrong?"

Rozalia stood still she put her hand to her mouth as if afraid to say anything. Sensing that something was terribly wrong, Sasha pushed her aside and headed into the bedroom. He stopped at the sight of Anya lying on the bed, very still and very pale. On the floor beside her were his three children. Beside them was a Russian Wolf Hound puppy sitting quietly looking at Sasha as if wondering who this man may be.

Motioning to the frightened children to be quiet, Sasha quickly walked to the bed and gently whispered to Anya, "*Maja Anya ja Cibie Miluju!* My Anya, I love you!"

Anya opened her eyes. "Sasha?" she whispered. She blinked her eyes and opened them wide again. "I am not dreaming?"

Sasha enfolded her in his arms. "No, you are not. I am home now." His trembling hands stroked her hair as the tears flowed down his cheeks into the overgrown beard and down on Anya's face. She wiped the tears from his eyes and called to the children, "Your father is home!"

Without hesitation, Nicolaj ran into his father's arms. Marina, not sure at first, followed Nicolaj. She stood in front of him and looked deeply into her father's eyes as if making sure it was he. Recognizing the smiling cornflower blue eyes, she reached out and wrapped her arms around his neck, kissing him all over his face. Katrina quickly followed her sister. She, too, was not sure of this bearded man. However, she cuddled up to him, looking curiously at his unshaven face and filthy, dirty clothes. The puppy followed them, wagging her tail and sniffing Sasha's shoes.

"What is her name?" Sasha asked, reaching out to pat her furry head.

"Layka," Nicolaj answered.

"Layka is a nice name! Who named her?"

"I did, Papa," Katrina blurted out excitedly. Sasha turned to Katrina and stroked her hair. "Katrina, you chose a fine name. I am very proud of you." He leaned and kissed her rosy cheek.

"Where did you get her?" Sasha asked.

"We found her abandoned in the fields," Nicolaj answered. "Mama said that we could keep her because Misha is getting very old."

As if knowing they were discussing her, Layka leapt on to Sasha's lap and licked his face. Sasha laughed and scratched her behind her ears.

Tears streamed down Sasha's face as he held his beloved children and the puppy. With Marina still in his arms, Sasha sat on the bed next to his

Anya, studying her face. Her sorrowful look told him: the baby had died. Tears filled her blue eyes and ran down her pale cheeks.

Sasha put Marina down and gathered Anya into his arms. He held her until her tears ceased. "Anya, what happened to the baby?"

Anya went still in his arms. She lifted her head and looked deep into his eyes. "The baby lived only a couple of hours. He was born with the umbilical cord wrapped around his neck. My mother tried to revive him, but it was too late. Oh, Sasha, we had a baby boy." Sasha sucked in his breath and buried his head on Anya's shoulder. Sobs of grief wracked his body. She held him until he could cry no more.

"Did you give him a name?"

Anya nodded. "Yes, I named him Johnny."

Anya's grief for her little Johnny had consumed her. Her mind felt dull, wrapped in flannel, like the white flannel shroud one wrapped a child. She had held him for such a short time, his dark blue eyes looked into her blue ones just once, as if recognizing his mother with the want of memorizing her. Then the convulsions began, shaking his little body, making his blue lips tremble. He closed his eyes and never opened them again.

Anya's mother, although she was a midwife, did not know how to save her tiny grandson. She wrapped him in a warmest blanket so that he would not be cold in his wooden little coffin. It was foolish, but it gave her comfort to know that he would be warm. His little body was so thin and frail under her hands as she touched him for the final time. They quietly buried him. Nicolaj, Marina and Katrina stood next to the little casket, crying for the loss of their baby brother as Anya's mother whispered some prayers for his departed soul.

Sasha kissed her brow. He mourned the son he would never know, nor nurture to manhood. He closed his eyes and promised himself that he would survive regardless of what may happen in his life. Somehow, he would find a way to bring his family to a better place where there is peace and freedom.

Anya touched Sasha's gaunt face. His cornflower blue eyes, once sparkling and bright, were now sad and dull. "Sasha, we thought that you were dead. No one would tell us anything, and we did not ask too many people for fear of drawing attention to us. Tell me what happened to you and where you were all this time."

"I will tell you everything when the children are in their beds and asleep. I do not want them to know anything in case they are questioned by the authorities."

Nicolaj was curious as to where his father had been. "Please, Papa, you can tell me." He stood up straight, showing how tall he was. "I took care of Mama and my sisters while you were gone. I am not afraid of anyone!"

Sasha ruffled his hair. "Nicolaj, you are a good son and I thank you for taking care of everyone. However, I want you to understand that there is a very good reason why I do not want you to know certain things. It is better that way. You must trust me." Nicolaj's face took on a stubborn look. "Nicolaj, take that look off your face. I am trying to protect you. You must believe that."

Nicolaj's eyes filled with tears. He nodded his agreement and smiled at his father. "I believe you, Papa."

"Did your sisters listen to you?"

"No, the girls didn't always listen to me, but they were very good and behaved most of the time."

Sasha laughed and kissed his son's forehead.

Sasha looked at his Marina, so beautiful with those dimpled cheeks. He knew that this daughter of his heart would be the caretaker of her siblings all her life. He kissed her cheek tenderly and told her to take his sweet Katrina to bed.

Anya's mother ushered the protesting children and the puppy to the one bedroom they all shared leaving Sasha and Anya alone together.

"Anya, I know you are not well, however, we must leave here for awhile. Our friend Ambroz is one of the Partisans." Shock and surprise appeared on Anya's pale face. "I was astonished to see him also. He acted as if he never knew me and treated me as a traitor," Sasha said bitterly. "He and the other henchmen will be looking for me. If they find me, they will kill me and kill all of you as well." He stroked her hair lovingly afraid for all of them. "We must make plans and leave as soon as we can."

76

"Sasha," Anya whispered. "It is hard to believe that Ambroz would join those thugs. I saw his sister just the other day, and talked to her. She didn't say anything about Ambroz being gone. Maybe she does not know of his activities. I wonder if his parents are aware?" She thought for a moment. "They would be devastated. I know that they don't agree with the Communists forcing us to their beliefs." She grabbed Sasha's hand, holding it tightly. "We must be very careful, Sasha. It won't take them long to catch up with you here."

He held her close. "Anya, we will do whatever is necessary to stay alive." He kissed her lips. "We must leave in the morning. Maybe we can go to your mother's home for a while. I can hide there until they stop searching for me. Speak with her. Get her advice."

"It would be good to go home again. My brothers will help hide you."

As if sensing her daughter's impending request, Anya's mother entered the room "Anya, I was thinking. They will be looking for Sasha before long." She stood and chewed her lip pensively. "Come to our house and stay until they give up the search. We built a basement for hiding. Sasha can hide there when danger approaches."

Anya looked at her mother gratefully. "Thank you, Mama. We will try to be no burden to you."

Rozalia walked over to her beloved daughter and gently kissed her thin cheek. "Anya, my child, you don't have to thank me. But we must hurry and leave soon."

Sasha and Anya awoke early and with a sense of urgency packed their belongings. Anya's mother tended to the children, urging Nicolaj to hurry and help with the packing. They ate a meager breakfast of bread and butter and shared two eggs.

Nicolaj helped his mother and grandmother load the wagon while Sasha harnessed the horse and hitched the wagon. They covered their belongings with burlap bags, stacks of hay and bags of potatoes in case the authorities spotted them. Anya and her mother sat between piles of hay and placed the children on their laps covering them with blankets. Sasha lifted old Misha into the wagon and Layka followed happily wagging her tail and licking the children's faces.

"Papa," Nicolaj insisted, "I want to sit up front with you." His eyes were big with excitement. "I will drive the wagon in case you need to hide. I know how, after all, I did all the driving when you were gone."

Sasha's eyes clouded with tears. A son of his has taken on the responsibilities of a man at such a young age. How proud he was of him. He ruffled his blonde hair. "Nicolaj, you can drive until you get tired, then I will take over." He took his son's face into his hands and looked deeply into his eyes. "You have been very busy taking care of everyone. Now it is time for you to sit back and spend time with your sisters."

Marina heard the conversation and with some excitement tugged at her father's sleeve. "Papa, Nicolaj is teaching me how to read. I can write some letters and draw a flower!" Her smile melted Sasha's heart. "When can I go to school, Papa? I want to learn about Stalin, too. Nicolaj said that Stalin is our protector and our God. Is it true, Papa? Do you pray to Stalin?"

Sasha was appalled at hearing his little girl say such things. "Nicolaj, what is this I am hearing? Did your teacher tell you this?"

Alarmed, Nicolaj replied, "Yes, Papa. The teacher told us to pray to the God that we believed in and ask for bread and butter. We all prayed... and prayed... there was no bread given to us. We were hungry and were waiting for our breakfast. The teacher said that God did not want to bother with us and that he forgot about all of us. Therefore, the teacher told us to pray to Stalin. We did. The school workers brought us freshly baked bread and fresh creamy butter and big glasses of fresh milk. It was so good. Then, she told us to say thank you to Stalin. The teacher said that we must pray to him as we did to our God. She said that our God does not exist anymore. We all must be very thankful to Stalin. He loves us like a father. Does he Papa?"

Sasha could not believe what he was hearing. Yet, he was not surprised. He heard of these stories from other people.

Anya and her mother were listening to the conversation and they looked at each other with horror in their eyes. Could this be true? Was the government using such techniques to brainwash the children?

"You should not believe what they tell you about Stalin," Babushka said to Nicolaj. "Listen to your Mama and Papa. They tell you the truth."

Nicolaj gave the reins to his father and crawled into the wagon where he laid down and closed his eyes, thinking and trying to make sense of it all.

Carefully and quietly, they made their way through the village as the sun rose behind them, the creaking wagon jostling over the narrow, cobblestone road. As Sasha guided the horse through the back roads, the children and Anya slept despite the wagon bouncing over tree roots and muddy tracks in the ground.

The last golden rays of sun shone through the clouds as dusk descended on the weary travelers. Trees extended their branches high into the sky, casting eerie shadows along the dirt road, and gusts of cold wind mixed with rain chilled the children. The shadows and cries of animals in the forest scared them.

Dusk turned into velvety darkness. Poor visibility slowed them down and there were two more miles before they would reach the road leading to Anya's girlhood home. There seemed to be no end to the dense forest. Fear gripped Sasha's heart. Was he lost? In the distance he heard the howling of the wolves. "Dear God," he prayed, "let me find my way out of here soon." As if in answer to his prayers, slivers of moon streaked through the trees illuminating an open field and a road. Sasha's eyes opened wide, a big grin formed on his gaunt face.

"Anya, I see the road!" He almost shouted with excitement and urged the horse to go faster. The horse, as if recognizing the lane, shook its great head, snorted, and quickened its step.

As the house came into full view, Rozalia cried out in happiness at being home. The wagon slowly came to a stop in front of the house. Sasha jumped off the wagon with Nicolaj behind him. Together they helped the children, the women and Misha, as Layka jumped off barking happily. She had spotted a rabbit and bounded after it into the woods.

The front door creaked open slightly. Antos peered through the crack, afraid of whom it may be. In the shadows of the night, he saw a wagon and movement with a man, two women and children. Puzzled, he opened the door wider. He could not believe his eyes. Was it his family unloading their baggage? He ran to them.

"*Mamushka*, what has happened? Why are you here in the middle of the night?" Astonished and full of questions, he turned to his brother-in-law. "Sasha, you are safe! We thought you were dead or sent to Siberia. What happened? Where were you?"

Sasha grabbed Antos in a bear hug. "Antos, I will tell you as soon as we make the women comfortable and feed the children. We will talk and make plans for us to hide for a long while."

Antos placed his arm around Sasha's shoulder, feeling the thinness of his body. Together, they unloaded the meager belongings from the wagon.

"Nicolaj, come here. I want to look at you," Antos called to his nephew. Nicolaj quickly ran down the steps and stood in front of his uncle. "You have grown! I almost didn't recognize you. Can you take charge of bringing these things into the house?"

Nicolaj, feeling very important, gave Antos a big smile. "I know how to take care of things, Uncle." He handed a few light items to Marina to carry and a small parcel to Katrina. They ran up the stairs gladly helping their big brother.

The house inside was comfortable enough. The furniture, which the Party did not take, was still in good shape. The burning fireplace warmed the house from the October chill.

Trying to warm her hands, Anya sat on the sofa in front of the fire while her mother warmed some milk for her and the children. Antos and Sasha settled in the library. They needed a plan: how to keep the family safe from the Partisans.

"I, too, have escaped the Partisans," Antos said. "They are searching for both of us. Our family must go into hiding Sasha. If one of is caught, they will send them to Siberia and we will never see them again."

"I agree Antos." Sasha stood up and paced the floor restlessly. "Where are the rest of the family members?" he asked.

"My two brothers were killed by the Partisans and Marina was sent to Siberia with her family." His voice broke with grief. "Only Juzia is here."

He took a deep breath. "What has happened to your family, Sasha? Have you heard from Martina or Irena?"

Sasha shook his head. "We have not heard from Irena." Tears glistened on his eyelashes.

"We did received a letter from Martina. It took several months to get here, but in it she told us of her plight. She and her two little girls managed to escape from the train at one of the stops in Siberia. The labor camp where she believed her husband might be was some distance away. She set out with the girls on foot, trudging through the wilderness covered in snow and ice. I do not know how she managed to stay alive." Sasha shook his head in disbelief. "She did make it to the camp, only to find out that her husband had died. She decided to remain in that camp. That is where she is now." Sasha wiped a tear that found its way on to his cheek. "I don't know what happened to Irena and her husband."

The two men sat for a minute in deep and sad thought.

"Sasha, there is a hiding area in the cellar that we dug. Let me show it to you." Sasha followed Antos into the kitchen. "Help me with this," Antos said. The two men pushed a credenza out of the way, revealing a small latch that looked like a piece of loose wood. Antos raised the latch and pulled the hatchway door toward him.

Sasha peered into the cellar while Antos retrieved an oil lamp. *This may do,* he thought.

He followed Antos down the ladder into the musty, damp basement. There was not much room; four people could just barely sit down. There was a shelf in the wall with food and a jug of water stocked on the shelf, and another oil lamp hung on a wooden peg. Sasha nodded. "This is good, Antos. In an emergency, this will do."

Antos agreed. "Now we must prepare the horses."

The two men went outside to check the grounds and horses. They had to be certain that everything was ready for an escape. Misha and Layka, back from their chase in the woods, jumped up at Sasha waiting for a scratch behind their ears. Sasha petted their heads lovingly.

"Go and lay down now, both of you." Misha and Layka reluctantly headed towards the barn, their tails between their legs. Their rejection was forgotten when they spotted scared chickens. They flew in a flurry of feathers, clucking in protest at being disturbed.

Antos checked all the windows and doors and together with Sasha walked around the house securing everything visible to intrusion. Once their inspection was through, they settled on the porch steps. Antos leaned back against the railing and looked pensively at the stars. "Sasha, what will happen to all of us?"

Sasha thought for a moment. With his hand, he pushed the hair off his forehead. "Only God knows what will happen to us. We have been lucky up to now. We are still alive and still have some family members here."

Antos stroked his mustache, as was his habit. "We will have to be very careful and stay hidden during the day. All our neighbors are frightened and will do anything to stay alive. The Partisans will stop at nothing. They are looking for both of us, and eventually somebody will report us to gain their protection. Until this drastic war is over, we will have to watch our backs."

Sasha nodded in agreement. "Yes, Antos you are right. I hope the war will end soon. For now we must tend to our families." Sasha turned to Antos. "Tell me of how you were caught by the Partisans. How did you escape? And how long were you in captivity?"

Antos sat quietly for a while thinking. Memories of engineering school and his work building the road from Minsk to Moscow flooded his mind. A sad smile appeared on his lips as he recalled that bittersweet part of that life.

"After I finished engineering school," he began slowly, "I was hired as an assistant engineer with a private road building company contracted by the Communist regime to build a road from Minsk to Moscow. It was a good job and I tried to stay neutral and not take political sides. I worked hard and very quickly was promoted to a top engineer position. An engineer from Moscow took a liking to me and we formed a friendship. He invited me to his home several times where I met a very pretty girl. She was his cousin. Her sparkling eyes and laughter captured my heart." Antos looked up at Sasha looking for approval. Sasha smiled and motioned for him to go on. "We saw each other often and fell in love. However, she was a

Communist supporter and pressured me to join the Party. I could not do it. It was against my belief and despite my love for her I could not betray my family."

Sadness appeared in his eyes and a tear found its way down his cheek. He wiped it with his finger and whispered.

"I quit the job and headed for home without saying goodbye to my Marina." He bowed his head and held it in his hands.

"As I was riding down a path in the woods one day, I ran into a group of Partisans. I tried to outrun them, however my horse was tired and lost his footing jumping over a ravine. He broke his ankle and I shot him. I tried to run, but they caught up to me with ease and hauled me away to a nearby camp." Antos gestured with his hand to his forehead where a red welt appeared close to his hairline. "I don't have to tell you how that happened." He smiled a sad smile. Sasha nodded in understanding.

"How did you escape those bastards?" Sasha asked.

"One day in the field where we were hauling hay, I hid myself in one of the hay stacks. I still don't know how they missed me at count down at the end of the day, but as dusk fell, I crawled on my belly to the edge of the forest and ran like the wind into the woods. And here I am. I made it home."

Sasha laughed heartily and told Antos of his plight. They sat in silent communion, each with their own thoughts of what was to come.

The two men joined the rest of the family seated at the kitchen table snacking on slices of smoked ham, boiled potatoes, and bread and butter that Rozalia prepared. She brought out extra ham to celebrate the family being together once again. She bowed her head and prayed, "*Spasiba Hospudzi*...for this food and all that you have given us. Keep us safe from the evil, which is so rampant in our land. Keep our children from hunger and give them strength to resist the teachings of Stalin. We thank you for your love. Amen."

Despite the gloom of war and the fear of the Partisans, after finishing their meal they went out on the porch and sat back quietly, each deep in thought. Sasha sat by Anya. He put his arm around her shoulder hugging her close to him, inhaling the presence of her. Closing his eyes, he hummed a very poignant Russian folk song, *Rozkwitali Jabloni i Grushy,* and then in his rich baritone voice, sang quietly and passionately while stroking Anya's beautiful hair. Anya leaned into his hard body and looked deep into his eyes with both longing and the terrible fear of losing him.

"I am terrified," said Anya. "I could not bear it if you were taken again. Nicolaj and Marina need you to help them understand the meaning of God and family. I am afraid that they will be brainwashed by the Communist teachings." She gestured toward Marina. "Marina is a very intelligent little girl who pesters Nicolaj to teach her what he learned in school. However, I can sense that Nicolaj is very unsure of what he is learning and does not know who to believe."

"Anya, I know what you are saying," Sasha nodded. "The Communists know that by brainwashing the children at a very vulnerable age, there will be little resistance from the parents. We must be strong in our beliefs and guide them away from their teaching. I will do my best to spend time with them."

For the next five months, Sasha spent much time with Nicolaj. He tried very carefully to nurture him away from the Communist teachings in school. Nicolaj was no longer as confused. And although the teacher kept insisting that Stalin was their savior, Nicolaj carefully listened but stayed noncommittal while in school.

Father and son sat together on the porch watching dusk descend. The late fall sky was cloudy and the wind blew cold swirls of air, whisking the leaves in circles creating mounds for the children to play in. He was humming one of his songs to his son who was eagerly listening.

"Papa, I saw some riders yesterday when I was walking home from school. I didn't recognize them. They looked at me and waved, but I kept on running home." Nicolaj's voice was quiet and worried. "I think that my friend, Ivanek Pavlovny, talked to them when they stopped him. They kept looking towards our house and followed me for some distance until I cut through the fields."

Sasha's heart skipped a beat. *Could it be the Partisans? They must be looking for Antos and me.* They had tried to be very careful. Antos did go into town a few times for supplies. He tried to avoid conversation with anyone while there. However, someone must have seen him, Sasha thought, and must have reported him to the Partisans to gain favor. Sasha put his hand on Nicolaj's shoulder. "Nicolaj, stay here with Misha and Layka. I will go and talk to your uncle Antos. I think he is in the barn feeding the horses and the livestock."

As he stepped off the porch, Misha and Layka jumped up, blocking him, their ears upright as they were listening intently into the still night. Sasha turned to his son, raising his finger to his lips. He stood quietly, intent on hearing what had alarmed the dogs. Within seconds, he heard the distant hoof beats of the horses coming in their direction. Misha growled baring his teeth, but Sasha knew his companion was now too old to fight and protect. He led him by the collar into the house with Layka beside him growling and protesting.

Nicolaj jumped up and stood by his father, straining his eyes to see the intruders. The first rider was a Partisan. Nicolaj pushed his father into the house. "Go to the cellar, Papa. I will talk to the men. Go!" His young voice was full of urgency and fear as he whispered in his father's ear.

Sasha was reluctant, however he knew that Nicolaj would be safe. He was too young for the needs of the Partisans. Sasha stepped inside the house, motioning silence to his wife and mother-in-law. He slipped into the kitchen, moved the credenza, and descended into the cellar praying that Antos had heard the horses coming and would soon be joining him or take cover in the woods.

The riders, a motley group of men out to kill and steal, thundered in, and quickly dismounted. "Hey! Boy! We want that bastard, Antos. Where is he? Is he hiding behind the women's skirts?" one bearded, longhaired Partisan shouted.

Nicolaj froze with fear, but stood firmly on the steps of this house that gave so much love and comfort. Trying to sound brave, he answered, "He is not here. He has gone to Minsk to look for work. I am here with my grandmother and mother. No one else is here." The men laughed and started to circle the porch with their guns drawn and knives glistening in their hands.

Nicolaj slowly backed away towards the door and with shaking hands held on to the doorknob. The men sensing a game of cat and mouse with Nicolaj kept coming closer to the porch. "Meow, little mouse, this cat will catch you!" The bearded Partisan jumped onto the porch and grabbed Nicolaj, spinning him around and throwing him against the porch railing.

Nicolaj felt his bones cracking as he hit the railing stunned at the ferocity of the man's brutality. He realized that these men were dangerous and would kill for no reason. "You are lying, little mouse!" the Partisan shouted. "We have been watching your house and you. Antos is here somewhere, and you better tell us where he is hiding or we will burn this house down with everyone in it!" He approached Nicolaj, his gun drawn.

Rozalia opened the door and gasped at the sight of Nicolaj sitting on the floor of the porch, his face bloody from a gash in his forehead. The bearded man stood over him, gun in his hand.

Rozalia stepped forward ignoring the gunman and reached for her grandson, ready to protect him with her life. But the man stepped in front of her, pushing her to the side. "Old woman, stay away from him and tell us where your traitor son is!" he yelled.

Shaken and frightened, she looked at the deranged, bloodthirsty man. "I do not know where he is! My son comes and goes as he chooses. He is a grown man. I do not control him. Take whatever there is left and leave us women and children alone!" Her hazel eyes were unafraid as she stared the man down, but inside she was panicked, praying that Antos would hear the commotion and run for the woods.

As she moved to straighten herself up, she glanced towards the barn. Antos was approaching the house unaware that the Partisans were in their yard. One of the men heard Rozalia gasp and noticing her stricken face turned towards the barn and saw Antos walking in their direction.

Rozalia screamed, "Antos, run! Run, my son! Do not let these deranged animals catch you!"

The bearded man grabbed Rozalia and slapped her face. "Old woman, you are asking for the same fate as your sons if you do not stop yelling! Or maybe I will give you to the men to have fun with you!" He pulled her to him. She smelled the stink of his breath; his body reeked of odor. She struggled to get free, but he held on tight. "Would you like that?" He leered at her, making vulgar noises with his lips.

Hearing his mother call out to him, Antos saw the Partisans, turned and ran towards the woods. The men ran after him. Antos stumbled and fell hitting his head against a tree stump. Dazed momentarily, he struggled to his feet and dashed for the heavy brush at the edge of the forest. Running swiftly, he avoided the trees standing quietly, their branches outstretched as if trying to shield the fleeing man. Breathless from exertion, perspiration dripped into his eyes blinding him. Antos stumbled against a boulder covered with moss and shrubbery. He fell against it, knocking the wind out of his lungs.

The bearded gunman caught up with him. He jumped upon him, grabbed his legs and held him down. Antos had no escape. Three of the men surrounded him, kicking him in the ribs. "You are a Communist informer! You will see what we do to informers!" they laughed viciously. "We cut their balls off! Take him back to the house! Let his mother and the rest of the women see a man with no balls."

Struggling to get free, he grabbed on to the tree roots and rocks with bleeding hands while they dragged him by his feet. He kept struggling, thrashing about with all the strength he had left in him. As he heaved himself up to get his leg free, his head hit a sharp edge of a protruding boulder. A big gash opened the side of his temple. Bright lights exploded in his brain as he lost consciousness.

Rozalia, Anya, and Juzia upon hearing the shouting and yelling of the Partisans, ran out of the house to see what the commotion was all about, fearing the worst. The men were dragging Antos bleeding badly from his wound. Rozalia tried to run to her son, but one of the men stopped her by pointing his gun at her head.

"Please spare his life! Take mine, but please spare his! Take whatever you want. Please, I beg you to spare him! Take me! Take me! Let him live!"

One of the men slapped her face hard and pushed her down to her knees, holding her head by her hair and turning it towards the men holding Antos. "Bitch, you will see what we do to traitors."

With the butts of their rifles, each man hit Antos on the head; the bearded man brought out his knife, plunging it in Antos' chest.

Rozalia screamed and fainted into a heap on the ground. Anya's face contorted in horror at the sight of her mother fainting. She made a move to run and help her, but Juzia grabbed her by the arm in an iron grip and hissed into her ear, "Anya, stay still or they will kill all of us! We have to think of the children and Sasha! Stay still!" Anya realized Juzia was right.

The two sisters held each other, afraid to make a move to help their mother or Antos, afraid that Sasha may come out of the cellar wondering what was happening.

Mission accomplished, the men mounted their horses and laughing and yelling obscenities at the women, galloped away.

Anya and Juzia waited until they were out of sight then quickly ran to their mother. Antos was dead. His handsome face and hazel eyes were staring forever.

"Anya, run in the house. Get Sasha and quiet the children. I will see to Mama." Juzia took charge.

Anya sobbing and grief-stricken stumbled to the house. On the couch was Nicolaj lying down and holding a kitchen towel to his head. "Nicolaj, they killed your uncle Antos. I have to get Papa from the cellar." Nicolaj nodded, his eyes opened wide with horror and fright.

She ran past him to the wall and with strength she did not know she possessed, she pushed the huge credenza to the side revealing the small door in the wall. She banged on it with her fist until Sasha opened it. She fell sobbing into his loving arms, her tears flowing freely as she told him what happened. Sasha held his Anya letting her sobs subside, then gently took her by the hand and led her outside.

Rozalia held her son, kissing his bruised face and washing it with her tears. "Oh, my son... my son...if only I could have warned you in time..."

Sasha walked to her and gently put his strong arms under hers, lifting her to her feet. "Come, *Mamushka,*" he said gently. "Anya, Juzia. Take your mother in the house and make her some tea. Put some brandy in it. It will calm her down." The women headed to the house while Sasha headed to the barn for a shovel to dig his beloved brother-in-law's grave.

That afternoon, after burying yet another son and brother, they gathered in the front room, somber and numb, each with their own thoughts. Sasha, shaken and pale, knew that his time was limited before the Partisans came back and found him. "You must leave, Anya. Go back to *Kolhozy*. I will hide in the forest for a time and will join you later when the Partisans go in another direction looking for others to recruit."

Anya and her mother agreed that it would be best to do that. At least they would have some rations of food for the children. They packed their meager belongings and once again loaded the wagon and began the journey back to Sorojevsko.

Anya went back to working at the *Kolhozy* while Nicolaj took care of the children. Occasionally in the middle of the night, Sasha would sneak into the cabin with some food for his family from Rozalia's garden. After five months of hiding, Sasha felt it was safe to return to his family and take care of them. Anya was heavy with twins.

Chapter Ten
1938

The kind, elderly couple waved goodbye from their steps, tears welled in their eyes. Anya and Sasha began their journey home with their new babies, Janushka and Alexandria, bundled beside them. As they neared the log cabin, Sasha saw Nicolaj outside feeding the hungrily clucking chickens.

Nicolaj, always alert for the sound of horses, spotted the sled and came running to greet his parents. He saw the babies immediately and jumped up onto the sled with curiosity. "They sound like kittens meowing like that." Nicolaj looked at his mother with questioning eyes. An anxious look crossed his face. At his young age, he worried about everyone, especially his mother.

She smiled tenderly. "Nicolaj, we spotted two little girls running on the road we were traveling. They were very cold, scared and tired. We stopped and asked them where they were going. They said that they were lost and were searching for a new home and family. So, we told them that we had two other little girls and a big, handsome, strong and loving brother at home and asked them if they would like to be their sisters? 'Yes!' they mewed. They would love to come with us and join the wonderful family." She smiled at her son who was not too sure of what his mother was telling him, his face puzzled. "We named them Alexandria and Janushka. Later, I will show you Alexandria's little foot. You will see that she has a frost bite on her foot from walking so long."

At ten years of age, Nicolaj did not really believe that story, but could not wait to hold his newborn sisters. Then his brow wrinkled with concern. "But now we have two more little girls to take care of."

Anya replied, "God will provide somehow. You will see."

Inside the house, Marina and Katrina were playing on the dirt floor with their rag dolls made by their grandmother. The sound of the door opening startled them. The girls jumped up and ran to the door to see what was going on. Entering the house was their father and brother, each carrying a bundle in their arms. Their mother, still worn from dual labor, walked very slowly behind them.

"What are you carrying? Did you bring us puppies?" Marina asked.

Sasha chuckled softly and placed Janushka on the one bed. Nicolaj laid Alexandria next to her and opened the blankets. The little girls squirmed and waved their arms. Marina and Katrina peeked at them.

"These are your baby sisters…Alexandria and Janushka."

"Look, Marina, Alexandria is going to cry!" Katrina touched the baby's face gently. "Don't cry baby," Katrina whispered. The little face registered alarm frowning. "Can I hold her?" Katrina asked her mother.

Anya laughed, picked up the baby and placed her in Katrina's small arms. "She is not heavy," Katrina said. She rocked her gently kissing her tenderly on her head. Soft brown hair on Alexandria's head tickled Katrina's nose. She giggled hugging her closely.

Marina was not to be left out. "Can I hold Janushka?"

Anya laughed again and placed the baby in Marina's arms. The girls held their little sisters with excitement. "Girls," Anya said, "the babies had a long journey and are very tired. Let me bathe them and feed them. You can play with them later after they rest." Reluctantly, Marina and Katrina placed the babies on the bed. "Would you help me bathe them?" Anya asked.

Marina squealed and Katrina jumped up and down with excitement. "Marina, get some towels and Katrina sit down next to the girls and watch them for me while I get the basin and warm water."

Within a few weeks time Anya could tell that the babies were very different from one another with very different personalities. Alexandria was very quiet and serious; her hair was dark like her mother's though she resembled her father. Janushka was blonde like her father, but resembled her. Janushka was the smaller of the two, but she was filling out very quickly. When there was not enough milk in her mother's breast for both of them, she drank cabbage juice from her bottle. Alexandria remained very frail and sickly despite the tender care from everyone. Nicolaj and Marina loved the twins and Katrina thought of them as little dolls to play with.

Anya went back to work while Sasha remained home taking care of the household chores and the children. The Petrosewicz household was once again full of laughter and false tranquility.

Commotion and strange voices outside the log cabin woke Sasha with a start, "Petrosewicz, open the door or we will break in!"

Anya jumped out of the bed, grabbed the babies from their crib and ran to wake Marina and Katrina. "Girls, get up and hide quickly behind the fireplace. Hurry now." She urged them. Nicolaj and his father dressed quickly, "Hold on! We will be right out!" Sasha shouted.

Sasha grabbed his son by the shoulders. "Nicolaj, I think they came to get me." Tears sprang into Nicolaj's eyes. Sasha held him tightly and looked at his tear-stained face. "Someone must have informed the authorities that I took the priest to safety across the border. You are too young to understand these things, Nicolaj, but if they take me then you must take care of your mother and the girls." He felt Nicolaj's body tremble with fright. He hugged him protectively. "The babies are only three months old. I will depend on you to somehow provide for them and help your mother to raise them. Promise me that you will do that."

Nicolaj's terrified face contorted with sobs deep within him. He looked at his adored father. "Papa, I will do my best, I promise." Sasha hugged him once again, "*Spasiba* Nicolaj." Then he went quickly behind the fireplace, and fiercely hugged his crying wife and daughters. He held his babies kissing them and whispering goodbye, then turned to Anya. Her face was a mask of terror. Leaning against the wall, her knees barely held her up. She tried to move her lips, yet they refused to speak. She mouthed, "No! Not again, Not Siberia!" She crumbled to the floor like a rag doll. Sasha quickly picked her up and held her against him. "Anya, my darling, you must be strong. Everything will be all right." He tried, in vain, to reassure her.

The banging grew louder. Sasha kissed Anya on her cold lips and reluctantly grabbed the door handle and slowly opened it. Three burly

Communist soldiers with pistols drawn, pushed into the house. Sasha staggered back against the wall and before he had an opportunity to ask what they wanted, they grabbed him by the arms and tied his hands.

"Petrosewicz, you are a traitor." A dark-haired, middle-aged, obviously well fed soldier yelled at him.

"*Tovarysz*, what proof do you have to accuse me?" he asked.

The soldier looked at Sasha with such hatred in his eyes that Sasha staggered back. "You dare to question me?" He slapped Sasha with the back of his hand and spit in his face. A dark red handprint appeared on Sasha's cheek, blood trickled from a split lip.

Anya, upon hearing this, ran from behind the fireplace still holding her babies. She screamed at the sight of her husband, placed the babies on the bed and ran to Sasha. She embraced him, then wiped the blood from his lip and kissed his mouth tenderly.

The soldier watching this display of affection sneered at them. He grabbed Anya and roughly held her tightly against him. "Sasha, your wife is a beauty. We could have fun with her!" He leered at Anya, saliva drooling from his big mouth. Foul breath assaulted Anya's senses and she wanted to vomit as she twisted and turned trying to get free from the soldiers grip.

Nicolaj came running from behind the stove. He saw his father pushed against the wall; a gun pointed at his head as the soldier held his mother. He jumped at him, hitting him with his small fists and crying. "Leave them alone!" he screamed.

The soldier laughed, picked him up by the collar and threw him against the wall. "You do that again and you will go with your father to Siberia!" He snarled at Nicolaj. "Better yet, we will take all of you and allow you to freeze to death on the way there!"

Anya bit her captive on the arm and ran to Nicolaj. He was not hurt, only bruised with a small cut on his forehead under his blonde hair. "Nicolaj," she whispered, "don't do anything. They will kill all of us. Papa will return to us. I know that he will. Be still, my child!" Anya turned to see her husband, struggling to get free. His eyes were upon her, filled with sorrow and love. She stood still, conveying her love for him with her eyes.

They pushed Sasha outside where five other captive men were waiting in the wagon guarded by six soldiers with guns drawn ready to shoot to kill if anyone tried to escape. Sasha was shoved onto the wagon and tied to the other captives. Sasha knew some of the men and their families. He nodded to them without showing recognition and pushed himself up deeper inside so he could better see from the side of the wagon.

The soldier in charge barked an order to the soldier driving the wagon. The driver grabbed the reins and the two horses pulled the wagon out of the driveway. Sasha struggled up to look back. He locked eyes with his wife standing in the doorway with Nicolaj, holding the hands of the girls. She swayed slightly reaching out to him, but the wagon picked up speed. They waved to him, holding onto each other for support. He nodded his head as tears rolled down his face. Anguish consumed him. He turned his head one more time in the direction of his home. And through eyes blinded by tears he bid farewell to his beloved wife and family. The wagon turned a corner and his Anya disappeared from sight.

Slowly the wagon made its way to the Communist soldiers' barracks and came to a stop in front of a log building surrounded by barbed wire. Still tied together, the men were dragged from the wagon and pushed inside the compound. Sasha looked around at the big room—bare log walls and empty of all furniture. After his eyes adjusted to the dimness, he saw that the room was crowded with men. They sat in small groups, their hands tied, quietly staring into nothingness. In a far corner of the room he saw a group of women scared and sobbing. Everyone knew that Siberia was a death sentence. Survival was slim. No one returned from Siberia. Thousands of men, women and children had perished in freezing below zero temperatures.

In the early dawn, the men and women sore and tired, their joints stiff from being cramped, their eyes red and burning from lack of sleep, dressed in clothing filthy and soiled from bodily waste, were dragged to the waiting wagons that would take them to the railroad. On top of dirty, wet hay the captives were packed tightly together. The stench made them want to retch.

Sasha pictured Anya standing in the doorway, pale and frightened her eyes full of terror with Nicolaj holding her up as he always appeared to do, trying to be the man of the house once again. How will they survive? The twins were only three months old and left without their father. Would he ever see them again? And what fate was he facing? Siberia was so far way. Would he survive the journey there? Would he be able to escape? No one escaped from Siberia, he told himself. His mind screamed with injustice.

Finally, the wagon began to move; the horses strained pulling the heavy human load towards Toloczyn where the trains awaited. The ride was agonizingly slow. They could not move or stretch their legs. The stench of sweat and human waste got stronger as the day wore on. Women were getting sick—crying and begging for some time to stop. The soldiers would not hear of it. They made fun of them, pinching their noses to let them know how badly they smelled and kept on going.

Just before sunset Toloczyn loomed in the distance. Communist soldiers were everywhere, on patrol and in groups, talking and drinking vodka to hearty laughter and jovial camaraderie. As the wagons approached the town, soldier's rowdy and drunk sauntered over to the wagons. They spotted the women and leered at them, making lewd remarks, pinching them and stroking their bodies. Disbelief and horror showed in their tear-stained eyes as they tried to fend off the soldiers' hands, trying to squirm away, but unable to because their hands were tied to men who could not help them.

Sasha was hungry, thirsty, and in need of bodily relief. The trains up ahead to the right of the town were visible, looming dark and sinister. At the sight of them, the women began to whimper and cry. Sasha looked at his next transportation to hell with dread in his heart. He and the other men tried to comfort the women the best they could, but not much could be said to change the doom of their circumstances.

The wagons stopped alongside of the train. White plumes of steam *whooshed* from the huge locomotive that pulled dozens of boxcars filled with women, children and men, packed tightly together. The crying and moaning of these poor human beings was deafening; everyone was in agonizing fear of what was to come.

Chapter Eleven

It was early May. The weather was cold. The sky was full of heavy clouds and the wind gusts blew strong against the wooden cattle boxcar full of holes and cracks. The captives sat close together savoring the ineffectual body heat from one another, crying children huddled close to their mothers hungry and cold. The train rumbled along the rails with its wretched human cargo getting closer to the destination with each mile.

Each time the train stopped to let the captives relieve themselves, the soldiers unloaded numerous bodies of men, women and children who had perished from the abhorrent conditions. The dead were left for the wolves and other animals to feast on. No one protested after awhile as they were too weak to resist. Hope and the will to live faded. Sasha fought the fear and hopelessness by focusing on finding a way to escape.

Through a crack in the wall he studied the landscape every chance he got. Patches of snow were scattered throughout the barren fields, heavily wooded forest with huge pine trees stood dark and forbidding. And then one day, in the distance, he saw human settlers. Log cabins dotted the vast landscape, a few dispersed men and women were working in the fields with cattle grazing in the green grass that was peeking out from under the snow.

Sasha estimated there were fifty log cabins housing the people. Some were small, others big and long in structure, obviously barracks for the new arrivals that were used for interrogating and sentencing. At the end of the dirt road was a huge building where the soldiers were residing. Another large building was the headquarters of the *Narodny Komissariat Vnutrennikh Del*—the NKVD—or People's Commissariat of Internal Affairs Communist regime.

The train chugged along to the station located in the back of the village. With a noisy blowing whistle and the screeching of the wheels, it came to a stop. Although everyone was anxious to get off the train, they were also apprehensive about what was in store for them.

The heavy boxcar doors slid open.

"Get out everyone, out!"

The raggedy, filthy women and children who survived this journey could barely walk. Sasha tried to help very pregnant woman, however, a soldier hit him in the stomach with the butt of his rifle.

"You, mind your own business! If you try that again then you will be put in solitary confinement." Sasha fell to the ground doubled over in pain, unable to breathe for a moment. He lay in a fetal position, like a fish out of water, gasping for air. The ground he lay on was as cold as a grave must be. Into his gasping came a shivering that shook him ruthlessly.

"Get up!" Kicking him in his ribs with his boot, the soldier shouted.

Sasha lifted himself on his elbows. Pain made him lightheaded, but he pushed onto his knees and slowly he stood up swaying against another captive. The captive held him up briefly and stood him up, then quickly walked away afraid of the same treatment by the soldier.

Women, children, and men were segregated into groups away from one another. The women held onto their frightened children, embracing them and comforting them with soothing words, as tears fell from their eyes mixing with the tears of their children.

The soldiers grabbed one of the young girls. She had long, blonde, curly hair and beautiful brown almond shaped eyes. He began to toss her around like a rag doll making fun of her screams and her struggling. Her mother tried to protect her, but the soldier held on to her. He tore her blouse exposing her breasts and laughing made lewd remarks, "*Hadzi tovarysze.* Come, buddies, have a look at this!"

The men hooted with laughter while the soldier pushed the woman around making fun of her. Her young, frightened, daughter was thrown into a group of other children already assembled in a group. Then everyone was ordered to strip naked and go to the bathing room in the long building.

With lye soap they quickly washed in cold water. With rough homemade sacks they covered their bodies the best they could. A soldier ordered them to sit down on the floor until the NKVD commissar came in to sentence each person for their crime.

Sasha sat along the log wall with remainder of the captives. He closed his eyes for a moment relishing the feeling of being clean and the freedom of his untied hands. Anxious and nervous, they all waited for the commissar's decision on their fate.

The door opened and a short, round man with a circular face, brown squinting eyes, a nose with red-veined large nostrils entered. A menacing sneer appeared on his face exposing rotten teeth; saliva dripped from his thick lips. He wiped his big mouth with the back of his hand, wiped it on his trousers and waved it in the air shouting for everyone to be quiet. Stomping his feet on the wooden floor he bellowed, "Attention!"

The captives went quiet, fear passing through them like a storm. The children whimpered; the women cried. Sasha eyed him and assessed that this man was mean and loved the authority. He decided to be very careful when interacting with him. The man was dangerous.

"I am Commissar Ivanovich. I will hold the court and I will judge you and sentence you according to your crimes! All of you are here due to your wrong doings against the government. You will be sentenced to labor camps in the Ural Mountains accordingly."

Everyone gasped with horror. The Ural Mountains were forbidding and desolate. The living conditions were deplorable, and everyone knew it. The survival rate was no more than two years of living hell.

Sasha quietly listened to the proceedings of the sentencing of the poor wretches, his neighbors from home. He was one of them, waiting to be sentenced and start a life of misery and sorrow away from his beloved Anya and his family.

"Petrosewicz, Sasha, come forward," the commissar ordered.

Sasha stepped forward; his eyes riveted on the commissar, showing no fear.

"Petrosewicz, you are accused of aiding a priest. Therefore, you are working against the Communist regime. What do you have to say?"

Sasha gritted his teeth and lifted his chin. "I helped my cousin go to his family in Poland. I do not see it as a crime against the regime."

"Petrosewicz, it does not matter how you see it!" The commissar shouted with rage. "Your cousin was a priest. He was guilty of treason. I sentence you to ten years of hard labor in the Ural Mountains. Take him away!" He spat.

Hearing the sentence, Sasha's legs turned to liquid. Visions of ten years in Siberia whirled in his mind. *Ten years!* He could not breathe; his senses became dull. Slowly, he straightened his back and with his blue eyes locking with those of the commissar, he walked out vowing to survive and find a way to escape.

Sasha watched as a group of sentenced men and women were herded to the backfield. They were lined up at the edge of a huge pit. On signal from the NKVD commissar, the executioners placed their pistol muzzles at the victims' necks. "*Agon!*" he ordered. Bullets smashed their way out of the foreheads of the victims. The lifeless bodies toppled softly into the ditch. Any bodies still moving were stabbed with a bayonet.

Sasha shook his head to clear it, willing his mind to not show any fear.

Those sentenced to the Ural Mountains were loaded on the train and spent ten more days of travel through a very rough terrain. The forests were thick with tall pine trees stretching their branches as high as the eye could see. The winter snow still covered the ground; the cold wind blew relentlessly causing frostbite to those with exposed skin. Their meager clothing gave little protection from the harsh elements of Siberia.

Through a crack in the wall of the boxcar, Sasha could see the Ural Mountains looming in the distance. This was to be his home for the next ten years, if he survived. He shut his eyes tight against hot, flooding uncontrollable tears.

Once again the train pulled up in front of the desolate looking log buildings. It was the end of May and the weather was still cold and blustery. The wind blew with a vengeance. Strong gusts whirled around the men and women as they were herded off the train. Lack of warm clothing made them shiver and huddle together. Women were assigned two per cabin and mothers were allowed to take their tired and frightened children with them to the cold, log cabins. Thin blankets were issued, one to each person. Warm homespun coats, gloves, and hats were handed out with a warning that it was the only clothing that would be given to them during their tenure in the camp.

The cabins were just a structure of rough logs with a dirt floor strewn with damp straw. Against the wall, wooden cots with burlap bags filled with straw served as mattresses. One small window with bars over it shed dim light from outside. In the middle of each cabin a large, black cast iron wood-burning stove dominated the floor. The toilet facilities were outside– one long building to be utilized by all.

The commissar from the train gave the orders to the commissar of the camp and pointed in the direction of Sasha. The commissar nodded, barked an order to one of the guards. The guard grabbed Sasha by his arms and pushed him in the direction of a building on the far side of the camp.

On weak legs, Sasha stumbled. "What have I done?"

The guard grabbed him by the back of his shirt as if he was grabbing a dog and pulled him to his feet. "*Ty Huj!* You prick!" He pushed Sasha hard toward the building.

"Why are you taking only me? Where are you taking me?"

"Shut your mouth or you'll have no teeth left!"

They entered a very large log building with no windows. The heavy door opened and Sasha saw a long corridor stretching ahead with many doors on each side of it. The vile stench of rotting flesh and fresh blood assaulted his senses. He couldn't breathe. The soldier, used to the stench, pushed him with the butt of the rifle. "Move!" he shouted.

They moved slowly past several doors. Moaning and screaming of the prisoners being tortured was heard as they passed open doors. The guard stopped Sasha in front of the second door. With horror in his eyes, Sasha fell to his knees. In front of him was a dead man seated in a chair with a bayonet sticking out of his mouth. A table next to him was covered with several decaying corpses. Sasha looked closer. They had been tortured. Their twisted fingers, putrefying toes, frozen stumps, and hungry blazing eyes were staring into space. Dry heaves attacked Sasha with vengeance. The soldier laughed and dragged him past another open door. There he saw and heard a man screeching in pain as a guard was kicking his testicles to a pulp. In the next room, torturers rammed needles under a man's fingernails.

Sasha was no longer able to walk. His legs turned to water. His stomach was retching and he no longer was able to function. The guard lifted him up slapped him and kicked him in the shins. "Stand up, you bastard!" he shouted. With all his strength left in him, Sasha struggled to his feet. The guard dragged him past another room. Sasha turned his head to the side, but the guard grabbed him by the chin and turned Sasha's head to face the open door. Sasha felt faint. Through a haze in his eyes he saw a girl, not more than eight years, old hanging from a hook on the ceiling. The signs of rape and torture were visible on her little body. Beside her was a female corpse. One of her breasts had been cut off and her abdomen had been cut open revealing the head of an unborn child sticking out of her. Sasha retched and his stomach heaved violently expelling green bile. The guard laughed and dragged him to the room where he was to serve his sentence.

It was a very bright room painted with white wash. Small cubicles were built into the walls with benches within. Large light bulbs glared against the whiteness, blinding the occupant's eyes. Sasha heard of this type of punishment, widely used by Stalin supporters. With horror, he realized that he was facing the same fate.

Sasha squinted, trying to shield his eyes with his hands. The guard slapped his hands away and shoved him into one of the cubicles.

"Petrosewicz, you are going to pay for the insolence you showed to the Commander in the other camp. He was not pleased with you." He shouted with glee in his eyes and his mouth twisted in a sneer. "You are sentenced to seven days in this punishment room. There will be no sleep for you. The whitewash will be dripping all day and night. And there will be no rest for you! Now strip!" he shouted.

Sasha removed his clothing and sat with his head bowed, not daring to say another word. The guard glared at him and left, the door banging shut behind him. Sasha was in a world of whiteness.

The room was small, barely big enough for him to sit in it. Cramped and cold, his teeth chattering, he did not know when the day ended or the night began. Sleep was fitful and short from the never-ending bright lights.

Striving to fight fear with reality, he began to count, as in childhood, all the secure things in the room. The drops of the whitewash....drip ....drip....drip.... were relentless. He counted them over and over until he screamed with frustration and anger. Then he counted his fingers on his hands, his toes on his feet. What now? Nothing else existed in the room, only the dripping whiteness.

I must focus on my hands and feet to keep some semblance of color. My eyes will go blind otherwise. What day is it? How long have I been here? Is this the way I must die? Why this torture? Why the cruelty? Hospudzi....! Hospudzi....! I cry to you! Why are you not hearing me? He was floating, floating away. He knew he would go mad soon if he didn't control his mind. *Concentrate on Anya! Picture her on your wedding day. Feel her soft arms around you.* The longing to look at her beautiful face brought him back to reality.

The shuffling of feet sounded in the hallway. Through an open slit at the bottom of the door a guard pushed in a tray with food. On his hands and knees Sasha crawled to the door and grabbed the tray. He looked at the food—cabbage and turnip with stale moldy bread. It made Sasha want to retch. He concentrated on controlling his stomach, sat on the floor and forced the food down his constricting throat.

I will eat and drink whatever they give me to nourish my body. I must stay alive and plan my escape! My Anya needs me! Is she waiting for me? Or does she think that I am dead.

On the seventh day he heard scratching and shuffling at the door. The handle moved. He strained his feverish eyes. A cold, sick sweat broke out on his forehead. The handle moved again. Door hinges squeaked as it opened revealing the commissar. "Follow me!"

Sasha, weak and barely able to stand, stumbled out of the bright, white room. His eyes blinked adjusting to the darker light. He shielded them with his white hands and slowly followed the commissar outside.

The fresh air assaulted his senses. He breathed deeply, filling his lungs to capacity. He looked around at the green grass, the budding trees and he could hear the birds singing. The cold wind was biting into his nakedness.

He was shivering violently. The commissar handed him a military blanket; he quickly covered up and with a strained grateful smile on his face, made his way to a building that housed the bathing room and the canteen where everyone gathered for meals.

"Now, you begin your ten-year sentence in the Siberian Mountains."

The forbidden, dreaded Ural Mountains loomed darkly through the early morning mist. Below, slivers of sun shed light on a miserable looking group of captives, chained to one another by their ankles. Hobbling and dragging their feet, they were on their way to clear the boulders and rocks in the open field for the early spring planting. Watching them closely were soldiers on horseback with huge whips and rifles on their shoulders. Insolence from any of the captives was punishable with torture, whipping and days in isolation.

Shuffling along with the rest of the men, Sasha, bearded and gaunt kept his head down. Each day at four in the morning, he awoke to the siren blaring throughout the camp. He dressed quickly and ran outside to join the rest of the miserable captives. Laughing, the guards shackled their ankles and they hobbled to the mess hall for their morning meal of warm oatmeal, a piece of stale bread, and hot water. Keeping their heads down, they ate eagerly. Their next meal was after twelve hours of inhuman hard work. Then they would receive another piece of black bread and potato soup. To keep alive and sustain some strength, Sasha set traps for rodents, which were plentiful in their cabin and ate them raw. "I must survive. I will escape," he kept repeating to himself.

Each day ran into another with no hope or meaning. Socializing was forbidden so people kept to themselves. Sasha was shackled most days to a man who was at the camp the longest. Five years. Every chance they had they whispered to each other. "*Tovarysz,* how have you survived so long in this hell?" Sasha whispered.

"Like you, I obey the orders and eat every rodent or bug I can get my hands on. The soldiers leave me alone because I do as I am told. I do not resist them. Sometimes they let me walk around the compound as far as the

103

outer buildings where the deliveries of supplies are brought over by the village men. I talk to them sometimes."

Sasha was intrigued and a plan took hold in his mind. He became a model captive. Every day walking to the fields, he sang to the captives. The guards at first frowned on it, however their Russian souls loved their music and many times they sang along with Sasha. A trust was established between the guards and Sasha and after a year went by they allowed Sasha to go for walks around the compound.

Sasha observed the wagon full of supplies covered with straw arrive through the gates each week for next two years. The male driver of the wagon was a friendly sort, in his early forties with a stocky, muscular build, an angular face with a very prominent nose and a dark brown mustache dominating his mouth. A fur hat always covered his head and ears from the bitter cold. He was from a nearby village delivering meager food supplies such as flour, butter, and milk and, once in awhile, some bacon. Sasha waved to the man each time he saw him.

Today, the wagon came early giving Sasha a chance to walk carefully over to the man without being seen by the soldiers and greet the man. "*Zdrastwijcie Tovarysz, ka pozywajicie?*"

The man glanced at Sasha warily, hesitant at first to start a conversation. "I am very well. How are you?"

Sasha offered a brief sad smile briefly and responded, "As you can see, we do what we have to do."

The man nodded. "Yes, I know the difficulties with which you live. I wish I could help." He shook his head and carefully looked around. "But you know that I can't." He busied himself with the harness.

"*Spasiba Tovarysz.*" He extended his hand. "My name is Sasha Petrosewicz. I am sentenced to ten years here, so we will be seeing one another often."

"And I am Pasha Pavlov." He shook Sasha's hand, "I live in a small village down the hill. I was born here and have a wife and seven children."

Sasha's eyes became misty with tears at the mention of family. He did not know what happened to his Anya and their children. It had been the two years and time had not dimmed the memory of them, rather it made the desire to escape even stronger.

"My village is not big, only forty-three houses and maybe two-hundred-and-fifty people, counting the children," Pasha explained. "Everybody works in the *Kolhozy* and we live comfortable. The soldiers leave us alone as long as we do what they tell us."

"That is good, Pasha, that is good. You must be careful. Your family must not suffer." They looked at each other and both knew that in different times and places they could become good friends. "Pasha, I do not want to endanger you by talking to you too long, but it is good to talk to a free man." He paused. "Tell me, what is happening outside of Ural Mountains? How is the war progressing? Is the German army invading our country? Do you get any news of the war?" His eyes became cloudy with tears. "I have not seen my wife and children for two years now. My twin daughters were little babies when they deported me. I think that God has forgotten me." Sasha was rambling on hoping for news and some hope. Tears of sadness fell down his thin cheeks. Embarrassed, he turned his head to the side and wiped them away.

Pasha looked sadly at Sasha, "*Tovarysz*, I feel sorry for you. There are so many like you here. It is hard to know whom to trust. But I will tell you, the war is still raging. Hitler is killing the Jews and Stalin is killing our own people. Only God knows when it will end. But as you said, God seems to have forgotten us. I wish I could help you. You seem like an honest, God-loving man." He paused and looked directly into Sasha's eyes. "I do not think that you are here for a real crime. I will do my best to help you in any way I can. But I can't endanger my family and my friends."

He stood in silence as if thinking of something and then quickly he placed his finger on his lips to silence Sasha. A soldier was nearby. The soldier stopped and looked their way assessing the situation. Pasha quickly said goodbye to Sasha and walked back to his work area. A plan began to take root in his mind and he walked with a lighter heart.

Over time the men formed a light friendship and would try to converse for a short while whenever Sasha was given some free time. Sasha sometimes sang one of his favorite songs that always brought tears to their eyes. Sasha always insisted that Pasha tell him of his family. And the two friends always parted in silent communion of what they had to do.

One very early morning when Sasha was given a couple of hours off, Pasha pulled up with an unusually large load in his wagon of supplies, hay, and straw. Sasha noticed it immediately and looked at Pasha with a questioning glance. Pasha nodded his head quickly and turned towards the horse checking the harness. The street was deserted; most everyone was at his or her toil. Sasha looked around briskly and not seeing any danger he rapidly jumped into the wagon and sneaked under the straw as far in as he could. He covered himself with a couple of flour sacks and waited for Sasha to go. The wagon lurched forward, moving in a slow pace towards the headquarters to drop off the supplies. Sasha's heart was beating fast and in his mind he was thinking, *what if Pasha turns me in?* He would be executed in front of the prisoners to teach them a lesson that no one escapes Siberia.

Pasha unloaded the wagon, covered Sasha with more straw and quickly departed, walking slowly whistling a tune that Sasha taught him. They went through the gate. The soldier stopped Pasha, as he always did, looked in the wagon, saw the straw and motioned Pasha to keep going.

The village was quiet; everyone was at their job. Pasha came to a stop in back of the log cabin. He un-harnessed the horse, gave him some feed, and walked to the back of the wagon. "Sasha," he whispered, "stay here in the wagon until nightfall. I will bring you some bread and milk shortly. Later, I will come and get you so you can spend the night in my home. In the morning, you must go. It is too dangerous for us if you stay longer."

Sasha whispered back, "Pasha I am so grateful for your help. God will bless you for this."

Sasha's legs were cramped and his breathing was raspy from the dust of the straw. He was thirsty and hungry, but did not dare to take a chance of leaving the wagon.

The hours dragged on. It was dark and Sasha was desperately waiting for Pasha to come and get him. *Did Pasha betray me? Why is he waiting so long? Are they searching the house for me? They must know that I am missing by now. Will they come this far to look for me?* Sasha's thoughts were running through his mind over and over and fear was setting in.

"Sasha. Sasha, you can come out now," Pasha called quietly.

Sasha was dozing when he heard Pasha calling to him and thought it was a dream. But then he heard his name again, so he quickly opened his eyes and struggled to crawl from under the straw. Pasha grabbed his legs and pulled him out. Sasha's legs buckled under him as he tried to stand up, but Pasha's strong arms held him until the blood began circulating in his cramped legs.

Slowly they walked to the house and entered the kitchen. Sasha gasped at the sight that greeted him. The kitchen table was dressed with a pretty tablecloth and all the places were set with sturdy dishes. The aroma from fresh bread baking in the oven filled his nostrils. He inhaled deeply remembering his own home and his loving family. Pasha's wife and the children were seated at the table. She stood up when Sasha entered and greeted him with a friendly and warm expression on her round face. The children looked at Sasha curiously, but did not stop their chatter amongst each other. If their father brought a guest to their dinner table it was all right with them.

"Welcome, Sasha. Pasha has told me about you. I am Katlina." She had dark hair and a very pleasant face with striking green eyes. With a huge smile she motioned to him, "Please join us for dinner and then I will prepare a bath for you and show you to your bed." She smiled again at Sasha and showed him where to sit.

"*Spasiba* Katlina. The luxury of a bath has been forgotten by me," he said smiling.

Sasha joined them for dinner–drinking thirstily, eating the fresh bread with fresh butter, and savoring its goodness. He knew that it might be a long time again before he tasted anything so good. The long journey awaiting him was only a few hours away.

Chapter Twelve

In the early dawn, Sasha awoke to the sound of bacon sizzling and the smell bread baking in the oven. His nostrils had not experienced such wonderful aroma of food for over two years and his stomach was growling. He dressed and joined the family for breakfast. His blue eyes were sparkling again this morning with the anticipation of heading home—home to his children and Anya.

He quickly devoured his food. " *Spasiba*, Pasha, for all you have done for me. I will not forget that you risked your life to help me. Maybe someday, if I get back to my home, I will be able to repay your kindness." He took her hand in his and gently brushed it with his lips in gratitude. "Katlina, you have a wonderful family. God bless you."

He embraced Pasha and then Katlina. He put on the warm coat that Pasha gave him, took the satchel of food Katlina had packed for him, tucked the hunting knife into his boots, and with a spring to his step and a smile on his thin face he walked out into the morning sun. He waved goodbye to the two people that he would remember and be grateful to all of his life.

He reached the edge of the forest and smelled the fresh air. "I am alive!" he shouted to the trees. "I am free!" he shouted to the sky. As if in answer he heard the birds chirping happily flying in and out of the trees in unison. Sasha watched them and laughed his first laugh in freedom. He began his journey through the wilderness. It would not be easy. He had to cross Siberia and all of Russia to get back to Byolarussia. If he was to perish, then he would rather perish in freedom than in captivity.

Chapter Thirteen

He hid in the utility closet at the railroad station. Through a small, dirty window Sasha watched the train unload the sorry-looking human cargo. And with a heavy heart, he remembered his own arrival two years prior. He scanned the boxcars carefully, looking for features to which he could attach himself. The last car was different from the others; its structure was heavier and was carrying massive equipment that was being unloaded. Underneath the car was a long, steel plank supporting the hefty metal sides. A large handle was attached to a slider door with a rail attached to the bottom side. After examining the steel plank and how it was attached, Sasha put a plan together in his mind and waited for the train's departure.

He dozed for a moment and was startled when he heard the whistle blowing. It was time to make his move towards the train. He grabbed his sack containing a few belongings and Katlina's smoked sausage, salt bacon, and dried bread. Then he checked the huge hunting knife in his belt that Pasha had given him. He walked quietly out of the station. A few soldiers were walking around, although not paying much attention to people on the street and on boardwalk by the train. The consensus between the soldiers was that anyone foolish enough to try and escape would perish in the Siberian wilderness from cold, hunger, and wild animals roaming the forest and so they did not bother with possible escapees.

The train started its tremendous engines, blowing hot hissing steam into the cool morning air. The massive wheels squealing in protest started to slowly move, the engines making chugging sounds. Sasha ran to the side of the train and waited for a few cars to pass by him. When the last car arrived, he grabbed onto the back door and swung his body underneath the train, lying on the steel flat plank behind the wheels. The train picked up speed with Sasha holding on with all the strength remaining in his body. He hung on as long as he could and as soon as they were out of the village and past

109

all the log cabins and farm fields, he slowly and carefully slid himself from under the train, grabbed onto the rail, and lifted himself up to the slider door. He slid the unlocked door open and looked inside; it was now empty of the heavy equipment. He stepped inside and closed the door. Squinting in the darkness and with the help of some daylight streaming in from a few cracks in the wall, he was able to distinguish a few contents of the car: A few old potato burlap sacks and some old, worn out army blankets stacked alongside the wall with dry, fresh smelling stack of hay.

Sasha gratefully went over to the haystack and made a spot for himself in the corner of the car. He covered the hay with a blanket and sat down covering his legs. With a prayer of thanks to God he closed his eyes and wept until sleep overwhelmed his exhausted body and soul.

Sasha did not know how long he slept, but when he awoke it was total darkness. The night was bitter cold. He covered himself with more blankets and listened to the rumble of the train, moving as if through eternity. Once in awhile he could hear the howling of a wolf in the distance.

He slept again and when he woke it was morning. The train was slowing down. Sasha immediately was alert and prepared to flee. He found a crack in the wall and peered out of it. He could see some settlers and rolling green hills with cattle grazing in the distance; it appeared to be a small town. *The train is probably stopping to replenish its coal and water supply,* Sasha thought.

It came to a stop. Sasha sat in the corner of the car waiting for what seemed to be hours. No one came close to the car he occupied so he began to relax. Then, he felt the train lurch and the rumbling began again. Sasha was on his way home.

The train's engines kept a steady, clanking sound. Sasha listened until the rhythmic sound lulled him to sleep. Visions of home and his Anya floated in and out of his dreams. He awoke with fear in his heart that they would stop the train and find him hiding. The night seemed neverending. Finally the morning arrived; the sun peeking in through the cracks woke Sasha from a deep sleep. He sat up attentively and looked outside at the bright sunshine spreading its rays over a vast countryside.

They were approaching a small village. He saw a horse rider in the distance and cattle grazing in the pasture. The train slowed down. Sasha gathered his few belongings and stood by the door ready to leap off the train if the soldiers came near the car. He slid the door open slightly and looked toward the front of the train. The village came into view. He saw people leaving their houses on their way to feed the animals or going into the fields for a hard day's work. He waited until the train stopped and then he jumped off the railing of the car and ran behind the train and into the woods.

He hid behind some thick bushes, took out a piece of bread and munched on it while scanning the village for signs of soldiers. The workers were loading supplies of water and food items on the train. The street was almost void of people and the only soldiers that he could see were the ones from the train. He waited, hidden in the bushes, chewing on the bread and salt pork.

The morning air was warm on his face and he savored it. He stretched out on the grass and closed his eyes for a moment enjoying the song of the forest with its many wild occupants. Some hours passed; it was now late afternoon. Sasha decided to walk to the front of the train as if he was one of the villagers. He casually sauntered over to the train and pretended to be in awe of the huge engine. The conductor was preparing for the departure. Sasha struck up a conversation with him and asked, "*Tovarysz*, where is this enormous train going? It sure is a massive engine." He pointed to it. "I have never seen one like it. It must be difficult to run this and know where you are going!"

The conductor replied, "We are going to Moscow, and yes, it is very difficult to run this train." He looked at Sasha suspiciously. "One must know what to do and not take any chances." He turned away from Sasha not wanting to continue the conversation.

"I can tell that you are a very smart man and I give you credit for the job that you are doing." he walked closer to the conductor and quietly said, "*Spasiba Tovarysz.*"

A soldier overhearing the conversation between the conductor and Sasha came over to check Sasha out. Seeing him coming, Sasha said to the

111

conductor, "Well, I must get back to work before I am missed. I just wanted to see this train with my own eyes so I can tell everyone at work that I actually spoke with the conductor!"

The conductor was flattered and waved to Sasha with a smile on his swarthy face. He quickly turned around and with a swagger walked onto the street as if going back to work. He glanced back and saw the soldier stop, look at him, turn around and walk back to his comrades. Sasha turned to the right and ran back to the train, jumped in the last car and closed the door. The whistle blew; the train began moving slowly, picking up speed.

When he arrived in Moscow, he jumped out of the car and ran into the street without being noticed. Moscow was teaming with people, full of bustle and noise. Food vendors with all type of carts containing a variety of foods were set up on the sidewalks. The aroma of cooked food made Sasha's stomach growl and his mouth water. Soldiers were stationed at every corner watching for suspicious people, so Sasha was very careful not to bring attention to him.

With bowed head, he walked around for a time and then noticed a vendor who was selling grain and flour. The vendor was an elderly man with sun-worn, tired-looking eyes. *He must be a farmer and should be going home to his farm at the end of the day. Maybe I can get a ride from him,* Sasha thought assessing the situation.

Sasha sauntered over to the farmer, "*Tovarysz, kak parzywajicie?* How are you, my friend? I came to Moscow to visit a sick relative but my horse went lame so I had to leave him with my cousin." He scratched his head as if in thought. "I am looking for a way to get back home. Maybe you would be kind enough to let me ride with you as far as you go?"

The man cautiously analyzed Sasha, decided that he was no threat to him and agreed to take him along. They packed up the grain, harnessed the old horse, and Sasha climbed in back of the wagon on top of the grain sacks and finally relaxed a bit and hummed a song. Visions of his Anya and the children misted his eyes. He sighed deeply and dozed.

It was a small farm and under the control of the Communist regime. The farmer was allotted a portion of his harvest that he sold at the market.

The remainder went to the government. The farmer's wife was kind to Sasha and insisted that he eat well. And when he sat at the table to eat her potato pancakes with a piece of bacon, she beamed. "*No, Haraszo. Haraszo.* That is good. Very good," she said to him.

After resting in the barn on sweet smelling hay, Sasha set out on foot after thanking the farmer and his kind wife for their hospitality. The farmer watched him walk away with sadness in his tired old eyes. He suspected that this young man, as so many others, was on the run from the Communist regime or from the Partisans. He was glad to help and with hunched shoulders he went back to work in the fields.

Sasha continued on his journey, stopping for the night in deserted barns or under the stars with only the tree branches for cover. He stayed clear of the traveling roads and avoided being seen by the soldiers. On the fifth day of walking, he was near a dirt road. He thought that he heard someone singing. He listened and went closer. Peering through the bushes he spotted a very sturdy wagon full of hay. Obviously this wagon was from a very large farm and the man holding the reins was well fed and was very well dressed in clean and well-maintained working clothes. He appeared to be in his early thirties with thinning blonde hair and a very friendly face. He was singing a familiar Russian folk song, so he picked up the tune and started to sing along with him, as he walked out into the road. Sasha waved his hand and smiled.

The man pulled on the reins, "Whoa, *Szarny.* Whoa." The horse slowed the pace and came to a stop. The man jumped off the wagon seat and came forward, laughing and unafraid. "*Tovarysz,* you can sing!" he said to Sasha. "My name is Igor Czarnoff. I work at a very big and prosperous farm which is owned by one of the Communist Commanders."

Sasha stiffened, but Igor laughed and slapped him on the back. "Relax, *Tovarysz,* I can tell that you are on a mission and most likely hiding from some political party, however, I am not political." Smiling he said, "I do what I have to do to survive and keep my family from perishing. Sing with me! We do not have much else left in these hard times. The war with Germany is going on. Hitler is trying to take over the world and Stalin is killing off his own people. What can we do? Sing! Sing!" He laughed heartily. Sasha joined in laughter and song.

"My name is Sasha Petrosewicz. May I ride with you as far as you can take me? I am heading for Minsk and hope to find my family who lives not too far from there. I have been walking for several days and my shoes are worn out."

Igor slapped him heartily on his back again and laughing motioned with his hand. "Get in, Sasha, and join me in a song! We don't have far to go. You can hide out for a while pretending to be one of the workers." They became friendly and Sasha stayed on the farm for four days. Igor arranged another ride for him with another farmer who was traveling to Zostojo some hundred miles from Minsk. He provided Sasha with a jacket, a good pair of pants, and good shoes. In his sack he packed a sharp knife with food supplies that would sustain Sasha for some time. Sasha thanked him profusely and the two friends said goodbye.

The farmer left him in Zostojo and Sasha set out on foot again. He spent his days looking for passing farmers who could give him a lift. It seemed to him that he was walking into wilderness away from the direction that would lead him home. He was getting very desperate, looking for some form of civilization. But all he confronted was more woods and wild fields.

His food supplies from Igor were running low. During the day he picked berries, and when he came upon a brook or a river he caught fish and on a small fire he cooked it, savoring every morsel. It seemed to him that he had been walking for months, but in reality it was only five weeks. He was getting weak, his bones were tired and his knee was badly hurting him from a fall into the ravine when he tried to hide from a convoy of soldiers that were passing through. His shoes wore out and fell off of his feet. He took his jacket off, tore it into pieces and wrapped his bleeding feet.

He had not shaved for weeks; his beard was long and matted. Hair once fair and shiny was now shaggy and ridden with lice. The sunken in eyes lost their glitter, they were dull and lifeless. His once muscular body was a skeleton now and his spirit was shaky and he wondered how he could go on like this too much farther. But the vision of his Anya and his children kept

114

him moving on. *I will survive! And I will find my way home* He kept repeating this to himself with each step, and each step took him closer to home.

Nicolaj was feeding the chickens in the yard. A stray chicken clucking noisily ran into the road and Nicolaj chased it with a stick trying to get it back into the yard. He glanced down the road and spotted a raggedy beggar coming toward their house. He let the chicken go and ran to the house, opening the door he yelled, "*Mamushka! Mamushka!* Come and look at the beggar walking down the street! He looks really bad and is coming toward our house!"

"I will see who it is. Don't worry, son." Wiping her hands on her apron, she opened the door and she looked out. Under a cloudy sky with rain threatening to spill any moment, the raggedy beggar was heading toward the house. She wasn't afraid. Beggars were a common sight and the villagers opened their doors to them with offerings of food and rest. She stood in the doorway watching the beggar come closer. His head was bent in dejection and resignation. The beard was long and hanging in matted clumps on his chest, and his hair under a dirty worn out hat was hanging in strands like dirty straw. The threadbare clothes hung on his emaciated body and his feet were wrapped in rags. He was limping badly; each step relying on a walking stick made from a thick branch. Yet, there was something about him that Anya could not distinguish at the moment.

Anya looked deeply at the beggar again. Something was very familiar about him. He staggered to her. The searing gaze in his blue eyes seemed to burn right through her heart. She froze in the doorway as if an arctic wind swept over her. She did not dare to hope, though excitement crept into her heart. "*Zdraswicjca tovarysh,*" She greeted him. "Who are you?"

The beggar did not reply as though he did not hear her, but kept on limping toward her. Anya was unsure of what to do. He seemed in need of help. She placed one hand on her heart and felt it beating rapidly in her chest as she took a step down and waited shaking with anticipation.

"Are you hurt?" Anya asked. "I see that you are limping badly. Is your leg broken?" The stranger still did not answer, just kept his eyes on her face as if there was nothing else in this world for him to see.

"Please come in. My son, Nicolaj, will help you."

She turned to find Nicolaj standing not too far from her watching the beggar with suspicion in his eyes. She motioned to him.

"Come here, son, and help this man into the house."

"But *Mamushka*, we don't know who this man is! He could be dangerous!" he whispered.

"Son, this poor man needs our help. We must help him. Now, help him into the house and run and get some water from the well for him to wash."

Reluctantly, Nicolaj agreed. He still wasn't convinced he should help the beggar. Many times they turned out to be spies for the Communists or the Partisans. He decided to do as his mother wished.

"Here, lean on my arm. It will be easier for you to walk."

The beggar's body shook slightly as Nicolaj gently took his arm for support.

"This is my son. My son is helping me and does not know he is helping his father, he thought. He stifled a sob in his throat as he stared at his son, studying his every feature. How he had grown in two years time!

He limped to the doorway where Anya was standing. Weak and unsteady he stood in front of her, his eyes devouring her. Nicolaj propped him up against the wall and ran to fetch the water.

Anya stared at the beggar. His lips were dry and cracked; his blue eyes dull, tired and red-rimmed from lack of sleep. Deep-etched lines at the corners of his eyes showed the harshness of his life he must have endured. But strangely, she was not afraid of him.

He stood bent over, thirsty for the sight of her, longing to hold her, but his strength left him. He leaned against the door for support and with calloused hands held on to the door handle. Looking into her blue eyes, his raspy voice whispered, "Anya, my Anya, don't you know me?" His voice broke into sobs. "It is I. Sasha."

Anya's eyes opened wide, she felt faint and her knees threatened to give way. She leaned into the wall for support. She wasn't sure she heard him correctly. She shook her head trying to clear it, her body swayed slightly. She peered intently at him.

"Sasha, can it really be you?"

The beggar smiled and nodded.

She reached out to him and touched his face. It was thin, his cheeks were sunken in and once prominent bones stood out skeleton-like. His skin felt dry and sunburned.

"We thought you had perished in Siberia." Her eyes misted over with tears. "Oh Sasha..." she cried. With the last ounce of strength left in him, Sasha held out his trembling hands to her, steadying her, and pulled her into his arms.

Nicolaj came back with a pail of water. His eyes took in the sight of his mother being held by the raggedy stranger. Hr thought that he heard his mama call this man who was embracing her *Sasha. Could it be my Papa? Is it really he?* He tugged on his father's arm. Sasha looked at him and smiled.

"I am home, Nicolaj my son. I am home."

"Papa!" Nicolaj cried. He grabbed his father in a fierce embrace feeling his father's bones through the thin clothing and hugged him hard, not wanting to let go forever. The love between father and son was like a shining jewel, they smiled at each other as Sasha stroked his son's hair.

"Papa, I will run and tell the girls that you are home." He hugged him one more time and with excitement ran outside to find Marina and Katrina.

Moments later the girls followed by Layka came running and stopped at the sight that greeted them—a raggedy, dirty strange man holding their mama in an embrace. This was not the Papa they remembered.

"Papa?" Marina said in a shaking voice.

Nicolaj put his arm around Marina reassuringly and took Katrina's hand in his. "It is Papa. Don't be afraid."

Sasha looked at his children. "Oh! How you've grown!

"Nicolaj, come here son. Let me look at you." Again he embraced his first-born son who had become the man of the house at such a young age and without a complaint. He held him close to his heart, kissing his forehead, brushing the fair hair away from his eyes.

Nicolaj noticed that his Papa was swaying slightly, ready to collapse.

"Come, Papa, you must sit down and rest." He helped his father to a chair.

"Son, you still worry about everyone. Thank you, I will rest my weary feet."

Layka sat next to Sasha, licking his face. He gently scratched her behind the ear.

"Nicolaj, where is Misha?"

Nicolaj looked down. "Misha died shortly after you were deported."

A tear found its way onto Sasha's cheek. In his mind he could see her bounding after him through the fields and forests chasing rabbits, and when he spotted Anya running toward them, he ran like the wind to greet her. Yes, Misha was a great friend and companion. He would miss him. He wiped away the tear and hugged his son again.

Then he looked at his beautiful daughters. Katrina was still being cautious. She slowly inched her way to him. She looked into his eyes very seriously.

"Papa," is it really you?" Katrina asked.

"It is your Papa. See…" He parted his beard and pushed it aside so she could see some of his face. Katrina giggled and snuggled into him holding on tightly. Sasha could not contain his happiness or the tears that were freely flowing.

Marina was now hugging her father, too kissing his bearded cheek. He held his children close, and then remembered that there were two more when he was captured.

"Anya, where are Alexandria and Janushka?" he asked.

Anya took his face into her hands, looked into his tired blue eyes and said gently, "Sasha, Janushka is taking a nap right now. She is a beautiful little girl. Very active and always running after Nicolaj," she chuckled. "She loves the horses and the animals and many times I find her in the stables sleeping under some horse. They seem to sense that she is only a child and don't harm her."

Anya rambling on and on about Janushka and her antics, but Sasha

118

sensed that something was wrong. Fear gripped his heart and in an emotional voice he asked, "Anya, there is something you are not telling me. Where is Alexandria?"

Anya looked away from his eyes. "Alexandria died six months ago from pneumonia," Anya spoke sadly. Pain rose from inside her heart. She took a deep breath. "She was a happy child with a sweet face. But she was very sickly. We tried to keep her healthy by giving her more food and pampering her all the time but she did not have the spirit and the fight in her like her sister, Janushka. My mother tried to cure her with her herbs, but she did not respond to any of them. The doctor from Toloczyn came too late." A cloud of sadness passed her eyes. "She died in my arms. We buried her with the other children."

Sasha was grief stricken. He remembered her birth on the sled in the snow, how very tiny she was. She was only three months old when he had seen her last. And now, she was gone forever. He will never hold her again or sing to her. He did not get to know her and he was not there to help. Tears were falling down his dirty face into his beard, and sobs deep inside were shaking his thin body. Anya held him close.

"Janushka is different as you will see. As young as she is, she tackles anything that comes her way. Nicolaj has his hands full with her. She follows him around like a puppy, and at times he gets very fed up and chases her away, then she comes in crying and complaining. I try to explain to her that Nicolaj is a boy and needs to be doing things on his own. But she still tags along with him," Anya said laughing through her tears.

Then, as if on cue, the bedroom door opened slightly, revealing a little face peering out.

"Janushka, come here." Anya motioned for her to come closer.

Janushka shrank back, frightened by the scary-looking man in their house.

"Janushka, don't be afraid. Come. This man is your father, your Papa. See? Nicolaj is not afraid. Marina and Katrina are not afraid. Come here, it is your Papa." Still, Janushka was wary. She was only three-months old when he was taken away. She did not know her papa.

119

With tears in his eyes, Sasha called to her, "Janushka, come here. It is all right, my child. I know how frightful I look to you now, but you will get to know me." In a soft voice he said, "I am your Papa." He motioned to her, "Come here, I will sing to you."

Janushka slowly inched her way toward her mother and brother. She stared at him and wrinkled her nose; he smelled badly. Sasha and Marina laughed at her distasteful expression. Her young mind was going in circles not able to comprehend what was happening. Sasha stared back at her with gentle, tired eyes. He smiled and held out his hand to her.

Janushka stood frozen, ready to flee like a little doe. Yet, something inside her made her look at him again. The kind blue eyes continued to stare back at her with love, almost pleading for her acceptance. She smiled and took his hand into her little one and held it.

Sasha closed his eyes. "*Spasiba Hospudzi,*" He leaned down and kissed her forehead. He turned to his wife. "Anya, the children are beautiful and so well taken care of. How did you manage to do all that by yourself?"

"Nicolaj was my big helper, as always," Anya said. "He goes hunting with Layka and they bring back a rabbit once in a while. It is always a happy occasion because we do not get much meat from the *Kolhozy*. My mother comes over whenever she can and brings us vegetables from her garden during summer months. It is rough at times, but we manage." A sad smile formed on her lips as she continued. "Marina goes to school in the mornings with Nicolaj and I take Katrina and Janushka to work with me and leave them at the kindergarten." She looked down at her hands, they were chapped and her nails short and scaly. "God seems to provide somehow. And now you are home! Oh, Sasha. How we worried, wondering if you were alive." She hugged him.

"So many people have perished. Almost every day we hear of another neighbor being deported. Stalin is relentless and Hitler is coming closer. Times are bad and will get worse." She shook the horrible thoughts from her mind and took his hand in her own. "Come, my love, let me get a bath ready for you."

She helped him up and brought him into their bedroom. Sasha sat on the one chair in the room. Nicolaj brought in the big tub they used for bathing and filled it with warm water.

"Papa, let me take the dirty rags off your feet." Leaning down he slowly removed the filthy layers of cloth. He sucked in his breath at the sight of his father's feet. Raw sores were oozing pus and caked-on blood covered his feet. His toes were black, he wasn't sure if it was from dirt or poor circulation. Nicolaj glanced up at his mother who was standing next to him. She was looking down with horror in her eyes at the sight of the sores, and quickly got a pail of warm water and placed his feet in it.

"Sasha, let your feet soak for a while," she said. "I will get the salve that my mother made from her herbs and bandage the sores."

She looked lovingly at him. "You must be starved. I will prepare supper, and get your clothes which are still in the closet." She rushed around the room nervous and light-headed, while Sasha was enjoying the soothing warmth of the water on his aching feet.

The girls kept running in and out of the room, curious to see what their Papa was doing. Anya gathered them to her. "Children, go outside and play while your father bathes. Son, can you get some potatoes from the garden? And get some cabbage. There is some smoked sausage, bacon and a cured ham in the cooling storage, please get it for me."

Sasha finished soaking his feet, took off his lice-infested clothes and handed them to Anya to be burned later. He slowly entered the tub on unsteady legs and sank into the hot water, luxuriating in its warmth. He scrubbed his head with lye soap to get rid of the lice. Anya sat on the edge of the tub and cut off his long matted strands of hair and his long beard. She noticed the thinness of his body and many scars all over his back.

"What are all these scars?" she asked. "How did you get them? Did they whip you?" She shivered with worry.

Sitting in the wooden tub absorbing the warmth of the water and the feel of Anya's hands on his back, Sasha's mind quickly scanned the horror of his capture.

Yes, they whipped me and tortured me, but Anya must not know that.

"Those are only scratches. Several times I fell into a ravine and the

121

branches caught me with their gnarly fingers!" He chuckled, making light of it. Anya didn't really believe that, but didn't want to press him for the truth. *He will tell me when the time is right.* She knew her Sasha. He couldn't keep anything from her.

"Anya, tell me how you managed all this time alone? Did the children give you a hard time?"

Anya thought for a moment and then smiled, "Nicolaj was very upset when you were captured. He was depressed for a long time. I tried to help him out of his depression, but he had to do it his own way. After a while he realized that, so many others had been taken with you, that he was not alone in his grief.

"He made friends with one of the boys from a nearby village. And one day he brought him home to meet me. It was a boy from a family whose father was an officer in the Communist regime. I was not happy about it, and tried to tell him how wrong it was for him to be friends with a Communist. He could not understand my reasoning for a while. Then, my mother intervened, took him to her house and kept him there until he came to his senses. It was very difficult for all of us for a time, but with my mother's help, we survived." She sighed deeply. "The girls have been no problem. Marina helps with chores and takes care of Katrina and Janushka. My sister, Juzia, works with me at the *Kolhozy* and we walk to work together every morning." She was quiet for a moment. "It has been very lonely, but the children keep me busy. It is not the same as having you here." She stroked his thin cheek. "We miss your singing."

Sasha grinned. "I will sing to you, my love, right now!" And his weak voice burst into one his favorite tunes. *Oh Kalinka, Kalinka, Maya.* Anya's dreamy eyes misted with tears.

She scrubbed his scarred back and massaged his tired muscles. Sasha was luxuriating in the feel of her hands. "Anya, I forgot how soft your hands are. I missed you so." He grabbed her hand and pulled her closer to him. She lost her balance and almost fell into the tub with him. She pushed him away laughing. "Sasha, it has been so long since I have actually laughed. I am so glad to have you home, my darling." She leaned and kissed his clean cheek. "Now, finish washing. The children are anxious to be with you."

The water-cooled and he slowly got out of the tub careful not to strain the knee, and stepped onto the wooden floor clean and refreshed. It was good to be clean and feel human again. Sasha turned and looked at his Anya. She was waiting for him with a towel in her hands. Her glorious chestnut hair was loose, hanging down her back. Her eyes were sparkling with desire for him and her tender mouth was curved in a smile that promised much more when the children were in bed. She towel dried him and handed him his old familiar clothes. He dressed, noticing the looseness of the clothes on his body. He was very thin. Then he reached for her, wrapped her in his arms and buried his head in her neck savoring her scent.

Anya called the children in for the supper she had prepared with great fanfare to honor Sasha. Baked *Babka* with fried sliced pieces of salt pork, fried onions, garlic, and melted butter was in the oven alongside the ham. Aroma of fresh bread baking reached Sasha's nose making his mouth water. Anya was setting the kitchen table humming a song while Janushka watched her father carefully, as if not believing that he was her Papa.

Sasha smiled at his youngest daughter with such warmth and love that Janushka lifted her arms to him. He held her, gently stroking her fine, blonde hair. Janushka looked into her papa's eyes. Even at so young an age she recognized his love and strength, and somehow knew it would sustain her all her life.

The gentle but illuminating glow of the lamp cast warm shadows over the family enjoying their dinner. They were full of happy chatter and when the dinner was over, the dishes cleared and washed, Sasha, though totally exhausted, sang passionately to his children holding them closely to his heart. Anya sat beside him marveling at the strength of this man who was her husband and the father of her children.

For the next three-and-a-half years Sasha and his family lived normal lives. Anya continued to work at the *Kolhozy* and Sasha worked mostly for different farmers, trying to keep low profile. Although he did not think that anyone would still be looking for him, he did not take any chances.

The following year, Anya delivered another girl. They named her Anya. She lived only one week and another child was buried; Anya and Sasha were once again filled with grief and sorrow.

The war raged on throughout Europe. Horror stories of atrocities being done to the Jewish people had everyone panicked and full of apprehension of things to come. The German soldiers were making their way to Byolarussia. Each day more Nazi's came through the village on huge tanks and on foot, setting up camps outside the village.

The Jewish people that lived in the village or in nearby villages went into hiding or looked for ways to escape. Every night the Nazi's came into the village searching homes for the Jews. They forced them out of their hiding places, ordering the village men to dig trenches.

On those nights Sasha would gather his children and softly sing, trying desperately to block out the sound of the shovels digging into the earth and the horror of screams and moans that would follow.

When the trenches were dug, the soldiers lined up the distraught women and children. Mothers pleaded and begged to spare their lives. But the soldiers, with bloodthirsty faces ignored them, and pushed and dragged them to the edge of the trenches. With machine guns they gunned them down until they all fell into the trenches either dead or wounded. Frightened children were grabbed crying and screaming from their mother's arms and tossed around by the soldiers like rag dolls. They tore apart their arms and legs and threw them into the trenches with their deceased mothers. People from the village were forced to stand and watch the atrocities, then ordered to bury them. Most were dead, others moaned with life left in their bodies. The sand on top of the buried moved eerily as those still alive tried to get out from under the ground.

Some managed to crawl out and escape into the woods, only to be found in the morning and killed.

There were those who were loaded onto German trucks like cattle and taken to concentration camps where they were gassed or killed by other means. These were some of the darkest days of Sasha and Anya's lives.

Sasha helped by hiding people in the food pantry behind bags of grain and flour. Under the dark of night he guided them in the thick pine tree forest and prayed for their survival.

In the fall of 1943 the Germans began their retreat back to Germany taking with them all the men they could capture. Word spread throughout the village and the men went into hiding. Sasha hid in the food pantry during the day, coming out at night only for supper.

Anya had given birth to another healthy, beautiful baby girl, named Alexandria after the twin sister who had died. Nicolaj, now fifteen years old, went to work with Anya every day; once again taking on the role of the man of the house. The young village girls, taken with his good looks and charming smile, followed his every move with their eyes, giggling and flirting with him at every chance.

"Nicolaj, you are a charmer. Before you know it you will find yourself a wife," Anya teased him.

Janushka was five-and-a-half years old now and begged to spend time with her brother, wanting to tag along wherever he went. Nicolaj did not want his little sister with him, and complained to his mother.

"Nicolaj," she laughed, "take Janushka with you. The girls will not mind. They will have much respect for you and say what a nice brother you are!"

Anya had prepared potatoes with a little fried salt pork with onions, and boiled turnip. Everyone ate hungrily. That evening, Sasha entertained his family with folk songs, all the while bouncing Alexandria on his lap when the door opened with a great force. Janushka screamed as a German officer, big and menacing, stood in the doorway scanning the room. His powder blue eyes went straight to Sasha.

"Get your things right now, Petrosewicz. You are coming with us! *Schnell! Schnell!*" The soldier pushed Sasha with such force making him stumble and fall.

Anya screamed in fear and the children cried in protest and ran to their father holding on to him as he scrambled off the floor. Sasha put his finger to his lips signaling them to keep quiet. It was a familiar signal, and the little ones slowly quieted down, muffling their sobs with their hands.

Anya stood frozen to the ground, and in her mind she pleaded with God. *This cannot be happening again! Dear God in Heaven where are you? Why have you forsaken us? Please don't let them take my Sasha again! Holy Mary Mother of God please help us!*

She stood there sobbing with a pleading look in her eyes at the soldier. The soldier had no pity for the likes of these people. He stood in the doorway blocking it with his feet spread apart and arms crossed on his chest, a smirk on his face; he had nothing but contempt in his eyes.

"*Schnell, Schnell!*" He pointed a gun at Anya. "Help your husband pack his things or I will do it, and not in a nice way!"

Together, Anya and Sasha they gathered his few belongings from the closet into a pillowcase and tied it into a knot. Sasha looked at his family. Anya's face was ashen; she stood beside him overwhelmed with grief. The children were peeking from behind the massive stove crying and afraid.

The soldier walked over to Sasha and with the butt of his gun pushed him forward making him stumble. Sasha looked back one last time at his family, and with resignation walked out with the officer.

As the door closed the children cried and sobbed uncontrollably. Anya held them close, trying to comfort them despite being overwhelmed with her own grief and fear.

"Quiet.... children, do not despair. Papa will be back. He always comes back because he loves us so much! God will guide him again and he will return to us."

Nicolaj put his strong young arms around his mother, and guided her to a chair. "Mama, I will take care of you and the girls don't cry. I am here and always will be."

Anya hugged her first-born son fiercely, looked at her girls and sat there with the sadness of being alone again.

Chapter Fourteen

The German officer shoved Sasha toward the military truck filled with men from the village. A soldier grabbed Sasha's hands roughly and tied them behind his back. With a vicious push against the truck, he was ordered to climb in with the rest of them. He crawled in and sat next to a neighbor whom he knew well.

"Pavel, they got you too? I thought that you were gone to Minsk? You should have stayed there."

Pavel smiled sadly at Sasha. "We can't escape any of these madmen. The world is turning upside down it seems, creating all these killers. Unless we join in the killings of women and children, we are not safe anywhere." They looked at one another with sadness, nodding their acknowledgement, afraid to say another word.

More men and some very young boys were brought and loaded onto the truck. It was filled to capacity. Sasha noticed a young boy who was friends with Nicolaj. "Yuri? How did you happen to be picked up?" Sasha whispered.

Yuri whispered back, "They came for my father, but he was gone to Toloczyn. My mother tried to tell them that he wasn't home. They only laughed and said that if he wasn't home then his son would do. They grabbed me and here I am."

Yuri wiped a tear from his eyes and thought of his mother and three sisters at home. His dog, a mix of Russian wolfhound and wolf, tried valiantly to rescue Yuri from the clutches of the Nazi's, however one of them put a gun to his head and shot him. Yuri collapsed on top of his dead dog with grief, holding his great head and lovingly said goodbye to him. His mother screamed and cried when they dragged Yuri away, begging the soldiers to take her and leave her son home with his sisters. But her pleading was ignored, as if she was just another bothersome insect. Yuri would not see his mother or his sisters again.

Sasha leaned against the wall of the truck. This was the third time this has happened to him. When would this end? His family was again left alone. *Dear God in Heaven, where are you? Why have you forsaken us?* No answer came to him. He looked back toward his home and pictured Anya surrounded by the children, forlorn and sad. *What will become of my family now? Anya has endured so much already. How will she survive? And what will become of me? Will I be taken to the gas chambers?*

Sasha knew that one did not have to be Jewish for the Nazi's to kill you. Many had perished simply by being at the wrong place at the wrong time. If you had a dispute with someone or if a soldier did not like you for whatever reason, it was reported to the authorities that you were suspected of being Jewish and off to the gas chamber you went. Neighbor was afraid of neighbor, friend of a friend, brother afraid of a brother.

Vengeance built up in Sasha's heart like a raging storm. He looked to the sky and cried: *God, I will find a way to escape again and I will find a way to bring my family to a better life. I will survive with your help. Please guide me and take care of my loved ones until I return.*

The truck moved out, sputtering plumes of smoke from the rusted exhaust pipe, the wheels bounced up and down over ruts in the dirt road causing the truck to rock from side to side. The men bounced in the rear of the truck like rag dolls; unable to brace themselves with tied hands. Sasha's head kept hitting the side of the truck; he hit his head with a force so hard that blood spurted from a gash on his forehead. As the blood dripped slowly down his forehead it mixed with tears etching a deep wound in his heart.

The sky was gray with heavy dark clouds and large drops of rain began to fall. It was as if the sky was weeping for the poor men huddled closely in the traveling truck. The men were getting soaked to the bone. For hours they traveled, with each mile they grew hungrier and thirstier. Some men desperately needed to relieve themselves. The soldiers refused to stop, wanting to arrive at the camp before nightfall.

128

Sasha knew they were nearing the camp for the road was less rutted and the ride smoother. He sighed. At least now they could stretch their legs, quench their thirst, and possibly get some food.

Sasha was exhausted and his stomach was growling. The dried blood on his face made him look sinister. He looked around at his neighbors; he saw that they were just as distraught and bewildered as he. No one knew for certain what was in store.

The truck stopped at the iron gate manned with a guard armed with a machine gun. The truck driver and the guard exchanged some words and the truck proceeded through the gate. Sasha noticed numerous tents were set up in a circular order. Barbed wire surrounded the perimeter of the camp. All types of artillery were present—menacing-looking tanks with enormous long-necked guns protruding towards the sky, ready to spew destruction. He saw captives shackled with leg chains, groups of men working on trucks and other artillery. The Nazi soldiers carried threatening-looking machine guns, guarding the ammunition and the men. The truck with fresh cargo of captives continued on toward a large, long tent. The truck stopped in front of the tent.

The soldiers barked. "Out!... Out!" The men tumbled out of the truck their legs cramped and stiff.

They were herded inside not knowing what fate awaited them. The tent was full of men shackled, their camp work clothes hanging loosely on their wasted bodies, their eyes vacant as they ate the meager rations of boiled potatoes and turnip. A huge cast iron pot was on the stove with rising steam sending an aroma of boiling meat and vegetables throughout the room. The smell of food assaulted Sasha's nose. He inhaled deeply, remembering Anya's cooking and the happy times at the table with his family begging him to sing and he would say to them, *you must eat first, my flowers, and then I will sing to you your favorite songs.* The memory of his children eating hurriedly brought a smile to his face.

Now in this wretched camp, far from his family, Sasha soon would be shackled like the rest of the captives. For how long, he did not know. The German Army was retreating, taking all the captives with them to labor camps in Germany. Sasha knew that most likely this was to be his fate. He knew, too, he had to find a way to escape.

He sat along side of other captives and hungrily reached for food. He must eat to keep up his strength and stay healthy. No one dared to talk for fear of retribution from the soldiers. Sasha watched the guards closely. Their hatred for their captives was evident from the contempt in their eyes. These were dangerous men, men who would kill or torture for pure pleasure.

Before the men could finish their meager rations they were herded outside.

"Get outside! Move!" the soldiers ordered. The language barrier frustrated the soldiers. Sasha and the others were shoved and pushed across the compound and into another tent. Sasha saw immediately the huge table laden with chains and shackles.

"Lift! Lift!" the soldiers shouted, pulling up their own pant legs indicated what they wanted. A frail elderly man did not move quickly enough, he was shoved to the floor, roughly shackled, and then thrown into a corner with the rest.

It was Sasha's turn. He walked over with his head bent not wanting to show his face directly and allowed them to shackle him without protest. Anger deep inside was building like a volcano, yet he fought to suppress it and meekly walked away. Let them think he was a submissive farmer afraid of authority. The men sloshed across the rain-soaked compound, mud caking in their leg-irons, adding weight and discomfort.

The work areas were at the far end of the camp. Sasha observed heavy dump trucks moving debris into the woods. Other trucks hauled damaged vehicles for repair or dismantling. Sasha and another man, Igor, were assigned to dismantle the tanks and other badly damaged artillery. The parts that were not damaged were used for repairing other vehicles. Igor and Sasha worked together daily, and cautiously established a friendship. The two men had much in common; both were burning with the desire to escape. One tank was badly damaged by a grenade and was left in the back of the yard. Sasha and Igor were assigned to strip all the workable parts off of it. As Sasha was pulling on a difficult part to release it, he glanced toward the wire fence and noticed that there were several broken links in it.

"Igor, come here and see what I found. Quiet, do not say anything; just watch me. I think that there is some weakness in this fence. It looks old and rusty. If you and I work on breaking the wires, we can make an opening big enough for us to squeeze through. What do you think? Do you want to take a chance?"

Igor nodded his head with excitement and anticipation. "I will check the fence while you stand guard. I don't want to stay here helping these butchers a moment longer." Igor made a disgusting face and spit on the ground letting his feelings known.

Sasha said, "All right, then Igor, let us get to work."

Every day for three months Sasha and Igor took turns working on the fence wiring. Each broken link gave Sasha and Igor an exhilarating feeling of freedom coming closer. They worked diligently, one standing lookout while the other crawled over to the fence to loosen another link, covering it with leaves and branches, and crawling back to their job.

While the two friends were loading a truck with army supplies, Sasha whispered to Igor, "I tried to crawl through the opening today. I think that it is big enough for us. It looks like it may rain tomorrow. It will make a good day for escape. Save some of the bread from dinner and I will see if I can find a knife or some sharp utensil. We will need it in the forest. When we walk to our job, I will fake a twisted ankle and you will do the same. We will make sure to be walking together and when the guard takes off the shackles, I will jump the guard, disable him and we will make a run for it."

The rain fell heavily in the morning, blinding their vision, yet the soldiers were relentless in their mission to get the parts ready to ship out to the front. Sasha and Igor were ready to pull their scheme. Igor walked very close to Sasha awaiting his signal. As they neared the end of the compound the soldiers ran quickly into the tent. Sasha edged as close to the tent as possible without drawing attention. He heard the soldiers laughing; the sound of playing cards shuffling. Sasha signaled to Igor that it was time to make their move.

Sasha stumbled, knocking Igor off his feet and the two of them rolled around in the mud moaning in pain, holding on to their ankles. The soldiers, hearing the moaning and yelling, peered out of the tent to see Sasha and Igor on the ground holding on to their ankles, obviously in great pain. Not one went to their aid, preferring to stay in the dry tent playing cards and drinking liquor.

The men screamed again. The commander pointed to one of the soldiers. "You, go and see what all this noise is about."

The soldier, irritated that his card game and drinking had been interrupted, kicked the two men shouting, "Steinke! *Auf! Auf!* Up! Up!"

Sasha feigned pain. "*Ja nie mahu wstac. Maja noha.* I cannot stand up. My ankle hurts."

Igor added a piercing scream for effect and motioned that he could not stand either.

"*Praszu! Praszu!* Please! Please! Unlock the shackles." Sasha motioned to the soldier to remove shackles, which added to his pain.

Reluctantly the soldier fumbled in his pants pocket for the keys. Since Igor was screaming the loudest he unlocked his first, then leaned down to unlock Sasha's shackles. Sasha looked back at the tent once more then grabbed the soldier by the neck and knocked him over. Igor grabbed his machine gun and with the butt of it hit him on his head knocking him senseless. The soldier went limp.

Sasha pulled the keys from the soldier's hand and unlocked the shackles on his legs. They dragged the soldier under the tank and quickly ran for the hole in the fence.

The rain was still falling heavily, giving refuge for the two escapees from being heard or noticed. "*Spasiba Hospudzi,*" Sasha prayed as he and Igor ran into the woods stumbling and falling in the wet forest until they came to a clearing and visible pasture. In the distance they could see smoke from the chimney of a farmhouse.

"Igor," Sasha said, "I wonder if we should see if that farmer is friendly and non-political? I am so hungry that I am ready to take that chance. That bread you saved was not enough to sustain us. What do you think?"

Igor stopped and thought for a moment. "Sasha, I do not think that we should take a chance. It is too dangerous. We are better off to stop and rest until it gets dark. Then, maybe we can catch a rabbit and light a small fire to cook it on. I am hungry too, Sasha. However, we must not take any chances. The soldiers must be looking for us by now. We must keep moving."

The sun was setting now; the shadows of the forest shielded them and they decided to rest. They found shelter under a tree with wide heavy branches and thick moss surrounding the base. They sat on the moss stretched their tired and hungry bodies and waited for the night to give them the cover of darkness.

"Sasha, I hope we did not kill that Nazi soldier. I know that he may have deserved to die, but I do not want to be the one to do it. I prefer that God takes care of that." Sasha was dozing and not really listening to Igor ramble on. "Sasha, are you listening to me?" Igor was agitated with fatigue and hunger.

"Igor," Sasha said impatiently. "If we killed him, God will have to forgive us. He would have no problem killing us if he had a chance. This is survival, Igor. Evil is on a rampage and we must stop it any way we can. We must protect our families."

The night shadows and the song of the night creatures in the forest were eerie and frightful to the two men hiding under the tree. Wolves could be heard howling in the not-too-far distance making the hair on Sasha's arms stand up with fright. Wolves were thought to be very vicious and not too fond of human beings. The farmers hunted them killing and maiming them with traps. As a result, they hunted in larger packs.

"We must move on," Sasha said. "The soldiers can't be too far behind us."

They jumped up, weak from hunger and lack of water, and started walking along the perimeter of the forest to stay clear of the wolves that picked up the scent of man and were edging closer to Sasha and Igor.

"Igor, we must stay at the edge of the forest and be ready to run for the trees if we see any soldiers. It is the soldiers or the wolves. Let's hope we will escape both." Sasha's voice was weak and shaking.

Igor was limping from an open and bleeding blister on his foot. Mosquito bites covered their faces and necks. They walked until dawn, not certain if it was in the direction of home. Finally they spotted a village. They could hear a rooster crowing his morning song and the cows mooing; waiting to be milked. Sasha smiled at the familiar noises that he loved and recognized the log houses. He was home.

They broke into a run. Sasha ran toward his house with his heart exploding in his chest. As he got closer he saw Nicolaj outside raking the yard. He whistled to him. At first, Nicolaj wasn't sure if it wasn't the wind blowing through the trees. But then he heard another whistle. Nicolaj turned his head to look in the direction of the whistle. It was his Papa! He broke into a run and almost knocked his father down as he jumped into his arms.

"Papa, how did you escape again? We worried so much, and Mama cried all the time. The soldiers were here looking for you, questioning Mama and the neighbors." He frowned and caught his breath, "Mama was very frightened that they would take all of us to the labor camps without you. They said that they would be back." Panic was in his eyes. "You must hide, Papa!" Nicolaj was taking charge despite the severity of the situation.

Sasha grinned, "Nicolaj, you are a fine young man. I am very proud of you." He put his arm around him, realizing that his firstborn was growing into a man to reckon with.

They entered the house. Surprise and joy was on Janushka's face as she ran to him laughing and calling, "Papa, Papa we missed you. Do not go away again, Papa!"

He ruffled her hair, hugged Marina and Katrina, and lifted Alexandria into his arms. "Where is your Mama?" he asked Marina.

"Mama is at work. She will be so happy to see you." A cloud of sadness passed her eyes. "She cried almost every day worrying and wondering if you were taken to Germany." She paused. "Papa, it isn't safe for you to be here. I am very scared that they will be back soon." Big tears ran down her cheeks. "The Nazis came looking for you and threatened Mama. If she did not tell them where you were, they would take her to the labor camps without us. Somehow, she convinced them that she didn't know of your escape or your whereabouts. They don't give up on those who escaped."

"Marina, I know how dangerous it is right now. I have seen the soldiers everywhere, and I was able to hide from them." He sighed deeply, "I will stay very aware of my surroundings and not bring any attention to myself. Do not worry, daughter of my heart." He kissed her on tear soaked cheek and gently wiped the tears away from her blue eyes.

"Papa, I will prepare a bath for you, and make dinner." She wanted to sound very grown up. "You must be very hungry." She smiled up at him revealing the dimples that melted his heart.

"*Spasiba*, Marina, it has been days since I had any food. I will bathe and shave."

He stepped into the basin filled with hot soapy water and sank in, feeling the muscles on his body relax. He closed his eyes and dozed with troubling thoughts going through his mind. *Marina is a beautiful young girl, but I see fear in her eyes. She is afraid and very insecure. Rightfully so...she has seen too much in her young life. Hospudzi, help me find a way to find a better life for all of us. I must find a way.*

Sasha sat at the familiar wood kitchen table with the children surrounding him and begging him to sing for them. They all talked at the same time, making him laugh. "I have returned my little ones and when Mama comes home we will have dinner and I will sing your favorite songs to you. Let me rest for a while. Then I would like to walk towards the *Kolhozy* and meet your mama on her way home."

Nicolaj jumped off his seat and was by his father's side in an instant. "Papa, you can't go out there! You can't risk of being seen by the Nazis. I saw huge trucks full of soldiers making their way back to Germany. They are on the run. Whenever they set up camp, they scour the villages for men and young boys to take back with them to labor camps. You must not go out, Papa!" He was anxious and frightened.

However, Sasha was determined to surprise Anya and brushed off Nicolaj's warning. "Nicolaj, I must go see your mother. I can't wait another moment. I need to look at her and know that she is all right."

"Papa, I know how anxious you are to see Mama, but think about it. If you get caught, you may never see her, or us, again. This time, they will kill you. Please Papa, listen to me." He grabbed his father by his sleeve and tugged on it with urgency.

Sasha looked at his son thoughtfully. The blue eyes of son and father locked. The fear in Nicolaj's eyes was real. Sasha sighed with resignation and put his arm around his son's shoulders hugging him.

"You are right, son. I shouldn't risk the entire family. Your mother will be home soon enough. I will wait here."

Nicolaj smiled happily. "Papa, you could surprise her hiding in the house and we will play in the yard and pretend like everything is as usual. Then you could sing and she will wonder if she is hearing things." Nicolaj's face was beaming.

"What do you think Papa?"

"I think it is a brilliant idea." Sasha smiled. "I will do that, Nicolaj."

As Anya walked home from the *Kolhozy* thoughts of Sasha weighed heavily on her mind. She feared it was a premonition; that news of Sasha's fate awaited her at home. She walked, her head bent watching for stones in the dirt road. She began kicking them out of her way, to distract her mind from her fearful thoughts.

She was almost home. The dirt road narrowed and she could see the buildings up ahead. She hurried her step as if something was edging her on. As she came closer to her house, she saw the children playing in the yard. She smiled as she always did at the sight of them. There was Nicolaj, like a good shepherd watching his flock. *How fortunate I am to have this boy help me. God, thank you.*

The children spotted their mother walking slowly toward the house. "Mama is home! Mama is home!" Janushka called to Nicolaj excitedly.

He gathered the children to him. "You must be quiet. Mama must not suspect anything." He straightened up and motioned to Marina. "Run and tell Papa that Mama is almost here. Go on, run quickly."

Anya waved to Nicolaj as Janushka ran to meet her. She bent down and kissed Janushka's fair hair and took her by her hand as she skipped along beside her mother. They entered the yard. Anya's heart skipped a beat. She could have sworn that she heard singing in the house. Puzzled she glanced toward the door. The door was closed. She looked at Nicolaj. He was busy playing with Alexandria. But, there it was again, Sasha's voice as clear as if he was in front of her. She wiped her face with her hand as if wiping away the illusion, and then she noticed the door opening slowly and the vision appeared. It was her Sasha! He was here!

She flew to the door as he stumbled down the steps toward her. Sasha held her close and kissed her starving lips, tasting her salty tear rolling down her cheeks.

"Sasha, my Sasha, I have missed you so." She touched his face, as if to make sure he was real, and smoothed his fair hair off his forehead. "How did you escape?" she asked. "I hear that the Nazi's are very vigilant and not many people have made it out of the camps."

Sasha could feel her fear and agitation. He held her closer, protectively. Looking deeply into her eyes he said, "Anya, I was lucky to flee the long arm of the Nazi's. My friend and I managed to outsmart the devils." Remembering the escape, his eyes clouded over and he shivered inside. "I will tell you more of all that has happened later."

"Oh…you must hide Sasha. The Nazi's will be looking for you. It is not safe for you here. What are we going to do?" She held on to him, her body quivering; worry etched her tired face.

Sasha's heart ached for his Anya. *She has endured so much already. When will all this end?* He inhaled her lavender aroma. "Anya, I know that they are looking for me and how dangerous it is for all of us. I will hide and you go on with your activity as normal. No one must suspect that I am here." His hands moved to cup her face. He looked tenderly into her blue eyes. "I have missed you so, my Anya. But tonight let us go and prepare dinner and I will sing to the children. I promised them that we would sit together like we used to and be a family for this night."

Chapter Fifteen

The people in the village were restless and worried. The retreating Nazi army was causing destruction in its wake; burning homes, taking men and women with them to labor camps in Germany. They did not tolerate resistance. Machine guns were poised and ready to shoot down anyone that refused to obey their orders.

Sasha spent most of his time hiding in the food pantry where Anya made a bed for him. She slept in the pantry with him, refusing to sleep alone. In the early morning hours he quickly did indoor chores while Nicolaj took care of the animals and did the outside work. Marina was sent to school and the younger girls spent their days with their Papa, enjoying his full attention. Anya went to work every morning and in the evening she would bring news of what she heard about the war, and who was taken away to the labor camps in Germany.

Once the children were in bed Anya sat with Sasha. She looked particularly troubled. "Sasha, I have bad news from the village. There are many people who are getting sick. Everyone thinks that it may be typhoid fever." She paused, clasping her hands tightly together. "People are panicking, and I am scared. Several people have died already." Sasha was alarmed. Anya worked in the environment with all these people. He had seen outbreaks of such sickness and knew that there was no cure for it. "Sasha, it is spreading rapidly and there were some workers that fainted today and were sent home. I was exposed to these workers!" She pushed a few strands of hair that escaped from her braids off her forehead. "I am scared that I may come down with it and spread it to all of you!"

Anguish and fear were in her eyes as she looked at Sasha almost pleading for some miracle that would keep them safe. Tears rolled down her cheeks and onto her lips. She tasted its saltiness and bitterness; she didn't want to cry anymore! Sasha pulled her into his arms reassuringly and said,

"Anya, if you do get sick then we will have to fight it together. I will take care of you and so will the children. Don't cry. We have cried far too many tears already." He wiped her eyes, kissed her brow and prayed, *Hospudzi, how many tears must we shed? We have done nothing wrong, God. Why are we suffering so? My Anya has endured so much already please let us live in peace!* He held her for a long time until her tears subsided.

The following morning Anya was busy in the kitchen, kneading dough to make the bread, while Marina prepared eggs and bacon. Anya smiled when she heard her Sasha humming a song while shaving and washing. It was a peaceful morning, with sunshine filling the kitchen spreading its rays across Anya's face and warming Anya's shoulders as if embracing her.

It feels good to be alive today, Anya thought even though she felt very tired and light-headed. She didn't know why her hands were trembling slightly; she glanced at her pretty daughter. Marina seemed to have sensed her mother's gaze and turned to her and smiled noticing her mother's flushed face. *"Mamushka*, are you feeling all right?" Anya smiled back at her oldest daughter. "I am fine Marina; I think I must have eaten something that didn't agree with me. But, I will be all right. Do not worry."

Sasha strolled into the kitchen and as always was full of mischief and laughter. He picked Anya up in his arms and twirled her around the kitchen while singing and making her laugh with joy. Marina watched happily as the other children came running in to see the merriment their parents were creating. They sat at the kitchen table with anticipation of the baked bread and fresh butter.

"Hurry, Anya," Sasha was teasing. "We are starved. Are you going to watch your family starve?" He laughed heartily and winked at the children.

Anya turned to him and snapped her kitchen towel playfully at Sasha. He grabbed the towel and pulled her to him and kissed her forehead. He paused. It felt very hot to him. "Anya, you seem to be very hot. Are you feeling all right?"

"Yes, I am fine Sasha. I am just a little tired." She kissed him back and again playfully hit him with the kitchen towel.

Anya went back to the stove to take the bread out of the oven and as she bent down, she swayed and fell to the floor. Sasha ran to her, lifted her into his strong arms and carried her to bed. He felt her head; her skin was hot and dry. She was burning with fever. Her cheeks were flushed and she was having difficulty breathing. Sasha alarmed and helpless as to what to do quickly ran and got a towel, wet it with cold water, and placed it on her forehead.

"Nicolaj, get the wagon and the horse. Go quickly and bring *Babushka* here. She will know what to do," Sasha yelled to his son.

Anya was moaning and thrashing around on the bed with Sasha holding her down. Marina wet the towel with cold water and placed it on her mother's forehead. It seemed like hours passed before they heard the horse's hooves and saw Rozalia coming through the door. She quickly went over to see her daughter and felt her forehead, then checked her eyes and opened her mouth to check her tongue. She stood back looking very grave.

"Anya has the typhoid fever, Sasha. We must isolate her from everyone and hope that it is not too late. There are many people down with it and many are dying very quickly." She busied herself pulling out herbs and medicines she had mixed out of her satchel. "Cover her in cold blankets and keep the ice on her forehead. I will get some herbal tea for her for now."

Rozalia boiled some water, put the herbs in it, mixed and boiled the brew for ten minutes. Then she strained the brew, poured some of it into a bowl and went to Anya. She sat beside her and slowly poured the liquid between her dry and fevered lips making her swallow it. Her eyes would open slightly with eyelids fluttering as if the light was hurting her eyes. "If the fever breaks by morning, then she will be alright. We must pray." Rozalia said and they all knelt and prayed, begging God to spare her.

Rozalia and Sasha stayed by Anya's side all night changing the iced towels and talking to her softly, encouraging her to get well. The fever wasn't letting go. Anya was in a state of delirium, thrashing about the bed; mumbling and talking incoherently, her face flushed and dry. Rozalia feared that she might lose her beautiful daughter.

By the morning light Rozalia felt some moisture on Anya's face. She quickly felt her neck and felt perspiration on her skin.

She called to Sasha. "I think the fever is breaking. She will make it if it does."

Sasha took Anya's hand and kissed it lightly, feeling the moisture against his lips and knew at that moment that his Anya would make it. He fell to his knees thanking God for her recovery.

On the sixth day of Anya's recovery, Marina and Nicolaj awoke feeling ill. By afternoon both were down with fever. Rozalia went about taking care of them and brewing her potion. She poured the liquid between their parched lips and changed the ice packed towels. Anya stayed away, as she was too weak to help Rozalia and Sasha kept getting ice to keep the towels cold. As with Anya, Nicolaj's and Marina's fever broke by the morning and they were recovering while Rozalia was cooking, cleaning and making everyone comfortable.

Two days after Nicolaj and Marina fell ill; Sasha did not get out of bed that morning. Anya felt his head; it was burning with fever. She called out to her mother who was outside feeding the chickens. "Mama, come quickly. I think Sasha is sick with the fever!"

Rozalia dropped the basket of grain and ran into the house. She felt Sasha's forehead and knew that he, too, was down. Once again, she brewed her herbs and poured the liquid between his lips. Anya kept the towels cold with ice, and they kept vigil on him all day. By night the fever was getting worse. Sasha was burning up. He was in a state of high delirium, moaning and yelling, thrashing about, throughout the night.

He was drowning in the whitewash paint. It was filling his lungs, his mouth and nose. He was choking and couldn't breathe. The white wash was consuming him like quick sand. He was going down...down....caught in a vortex, spinning.... spinning...falling....to an endless bottom.

He was running....running....the monster train engine on his heels trying to envelop him in its billowing smoke. I must run faster...but his legs were like stones cemented into the railroad tracks. I must run faster....away from this terrible smoke....it is choking me! Anya! Help me, Anya! I can't move my legs! The train is upon me...I am burning.... The hot steam of the engine is burning me!

141

The Nazis are everywhere.... They are like black creatures crawling, engulfing the world.... We must run.... Anya, we must run from them....Anya!

The graves of all those little children gunned down by the Nazis...the soil on top of the graves is moving.... They are still alive! We must get the children! Children...children are crying.... The fire.... The fire is burning the children!

"I am burning.... *Hospudzi!*" Sasha screamed, thrashing about in his hallucination while the fever held on to him, burning the life out of him.

Both Anya and Rozalia were exhausted caring for him through the night. In the morning Anya decided to look for help. Sasha would not last another day with such high fever.

"*Mamushka*, I am going to look for the doctor. I know how dangerous it will be, but everyone is in the same predicament. Even the Nazis are sick." With a worried glance at her mother, Anya sighed and sat heavily on the chair at the kitchen table. Rozalia concerned for her daughter sat next to her and took her hand into her own, as she did when she was a little girl. Breathlessly, Anya continued, "They may let me through without paying much attention. I must risk being stopped. I can't let Sasha die without help."

Rozalia didn't argue with her strong-willed daughter. She knew the danger she may face. "Anya, you are still very weak from the fever and in no condition to travel on icy roads by yourself. Let Nicolaj go instead."

Anya shook her head in protest. "Nicolaj is not safe from the soldiers. They will pick him up and we will never see him again. He is blond and blue-eyed, just what the Hitler wants for breeding his blonde, perfect regime. No, *Mamushka*, I will go. I will be careful not to attract too much attention. I know the roads very well."

Rozalia nodded, resigned to her daughter's will. "I will watch the children and will do my best to keep Sasha comfortable."

Anya dressed warmly and walked over to the barracks where she worked. The streets were deserted only a few stray dogs and cats were scurrying about looking for scraps of food. Very few people were around; most of them were sick or had died from the fever. Anya walked quickly, slipping and sliding on the frozen ground, her worn out shoes not giving much support against the ice. She entered the compound and found the commander. "Is there a doctor that I can bring to see my husband? He is down with the fever and will die if I do not get help for him."

The commander, a stocky man of middle height with a jovial face, answered, "There is a doctor in the village north of here, but chances of getting him to come out here are very slim. Lady, you better go home and forget about it." He looked at Anya with compassion.

Anya refused to believe that and walked back to the house. With shaking hands she harnessed the horse to the wagon and, as weak as she was from the fever, she took the reins and urged the old horse to get going.

The village was like a ghost town. She passed several streets, before she spotted a man walking. She stopped him and inquired about the hospital. The man, with his head pulled inside his heavy coat, peered at Anya and pointed to a big building that was set up to house the sick. He quickly walked away from her with fear in his eyes.

Anya urged the horse to go forward toward the building. She pulled the horse over, tied the reins to the post and went into the building. It was dark and the thick air smelled of death. A tall man in a white coat was bending over a woman on a cot. Anya went straight to him.

"Are you a doctor?" she asked.

Tired and haggard he straightened up. "Yes I am a doctor. How can I help you?"

Anya started to cry. "My husband is sick with typhoid fever," she said through her sobs. "I just got over it, but my husband is very sick and I do not think that we know how to help him." She grabbed his hand. "Please, help him doctor. My children need to not lose their father. Please, you must come and help us."

Although weary from lack of sleep and caring for so many sick people, the doctor saw the desperation and love for her husband in Anya's eyes. He had done all he could for the people here in his charge.

"I will come with you." He picked up his doctor's bag. "I may not be able to help your husband. But I will come and do my best."

Anya returned with the doctor in the wagon and pulled up in front of the house. Layka, alert as always, came out barking not recognizing the stranger in the wagon. "Layka, it is all right, stop your barking."

The children inside the house heard Layka's barking. They ran outside and saw their mother with the doctor. *"Mamushka!"* Marina called out. "We have been so worried that you may not come back." Marina was sobbing and she was scared.

Anya jumped off the wagon and gathered her children into her arms, soothing them with loving words. "Don't worry, the doctor is here. He will help Papa. Now, come into the house and get warm. I will get some warm milk for you. Where is Nicolaj?" She looked around to see where her son was. He was sitting next to his father placing cold towels on his forehead while Rozalia was force-feeding him some chicken broth.

The doctor quickly walked over to Sasha, checked his pulse and placed his hand on his forehead to check the fever. He took out his stethoscope and listened to his heart.

"What are you giving him?" he asked Rozalia.

"I have healing herbs. I learned about them from my mother. She showed me how to use them."

The doctor nodded his head with approval. "We must take him and wrap him in a sheet. Then take him outside and cover him with ice and snow. It is the only way we can keep the fever down."

Anya and Rozalia hurriedly got the sheet and with the doctor's help dragged Sasha off the bed and outside. They covered him with ice and snow and kept him outside for over one hour. Finally the doctor said, "All right, get him back into the house. Rozalia get him some of your brew, heat it and put some vodka in it. We will make him drink it and that should cause him to sleep and relax his fever-wracked body. I will also give him the little medication that I have."

Sasha seemed to relax after drinking some of the vodka-mixed brew. The doctor stayed for another hour checking Sasha's breathing, his pulse, and his temperature for signs of the fever going down. Within a few hours Sasha was breathing easier.

144

"Anya, he should come through this," the doctor said. "I see some signs of fever releasing him. There is not much more I can do. Let him sleep and if he makes it through the night, then he will recover just as you did." The fear that gripped Anya released upon hearing the doctor's news.

After feeding the doctor a meal, Anya bundled up again and took the doctor back to the village. Rozalia, tired and worn out from taking care of everyone, sat in the chair and waited for Anya to return. Sasha was sleeping much more peacefully. The fever seemed to be leaving him. Rozalia was praying silently, *Hospudzi, Darahoj Hospudzi, please let him survive this terrible sickness. Anya and the children need him in these terrible times. Hear my prayer!* She wept quietly until she dozed to troubled dreams.

Chapter Sixteen

Life had again returned to a normality defined by the changing and uncertain times. Sasha and Anya recovered from the typhoid fever slowly. The fever left them weak and despondent. Anya's mother stayed on to help with the children and the house chores until Anya was able to go back to work at the *Kolhozy*. Sasha took longer to recover. Rozalia tried hard to heal him with her herbs, and finally after a month of healing, he became more alert and ready to start daily activities. The children were very happy to see their papa well because he was able to sing to them again.

Rozalia stayed on for another week. Then one morning she said her goodbyes to Anya and the family with a strong premonition that she may never see them again. She held her daughter in a tight embrace, kissing her cheek for the last time.

Four months passed with tranquility and normal day-to-day activity. Sasha and Anya almost believed that all was well with the world. News of the war was slow in coming to their village and everyone hoped that perhaps the Nazis had retreated and were gone for good. That tranquility was short lived.

Nicolaj was in the pasture caring for the horses when he saw the soldiers driving to the house. Running as fast as he could he got there only to see the Nazis holding his father with his hands tied behind his back while he was struggling to get free. The girls were huddled together on the porch watching their papa being taken away again. Nicolaj ran to the girls.

"Come into the house, hurry! Don't let them see you frightened." Nicolaj herded them inside. "Papa will come back again. He always does."

He closed the door, ran back out onto the porch and watched his papa being dragged to the truck. The soldiers ordered Sasha to get in the truck. When he resisted they grabbed him by his arms and threw him in like a sack of potatoes. He scrambled into a corner and glancing back at the house saw

Nicolaj on the porch, his young face frozen in fear and sorrow. Nicolaj's body was shaking. He wanted to run and grab the soldier's gun and shoot all of them, but he knew that it would only make things worse. At a very young age he learned to use his head and good reasoning. *Will this ever end?* He thought. *God, please let my papa survive again.* His eyes were dry; there were no tears left.

Anya saw the Nazi truck coming toward her as she walked home from the long day at work. She abruptly got off the road and paused. Her heart was pounding in her chest, afraid that the worst had happened. *Please, God, don't let it be Sasha in that truck!* She stood still, letting the truck pass by her. And as it did, horror of worst kind registered on her face. Sasha was in the back hanging onto the sides of the truck, blood dripped down his face. She stifled a cry and fell to her knees.

Sasha, through blood-soaked eyes, glanced towards his Anya. She was kneeling on the ground with her arms outstretched toward him, her face contorted with pain and heartache. She was losing him again. He nodded to her, forming the words, "I love you," and then he was out of sight.

With Sasha gone yet again, Nicolaj assumed the role of man of the house and Anya did whatever was necessary to keep her family strong, trying to find ways to provide them with food, which was extremely difficult to obtain. The *Kolhozy* gave rations of flour and potatoes to families with small children, but no meat was available. Once in a while an old chicken or rooster was killed and Anya would make soup. Their one cow, which the children named Mushka, supplied them with milk and butter.

Marina, able now to read and write, spent her time teaching the other children. As Marina settled Janushka and Katrina down for a story they were startled by a knock at the door. Anya opened the door cautiously. A young village boy handed her a note, then turned hastily and left without saying a word.

Anya opened the note. Tears sprang into her blue eyes.

"What is it, *Mamushka*?" Nicolaj asked.

"I think this note is from your Papa." She read the note carefully, not

147

too sure if it was from him. In these times one had to be very careful and not fall into a Nazi trap. "Nicolaj, Papa is not too far from here in the Nazi camp. He wants to talk to me. I must hurry and get there before nightfall."

Nicolaj took the note from her and read it. It seemed to be genuine; he recognized his father's penmanship. "*Mamushka*, it looks like Papa wrote it. I would like to come with you to make sure it is not a trap."

Anya thought for a minute, then said, "Nicolaj, you must stay and take care of the girls. Papa will want to see me alone. And if anything bad should happen to me and Papa, at least you will be here to take care of the family. You must be strong and wait for me to return in the morning." She kissed his cheek and dressed quickly kissed all the girls hugging them to her praying that she would be able to return.

Anya looked at the horse wistfully in the pasture and wished that she could saddle it and ride the four miles to the camp. But the horse, along with everything else, belonged to the Communists and she would need permission to take it. Briskly, she walked the four miles to the camp. At the gate a guard blocked her entrance, holding a machine gun over his shoulder. She did not know how to inform him as to her purpose of being there so she said Sasha's name and motioned with her hand that she wanted to see him.

The guard nodded, as if he had been expecting her arrival, and pointed to the tent on the far side of the camp. The flap of the tent opened and a soldier came out. Anya froze as the soldier looked her over.

"*Was Wolen zi?* What do you want?"

"I came to see Sasha Petrosewicz," Anya said. "I am his wife."

The soldier nodded his head and pointed for her to go in.

She walked into the dimly lit tent and searched for Sasha. She recognized several men from the village. One man nodded and pointed across the room.

"Sasha," she called out. In the dimness she peered at the men, but didn't see him. "Sasha," she whispered again. "Where are you?"

Sasha was sitting on the ground with other men and heard his Anya calling him. He jumped up and ran to her. "Anya, I am so glad you were able to come. I was so worried that the boy didn't get the note to you."

148

Anya cautiously looked around the room afraid at being overheard. "Tell me what is happening. I feared that you might have already left for Germany. They are taking everyone now. It is so frightening for all of us. Every day it seems more people are being snatched from their homes and families. We are being swallowed by the Communists and the Germans who are retreating and are roaming the country like wolves in packs." She paused wringing her hands in frustration.

"Anya, they are taking me to the labor camps in Germany. There is no escape from them now. I want you and the children to come with me. If you don't chances are that they will come and get all of you and we will be separated forever. If you come with me now, we will be together and face whatever comes our way with our children. And when the wretched war is over, we will come back."

Anya thought deeply while holding on to her Sasha. *I can't stay back here without my husband. We have been apart so much; I cannot endure another separation! I will go with him wherever life takes us.* She lifted her head and looked into her husband's blue eyes. "Sasha, I will get the children and we will go with you wherever you go. I vowed to be by your side until death. And so be it." She hugged him fiercely and put her head on his strong shoulder with resignation.

"Go home and pack some belongings. Come back here with the children. They will be shipping us out to Germany by nightfall tomorrow."

Anya walked back home. She gathered her worried children. "We must pack in haste, my children. We are going with Papa to Germany. It will be very hard for all of us, but we will be together," she said with sorrow in her voice.

Nicolaj looked at his mother with horror in his young eyes. "*Mamushka,* what are you saying? Can't Papa escape again? There must be a way we can get him out of there! I don't want to go to Germany!"

"What about Mushka, our cow, and the cat?" Janushka piped in. "We can't leave them behind!"

"*Mamushka,*" Nicolaj took his mother's hand. "Is there anything else that we can do to be with Papa?"

149

Anya's heart was broke at seeing her children so upset. "There is no other way. Papa and I discussed this situation and we could not find any other solution. We have to go."

Nicolaj bowed his head hiding the tears that were threatening to spill. "I will pack my things, Mama. What do we have to take with us?"

Anya told them what to pack. "Girls, get your things together. Son, get the wagon ready and harness the horse. I got permission to take him when I visited your Papa. Here is the paper in case we are stopped. Do not misplace it. We must hurry or they will take Papa without us."

Everyone rushed around grabbing clothing, the children gathered a few toys to take, and everyone helped load the wagon. Marina helped Janushka and Katrina onto the wagon, and Anya held Alexandria while she scrambled in. Nicolaj took the reins and with a clicking noise, they were off.

Anya looked back at the house knowing she may never see this home or her mother and sister ever again. There was no time to say goodbye. Dread filled her heart knowing they would be frightened, wondering what had happened to them. *Hospudzi! What is in store for us?*

The cow began mooing, almost forlornly as if saying goodbye to them and the cat ran after the wagon, meowing. "Mama," Janushka cried out, "we cannot leave our cat. Please, Mama, can we take her? She will die alone."

The tears rolled down her young face as she sobbed and screamed for the cat to catch up. Anya, sobbing too, tried calming her down.

"Janushka, she will be all right. *Babushka* will come and take her to her house." Soon the cat stopped following and sat in the middle of the road. Janushka focused on that place in the road until she no longer could see her beloved cat.

Sasha waited anxiously at the gate for his family. The wagon barely came to a full stop. Janushka jumped down and into her papa's arms. Within moments they were surrounded by the Nazis and ordered to grab their belongings and get into the waiting trucks. Nicolaj tried to comfort Marina, but the tears would not stop falling from her eyes. Katrina sat quietly not saying anything at all. Alexandria, too young to understand what was happening clung to her Mama, whimpering, scared and confused.

150

Sasha, with Janushka on his lap, sat next to Anya, his face pale and drawn, his once merry blue eyes were dull and worried. He spoke softly to Alexandria and held Anya's hand giving her comfort and assurance the best way he could.

The trucks moved out. The engines sputtered black smoke that stung the eyes, assaulted the lungs, causing everyone to choke and cough.

"Papa," Janushka cried, "I want to go home. I don't want to go on this truck. I don't like it! I want my cat...and my cow!"

"We can't go home. We have to find another home now. You must be patient, my little one. We are together and that is all that matters. We have each other."

On the outskirts of Toloczyn, a huge menacing-looking train waited. The trucks pulled alongside the train and the soldiers barked orders to get off the trucks and to get into the boxcars.

Confused and distraught, Anya said to her children, "Take each other's hand." The soldiers were pushing and shoving, not paying attention to the women and children who were crying and whimpering alongside the men. Anya and Sasha held on tightly to their children for fear of being separated.

The boxcars were filling up with the captives. All were stumbling and pushing to get in and get a place to sit down. Sasha helped his family into the boxcar, getting in last. It was packed full of crying children, sobbing women, and angry men. There was no room to sit in the dark, badly smelling cattle transporting boxcar. He ushered his family to a corner. "We will take turns sitting on the floor. Do not cry, girls. We will be all right."

The train blew its whistle and began its slow moving journey. For hours on end the train kept on moving without stopping for its cargo to relieve their bodily functions. Children could not wait. Some women and men relieved themselves where they were standing. The stench in the boxcar was unbearable. People moaned and cried from fatigue and lack of sleep. Many were getting aggravated and frustrated, yelling at others and pushing, shoving to get more space. Sasha knew that things could escalate into a very ugly situation. He kept his family in a very tight group, urging them to be quiet.

The day faded to dusk; yet the train kept on moving relentlessly. Several women and children fainted; others vomited from being in such close quarters with no fresh air. And then the train slowed down, its wheels squealing as the brakes were applied. It came to a stop.

An audible sigh of relief swept through the boxcar as everyone waited anxiously for the soldiers to open the doors. The lock clanked and the door slid open. A soldier motioned with his machine gun for everyone to get out. Everyone rushed to the door, pushing and shoving each other, jumping down and running into the bushes to take care of bodily functions. Sasha helped Anya, who was feeling weak and wobbly. The children followed Mama to a bush that shielded them from the rest of the people and quickly relieved themselves. Still shielded by the bushes, Anya took out some bread, smoked sausage, and a bottle of water from one of the bundles that she managed to pack. They ate quickly and sparingly; not knowing how long this food would last.

The whistle blew signaling it was time to board the train again. Sasha pushed his way to the same spot in the corner. The boxcar door slammed shut and the nightmare continued into the night. Too tired to stand any longer, strangers leaned on strangers. The stench of unwashed bodies assaulted the senses. Sasha worried about his Anya, so pale and tired. He kept his strong arm around her to hold her up.

The night ended with the sunshine coming through the cracks in the car. "Maybe the train will stop soon," Anya said. However, it kept moving throughout the morning and into the middle of the afternoon.

Through the crack in the wall, Sasha looked at the landscape trying to see any signs of people occupying the area. There was nothing but pastures and woods for miles. An hour passed, and then another. Sasha peered out again. This time he spotted a cow and a horse in a pasture. Maybe the train would stop.

Within moments the brakes squealed again and the train rolled to a slow stop. The doors opened and the soldiers again ordered everyone out. The human cargo stumbled out like cattle, the bright sun blinding them temporarily. Anya gathered her children and looked around for a private spot, but the soldiers ordered everyone to keep moving toward a large, windowless building; its wide door exposing a dark hall inside. There were many soldiers by the door and at the sight of them Anya shrank back and held on to her children with fear. She had heard the stories of gas chambers that looked like showers. The soldiers kept pushing them in the direction of the building. Anya held on to Sasha tightly with apprehension of what was to come.

A soldier stepped forward and shouted, "Take off your clothes all of you filthy pigs, and then go inside to take showers." Anya looked at the soldier aghast, grabbed Sasha's hand holding on to him with disbelief in her eyes. How could these people be so cruel and heartless? What had made them this way? She looked at her Marina, at ten years of age she was already getting to be a young, beautiful girl. How could she ask her daughter to undress in front of all these people? She saw the fear and humiliation in her daughter's eyes and wanted to protect her from this nightmare, but could not.

"Marina, don't be afraid, we all have to do as they say. You see, I will take my blouse off and you do the same." She looked at her younger girls who stood there bewildered, and at Nicolaj standing still as a statue. "Nicolaj, you must do as they tell you, or all of us will be punished. Just pretend that all this is just a dream in which we are playing games. Keep your eyes on other things. We will all undress without shame. Place all your things in the corner there." She pointed in the direction where others were doing the same.

"Schnell! Schnell!" The soldiers kept yelling. They were irritated and began pushing the women away from the men, grabbing them and making lewd remarks. Anya's hair came undone, falling down to her waist in silky waves. The soldiers started to grab at it, pulling it, wrapping strands of it around their fingers. Sasha stood there with hatred in his eyes unable to do anything about it. The other soldiers were armed with machine guns and anyone trying to interfere with their games would be shot on the spot.

They kept yelling and smacking the women on their naked buttocks. The children were crying as everyone was herded like cattle into the building. Men, women, and children went in the hall in total nakedness, family's holding on to one another offering little cover and protection. Men kept their eyes down, not looking at the women, and the women huddled close together to hide their naked bodies.

As Sasha entered he was handed what looked and smelled like lye soap. A weak attempt to keep people calm, he thought. Stillness came over the large room as they waited for the showers to go on. Sasha and Anya, thinking that they may be gassed, looked deep into each other's eyes as if saying goodbye. They held their children close to their nakedness, hugging them with love.

"If something smells bad, then just hold my hands and inhale deeply," Sasha told his children. "All of us are together that is all that is important. Mama and I love you, my flowers, and Nicolaj with all our hearts. We will be together forever. Do not be afraid." Sasha's voice broke as tears flowed down his cheeks and his family cried with him.

The wide door slammed shut. A whining noise filled the building. Men and women let out a cry of fear and frantically tried to run, to no avail. There was little room and no means of escape. They were trapped.

Sasha felt it first—drops of lukewarm water started to fall, caressing his weary body with a soothing sprinkle. The filth of the past two days began to flow off him. Remembering the bar of soap in his hand, he began washing. He handed the soap to Anya, who in turn used it on her children.

"It stings!" Katrina cried.

"I know, my little one, but it will be good to be clean again."

The water went off and the door slid open. The soldiers came in holding big black powder pumps. People coughed and sneezed as the vile smelling powder was sprayed over their entire body. When they finished, the soldiers motioned for everyone to put their filthy clothes back on. Sasha and Anya held on to the children and slowly found their way to the corner of the building where they left their belongings. They dressed quickly and got back onto the dirty train that reeked of urine and human waste.

The next four days on the train were unbearable. Sickness was rampant among men, women and children from the filth of human waste that

154

covered the floor. It was slick and wet from urine and piles of feces that were pushed against the walls. Intolerable stench was strong and unbearable. Women covered their children's faces with pieces of cloth torn from their garments while they retched and cried. Fights broke out for more space on the floor or to get more elbowroom. Tensions were high from hunger and thirst. Anya guarded her satchel that held some bread and a small piece of bacon. Without drawing attention she would take out a small piece, break it up, and give each of her children a small bite.

The train stopped once a day. Upon re-boarding they handed everyone some bread and water. The lice began to crawl again; feeding on thin flesh, and laying their eggs in everyone's matted hair. The children scratched relentlessly, making sores and scabs on their heads that would not heal. The misery on the train got worse as each day went by. Sasha and Anya talked to their children, trying to make them feel better while their hearts broke watching them suffer.

The horror of the train journey continued into the fifth day. Sasha noticed the train changing speed and slowing down. He peeked through the hole in the wall. "I think we are finally at our destination. I see farms and cattle grazing."

Anya gave a sigh of relief, even though she did not know what was awaiting her family.

The train came to a screeching stop. The doors opened and the soldiers stood at the entrance holding their noses shut from the stench that assaulted them and with hand signals they ordered everyone to get off the train. One-by-one people stumbled off like a bunch of filthy animals, unrecognizable from the dirt and starvation, then pushed and shoved into groups and ordered to walk to the waiting military trucks.

Marina, Katrina, and Janushka crawled up into the truck as their parents pushed to make room for them. Nicolaj held Alexandria, who was whimpering and crying in discomfort and hunger. He cuddled her on his thin shoulder and crooned a song quietly as he did many times at home. Anya, dirty and haggard, her once beautiful face was swollen on one side with an abscessed tooth. She was feverish and in terrible pain.

155

Sasha tried his best to comfort her. "Anya, I will have to pull that tooth soon. Let us hope that we come to a settlement long enough for me to do it. It will be very painful for you, however, it has to be pulled or you will be very sick. Can you bear it?"

She nodded her head. "It must be done, Sasha. I can do it."

The trucks moved out along a bumpy dirt road muddy from the heavy rain that had been falling since early morning. Everyone was getting soaked. "At least," Anya said, "some dirt is getting washed off of us!"

The bumps in the road tossed the people against the sides of the truck, leaving them bruised and sore. Anya clenched her sore teeth together holding her head in her hands trying to stop the throbbing pain in her jaw that felt like a steel nail being pounded in by an invisible hand. There were others that were sick on the truck. Moaning and crying was constant throughout the day and night like an eerie song that never stops.

It was nightfall when they arrived at their destination. "Sasha, where are we?" Anya asked.

Sasha shook his head. It was difficult to distinguish the area in the dark. He could make out a building looming in the distance. It was like a fortress that could swallow them forever. He wondered what was in store for his family again. Was it a gas chamber?

"Children, we are coming to a building that may have showers again. Do not be afraid, do as we did the last time, we will be all right together," he said.

The trucks came to a stop in front of a massive door. It had double sides that opened to expose a large hall lit with naked light bulbs casting a light over what appeared to be a circus hall, with trapeze swings hanging from the ceiling with nets underneath fastened to the walls. They were herded into the hall, afraid and unsure of what to expect. No one spoke the German language; therefore, there was no communication with the soldiers. They motioned for people to choose any area and place their meager belongings on the dirt floor. Sasha found a spot in the corner of the hall, laid out their one blanket, and arranged their belongings in such a manner as to offer some privacy. Hundreds of families were forced to share the circus hall and all were trying to find a secluded area. Fights began to break out amongst the men and women, who were exhausted and starving. The soldiers broke up the fights, using the butts of their rifles and threatening to shoot if order was not restored.

Anya sat down on the blanket, feverish and sick. "Anya, I will try to get a doctor for you. They must have somebody in their regiment that can help you. You need medicine." She nodded, too sick to protest, closed her eyes and lay down against the wall crying. Janushka sat next to her, her small arms embraced her trying to comfort her. *"Ja Cibie Miluju Mamushka.* I love you, *Mamushka.* Papa will be back soon with the doctor, he will help you."* She placed her pretty little head on her mother's breast and waited for Papa to return with the doctor.

Sasha walked the short distance to the Nazi soldier's barracks that were located behind the circus hall. Soldiers, who were busy unloading the trucks with stolen goods from the farmers, paid no attention to Sasha. He walked over to a building that looked like it may be the Commander's office. He knocked on the door apprehensively fearing that the Commander will be angry at being disturbed. He heard a voice say, *"Comen zi!"*

Sasha, his knees shaking from fright, entered the office and stood in front of a massive desk with a massive man seated behind it. His uniform was very impressive with many medals of valor on his breast pocket. When he looked up to see Sasha enter, his round heavy face was bland, expression free. The light hazel eyes looked directly at Sasha with contempt in them.

Sasha adjusted his eyesight in the dimness of the room and bowed to the man. "Commander, my wife is very sick and needs a doctor."

The Commander's mouth moved and in broken Russian he asked, "What is wrong with your wife?"

In a hoarse voice, Sasha said, "Her tooth is badly infected and her face is badly swollen from the infection. I think that it needs to be pulled. If she does not get help, she will not be able to work. She is a strong woman and can work very hard. You need strong women, you must help her."

The Commander sat still for a moment without any indication that he heard Sasha. The mouth moved again. "We have no doctor here. You will have to pull the tooth yourself." He turned to the soldier who was standing near the door and said, "Wolfgang, get some vodka for this man. Let him give it to his wife when he pulls the tooth. Make sure that she recovers. The *Fuhrer* wants healthy workers only. The gas chambers are filled with the Jews; there is no room for sick women. You, go and take care of your wife." He looked blankly at Sasha and motioned for him to leave with Wolfgang.

The soldier stopped at the canteen and brought out a bottle of vodka and handed it to Sasha. He followed Sasha to Anya, who was leaning against the wall holding her badly swollen face. Her eyes were closed shut from the swelling. Sasha tried to tell the soldier what the problem was with hand gestures. The soldier understood, nodded and walked away.

"Anya, I will have to pull the tooth now. It will be painful. Are you ready?"

She nodded weakly. "Go ahead and pull it. The pain can't be any worse than what I am feeling right now."

Janushka sat on the floor next to her mama wide-eyed and terrified. She closed her eyes, holding on to her mama's hand, trying to give her comfort, and wanting comfort herself.

Wolfgang came back and with some compassion in his eyes, handed a pair of pliers to Sasha.

He poured some vodka into a cup and handed it to Anya. With some reluctance she took it and taking a deep breath she drank some of the fiery liquid, swishing it in her mouth to dull the pain.

"Pull the tooth, Sasha," she said and opened her mouth wide. While the soldier held her head, Sasha yanked on her tooth until it came loose. She moaned quietly, however did not resist the pliers that were tearing apart her gum. Finally, after several painful yanks, the tooth came out along with gushing blood.

Janushka began to cry and so did Alexandria. Their mama was hurt and the blood was scary. The soldier handed a towel to Anya to stop the bleeding. He pointed to the bottle of vodka and with his hand he motioned to her to wash her mouth out with it. She swished the vodka in her mouth again and spit the blood and vodka into the towel.

158

Sasha gave her another swallow of vodka, made a pillow from their clothing and placed Anya's head on it. "Go to sleep, my Anya. You will be better tomorrow." She closed her eyes and with her head pounding and the gums throbbing she tried to find some relief in desperately needed sleep.

Morning arrived with the soldiers yelling for everyone to get up. Anya woke with her head aching and her mouth raw with pain. The left side of her face was swollen and black and blue.

"Your face is very swollen, but your fever is gone," Sasha said. "You will be better in a few days. I will bring the children outside so you can rest. Anya tried to smile, though it was impossible with her swollen face.

Sasha gathered the children. "Come with me. Mama needs to sleep." As the family exited the building, the roar of trucks startled Katrina. "Papa, the trucks scare me." Sasha put his arm protectively around Katrina's shoulder. "Don't let them scare you Katrina. It is just a lot of noise from the engines." As he was comforting Katrina, he realized that they were standing next to a crematorium. A cemetery was located to the left, its jagged gravestones like an old woman's teeth, chipped and worn with time.

Janushka screamed clutching her father's legs as three trucks came to a stop. At first look the cargo they carried was not clearly visible. But the oddly shaped cargo soon came into everyone's horrified sight. Human bodies were piled high like matchsticks—legs hanging in bizarre disarray, arms reaching outward to the sky as if in protest of the indignity and injustice of the death. Wasted bodies of children with still eyes staring into nothingness forever were scattered atop fathers and mothers, neighbors and strangers.

Human flesh rotting in the sun assaulted the onlookers with an overpowering stench. Sasha tried to shield the children from the sight, but it was too late. Marina stared with horrified eyes, swaying slightly as if about to faint. Sasha steadied her by taking her arm and pulling her towards him. "Marina, don't look. Go back inside the hall and check on Mama. She may need you. Take Katrina and Janushka with you."

Marina felt sick to her stomach. She turned her head away from the horror, then took her sister's hands and tried to take them back to the hall.

159

As they were making their way back, a soldier spotted them and yelled at them, "*Achtung!* Attention! Where are you going?" Marina and the girls froze with fear. They stopped and waited for the soldier to come closer.

"Where are you going?"

Marina swallowed hard feeling the bile rise in her stomach she answered, "We are going back to the hall to take care of my mother. She is very sick."

The soldier shook his head and said, "No. You go back with the rest of the people over there. They need your help." Marina and the girls turned around and ran back to their father, scared and crying.

The commotion caused people to rush outside. Faces froze with the same expression of horror, shock, and fear for their own fate. The soldiers appeared, too, and began shoving the men toward the trucks. Sasha tried to resist, but a soldier prodded him with the butt of his rifle threatening to shoot. Others reluctantly walked over to the trucks and started to unload the human remains of these unfortunate people who died with such horror.

Nicolaj was beside his father. "Papa, we must go and do as they say. We must be quick with unloading so the girls don't have to help. Come Papa, let us hurry."

Marina, Katrina and Janushka stood together huddled, afraid to let go of each other and watched in terror as their papa and their brother unloaded the bodies from the trucks, hauling them into the crematorium. Sasha, with tears streaming down his face, was gently carrying a little girl, with long, curly brown hair that cascaded down her back. Nicolaj was behind him with a body of a young woman who must have been very pretty. Her beautiful brown eyes with long lashes were open and staring, curly brown hair was braided in long braids. "Was she the little girl's mama?" Marina asked. The girls didn't want to watch, but the soldiers walked around with their rifles and kept poking those who were covering their faces to make sure that they saw the horror of their work.

The men and women continued their grizzly task for some time until the trucks were empty and the next load came. This continued for two weeks.

160

Chapter Seventeen

A month has passed since we arrived in this Hell. My Anya is worn out and listless. Her once sparkling blue eyes are dull with no life in them. The children are thin from lack of food. Their bodies are covered with sores from scratching the bed bug bites. My beautiful girls' hair is full of lice, dirty and matted. Nicolaj is quiet and I see accusation in his eyes for taking them away from home. Did I do the right thing by asking them to come with me? Should I have left them at home until the war is over? Hospudzi! Hospudzi! I should have left them behind, and survive this hell alone as I did all the other times. How can I bear to see my beloved Anya and my children suffer so? Hear me please! What are your plans for us? What journey are you sending us on? Answer me! Answer me!

Sasha prayed as he sat on a gravestone in the cemetery alone, his spirit broken. He covered his face with his callused hands as if trying to block out the world and all its suffering. Tears seeped through his fingers, and as he felt their warmth, he wondered how he still had any left.

The world is covered with tears; tears are everywhere I look. Each mother I see is crying for her children, children are crying from hunger, fathers are crying from helplessness, and not being able to take care of their families.

Deep sobs shook Sasha's body with despair.

He didn't hear Anya come up behind him. She saw her beloved Sasha broken and sobbing; she put her arms around him and held him like a child until his sobs subsided.

"Why are you crying Sasha? What has happened?"

Sasha wiped the last tear from his eyes and hugged Anya. "I am sorry for taking you away from home and bringing you to this hell. I can't bear to see all of you suffer so. Anya, if I find a way for all of you to go back, would you go back?"

The fear in Sasha's voice made Anya stiffened in his arms. "Sasha, what are you saying? How could we leave you? We are here together and that is how it will be." She held Sasha's face in both hands. "I will not go back without you. We will survive this nightmare, and when the war ends, we will go back. I will not let you go alone. You have suffered alone too many times. We stay together, my Sasha."

Sasha touched her face, very thin now, yet still beautiful. He kissed her gentle lips. "I love you, my Anya. I will always love you." They walked back together as husband and wife determined to face their destiny.

Inside the circus hall the conditions were filthy, unsanitary, and quickly deteriorating. The mass of people spread out on the floor on top of rags no longer cared about decency. The few who had a spare blanket to put up around their space were the only ones with any type of privacy. Sasha managed to find an extra military blanket down in the basement and hung it, separating one side of their space from another family. He used several very durable body bags under the blankets and utilized them as pillows.

During the day, the children played outside in the cemetery next to the crematorium. The older kids told scary stories about ghosts walking around at night. Janushka was very frightened by these ghost stories and began having trouble sleeping, or would awake screaming and crying from terrifying nightmares. *A ghost was chasing her from the graveyard! He came all the way to the door trying to grab her! The door was locked, and she tried to open it but it was stuck and the ghost was pulling on her dress and legs.*

The dream left her whimpering and crying in her sleep. Anya who slept lightly heard her daughter cry; she gathered her in her arms and held her to her heart. "Janushka, do not cry my child. We are here, Papa and I. Is it the same dream?"

"Yes, Mama," Janushka said through her tears.

"Look about, Janushka. You see? There is no ghost. Open your eyes and look."

Janushka cuddled up in her mother's arms feeling safe and secure and opened her eyes. Papa was there beside her mama smiling, humming quietly

162

one of his favorite songs. She closed her eyes again and soon slept peacefully.

The next morning Janushka with her friends Natasha and Jadzia decided to play in the basement of the circus hall. The huge door that led to the basement intrigued them and they were determined to find out what was behind it. It was heavy. But they pulled and pulled on the door until it creaked open. It was dark inside, only shafts of light streamed through the windows illuminating the basement. The children dared each other to go down. Slowly they crept down the stairs all the way to the bottom. The basement smelled of mold and decaying dead rats and mice.

Janushka slowly inched her way further towards a big pile of body bags. She pulled one off the pile, "Let's play hop, hop. Let's all get in the bags and see who can hop the farthest." She opened the bag and jumped in it pulling it up to her arms. She felt something inside. She quickly stepped out of it to see what it was. She reached inside and pulled out a human skull. The girls screamed in horror. It was the last time they played in the basement.

Chapter Eighteen

Labor camps in Germany should be better than this hell! Sasha thought while sitting on his favorite gravestone. *We must organize some order and church services. People need the touch of God's hand on their shoulder.* But, there were no priests at the camps. *Perhaps I should talk to the German commander and ask him if I can start prayer services.* Making the decision, Sasha walked back to the hall with a light, yet purposeful step.

He stood in front of the Commander. His body was straight and proud, yet he bowed his head in deference. "Thank you for seeing me, Commander. I would like to ask your permission to hold prayer services." The Commander eyed him skeptically, but Sasha pushed on. "The people in the hall need to have something to hold them together. You will need workers that are healthy in body and mind. It will be to your benefit, Commander." Sasha trembled inside as he waited for the Commander's reply.

The Commander turned and looked out the window, observing the fragile laborers. After what seemed like hours he turned to Sasha. "Petrosewicz, I think that you are right. We need to keep the people healthy in mind and body. I will allow you to hold the prayer services, but quietly. I don't want too many soldiers to know about this." He turned on his heel and left without saying another word.

An area in back of the circus hall was cleared and organized to hold the church services. Sasha built a small altar out of wood planks that he found in the basement of the hall. When he finished, he stood back and admired his work. But it needed something more. An old woman who was quietly watching him at work said, "You need a tablecloth for the altar."

Sasha nodded. "Yes. That is what is missing. It would be nice to have something special to cover the top, but we don't have anything that is worthy of our God. I will have to use one of the body bags from the basement. Some of them are in good condition. Our Lord will have to

164

forgive us for not giving Him better than that. After, all, the Lord Jesus Christ was a very poor man."

The old woman listened to Sasha and then hobbled closer to him. He could see her wrinkled face and kind, tired brown eyes. Her back was stooped and she used a cane to support her body.

"My name is Kasia. I am here with my daughter and her son. My husband and my daughter's husband were deported to Siberia. We were left in the village with many other women. And then the Germans invaded and forced most of the women with their children to go with them. We tried to hide, but it is hard to escape these devils." She spat on the floor and made a cross on her breast as if to ward off evil.

"I have seen you with your children. Your daughters are very beautiful and your son is a charmer, so full of life. He is a handsome young man. I have seen the young girls eyes stray to him with invitation for flirting." She smiled a toothless smile and patted Sasha on his arm.

"I have a scarf that belonged to my mother. It is pure silk. My father was in the Czar's service and traveled to the Orient during the First World War. He brought back numerous Oriental scarves and robes. The scarf has beautiful flowers embroidered on it. You are welcome to use it. I think that our God will be pleased with it."

Sasha was elated. Tears sparkled in his eyes as he reached out and hugged Kasia with gratitude. "Kasia, I am so thankful to you. God does provide in His mysterious ways."

Kasia patted Sasha on his hand and went to get the scarf.

News spread throughout the circus hall that Sasha was organizing the prayer services. At first the people were reluctant and afraid. But slowly they started to talk about it and looked for items to decorate the altar. A man donated a crucifix that he kept in his pocket. A little statue of Madonna appeared; a young girl gave Sasha her rosary.

He was grateful for the donations and hung the crucifix on the wall and placed the Madonna in the middle of the altar with the rosary around her feet. He stood back admiring his work. "*Spasiba Hospudzi*," he whispered.

On Sunday morning Anya braided Marina's thick hair. The girls put on

165

their clean dresses, and with Sasha leading the way proudly, they took their places at the service. He began the service by singing one of the many Litanies he remembered from his boyhood as an altar boy.

Each week more people joined in the worship. They needed the "Hand of God" to support them in their sorrow and to free them from this living hell. Sasha often would say, "If we forget Him, then how can He remember us"?

For the next two months life had settled into an unsettling routine. And still there was no news of being moved to the labor camps, which were preferable to the living hell they were in now. The heat of the summer was stifling, making the captives short-tempered. Fights broke out daily for extra space on the floor or for food. People accused each other of stealing. Arguments between husbands and wives were a daily occurrence. Children were constantly crying or yelling and everyone was bored from lack of activity. Sasha became somewhat of a leader and tried to motivate and counsel those who were at a point of breaking.

One morning the trucks came to the front of the circus hall roaring loudly, sputtering and coughing as if protesting the cargo they were about to pick up. The massive door was pushed open with force and soldiers swarmed in with guns drawn.

"*Schnell...Schnell*....Everyone pack up! You are being moved! Everyone get outside near the trucks!" The soldiers were shouting and waving their guns pointing them at the children and laughing.

Mayhem broke out. Mothers ran around trying to locate their children. Men tried to calm their wives with empty words.

"Anya," Sasha said, "Hurry and pack our belongings. I will gather the children."

She looked deeply into Sasha's eyes. He could see her fear. "I am so scared. Where are they are taking us?"

Sasha knew what she was thinking. To reassure her, he took her in his arms. "They must be taking us to the labor camps. Don't be afraid. God will take care of us. He always has." He kissed her brow.

She smiled at her brave husband. "You are right." Anya began to gather their belongings. "Janushka is playing with Jadzia in the graveyard. Hurry and find them. I will get Marina and Nicolaj to help pack."

Quickly they packed their belongings; Sasha quickly gathered the altar decorations and lovingly wrapped them in the body bags that were torn into pieces. He placed them with their other belongings feeling as if somehow they had a piece of God with them. Next they gathered the children and joined the other captives outside. An eerie quiet fell amongst them. Everyone milled around like robots, with frozen expressions on their faces. They obeyed their orders and boarded the trucks.

Nicolaj was the first to jump in. Sasha, Anya and the girls followed and settled on the small space Nicolaj saved in the corner. They held on to each other and Sasha tried to reassure them that everything would be fine. His strong faith in God did not waver.

At last everyone was on board. The trucks were full to capacity. Sasha glanced around him. He saw fear and desperation written on everybody's faces. It seemed like thick fog enveloped them and was slowly choking each everyone. He looked to the right and spotted Kasia. She was huddled with her daughter clinging to her. Her old wrinkled face looked pasty and gray. Her eyes were closed and her dry trembling lips moved in prayer. She reminded him of his own mother and his heart skipped a beat at the memory of her.

He crawled over to Kasia, placed his hand on hers and reached into his satchel took the altar scarf and handed it to her. She looked deeply into his blue eyes and with a curve to her lips that looked like a smile, she said, "*Hospudzi Pomiluj Cibie*, God Love You." Sasha nodded his head and quickly crawled back to Anya and the children.

He sat next to Anya, took her hand in his and closed his eyes. Her trembling hand was like a balm on his sore heart.

The trucks started their engines. With roaring noise and smoke coming out of the exhaust pipes, they moved onto the road full of potholes. Rotted tree roots were imbedded in the ground like old rheumatoid fingers.

As before, the trucks stopped once a day to let all relieve themselves and stretch their legs. Hungry and weary they crawled back in and the journey continued for three days.

They arrived at a Nazi labor camp in East Germany. Sinister barbed wire was surrounding the compound. A massive iron gate was in the middle with Nazi soldiers posted as sentries. Wooden barracks stood close together in a circle. A separate building different from the barracks and made of red bricks loomed at the end of the compound. There were soldiers sitting near it on benches and some standing around with rifles and guns in their holsters.

On the far-left side of the barracks stood a massive factory with tall chimneys spewing black smoke into the air. Its walls were covered with ivy, so at first glance it portrayed a deceiving impression of a serene atmosphere. Through the smoke-stained windows workers were visible and alongside them were children who appeared to be about ten years and older.

"My God! It looks like children are working in there!" Anya was aghast. "Sasha, will they take Marina?"

Sasha's face darkened with worry. "They may, however, we do not have much choice. We have to do as they tell us." He touched her hand as if trying to give her some strength. "Marina is strong and she will manage to do what she has to. We just have to wait and see what happens." His voice was confident and sure. He squeezed her hand reassuringly and guided her with the rest of the family off the truck.

Weak and unstable on their feet, they held on to each other while the soldiers pushed the families with children into small groups, and those who were alone, into another group.

"*Achtung! Achtung!* All of you will be assigned to the barracks where you will live. You were brought here to work in the factory, and that includes children ten years of age and older," the soldier spoke broken Russian. "You will be given food and some clothing. There will be no going back to your homes. The camp is secure and well guarded by the soldiers. Now go and register at the desk in the building ahead."

Sasha and Anya were assigned to the building on the left of the compound. The hall in which they were to make their home was separated

168

with several locker-type closets. The smaller side of it had four iron beds with iron coil springs under thin mattresses. The rest of the hall was assigned to twenty orphaned Russian young girls.

Military blankets and pillows were issued along with a large, thin basin to bathe in. Anya smiled. There was a wood-burning stove and a few pots and pans with some flatware. "Sasha, look, I will be able to make some potato pancakes and some soup, if they give us some rations."

Sasha was happy to see his Anya smile and with a tender smile on his face said, "We will see, Anya. I am sure that they will feed us. They need us to work in the factory."

Anya made the beds and organized all the meager belongings in the closets while Sasha and Nicolaj gathered wood for the stove. They filled the buckets with clean, clear water from the river that snaked its way in back of the camp. Anya filled the two big pans and heated the water on the stove, then filled the bathing basin and hanged blankets dividing the small area for privacy.

Marina was the first to bathe. The rest followed, bathing in the same water. Finally everyone was clean. They sat on their beds, too exhausted from the journey to venture out and explore the surroundings.

"Sasha, I think that we should go to sleep now. Tomorrow will be a very hard day for all us." Everyone agreed. Anya and Sasha went on one bed, Nicolaj on another bed, and the girls slept two to a bed. "Papa!" Katrina cried, "Look! The bed is big enough to stretch our feet!" With excitement in her voice she clapped her hands happily. The mattresses were not very comfortable, however it was a mattress and not the hard ground of the circus hall or the floor of the truck.

Dawn arrived with a loud speaker blaring. "*Achtung!* Everybody come outside and form a line on the side of the building."

Sasha and Anya quickly got out of bed and got dressed. Next they woke the girls who protested loudly, and Nicolaj who tried hiding his head under a blanket. Sasha sat on Marina's side of the bed and tried to tickle her. Then he softly sang to them.

"*Oh, Kalinka, Kalinka, Maya.*" Marina smiled, her dimples brightening

169

her face as she stretched her arms. She opened her eyes and looked lovingly at her father. Oh! How she loved him! Quickly she jumped up, dressed and followed her father outside. The morning was cool; the sun behind the clouds was just waking from its night's slumber sending golden rays to warm the captives who were lining up outside the barracks. Sasha and Anya with Nicolaj and the girls stood outside inhaling the fresh air. It was invigorating to look at the sky and the trees as though they were free.

The spell was broken when they heard the same soldier, who spoke to them yesterday. "Children under ten years old will stay in the barracks with one of the mothers to watch them."

He walked around and pointed to the children that were to go to work. To Anya's horror, Marina was one of them. She clung to her trying to shield her with her body. The soldier walked over to Marina and grabbed her by the arm. She tried to get her arm free, but he shoved her toward the factory making her stumble and scrape her knees. She got up and with resignation she looked straight ahead and followed the other children and women. She learned to accept what she could not change and would make the best of it.

"You," the soldier pointed to Anya, who shrank back frightened. "You will stay with the children." She nodded in acknowledgement, gathered the children and walked them back to the barracks. She glanced back at Sasha; he nodded and gave her a faint smile. With Nicolaj beside him they went to work with the rest of the men to the loading docks in back of the factory.

A routine was established with everyone going to work every morning. Anya stayed at the barracks and took care of the children. At sunset, Marina came home after ten hours of standing in an assembly line putting pins into the heads of the grenades. Her small hands were raw and bleeding at the end of the day. Anya washed her hands lovingly and hugged her to her breast with pain in her eyes, wishing to be able to change the circumstances in their lives. "Things will get better my children. The war will be over and when it is we will return home and claim what is ours."

The next day Sasha was sent inside the factory to work on a monstrous machine with huge blades that cut through metal easily. His job was to take sheets of steel and place them on the line under the blades to be cut into small pieces. It was very heavy work and extremely dangerous. One morning he went in and started the machine. He began his usual job of taking the steel sheets and placing them under the blade to be cut and as the blade was coming down; his hands slipped and dropped the steel sheet. He tried to hold on to it and as the blade came down, it cut off the tip of his middle finger on his right hand. The supervisor bandaged the finger carelessly. Sasha continued to work. His hand was in excruciating pain and he was barely able to lift the blades that became slippery from the seeping blood through the thin bandage. However, the supervisor paid no attention to those who were hurt. They were here to work.

The following morning as Sasha was changing the bandages, the sirens wailed their warning for everyone to go to the bomb shelter located on the far side of the camp near the railroad tracks.

Sasha yelled to Nicolaj, "Son, take your mother and the girls and run to safety. I have to finish changing the bandage. I will be right behind you."

Janushka cried, "I don't want to go! I want to stay with you, Papa. We will run together!"

"No, Janushka, I have to finish bandaging this finger or it will get infected. You must go with your mama. Now, hurry and catch up with them. Run!" Sasha took her by the shoulders with his one hand and pushed her towards the door.

"No Papa, I want to stay with you. Please! I always stay with you. I will run fast, you will see."

Sasha looked outside. The sirens were wailing, but there were no planes visible in the sky. "All right, Janushka. We may have a little time. But you must stay very close to me when we run. I will hold your hand. And you must hold on tight."

He quickly washed the ugly wound. The tip of the finger to the knuckle was gone. White pieces of bone were visible making Janushka gasp and turn white. She turned her head away. As he finished bandaging the finger, they heard the roaring of the planes above, swooping down like big vultures ready to snatch and destroy their victims as they dropped their bombs.

Sasha and Janushka opened the door; the noise was deafening making them pull back for a second. Slowly they made their way to the end of the building, sliding along the wall trying not to be seen by the pilots. When the planes made their turn to come back, Sasha held Janushka's hand tightly and they ran for the shelter.

Anya was waiting at the entrance, her face white with worry, her lips moving in prayer. They dashed inside almost colliding with her. Stumbling into Sasha's arms, she let out a sigh of relief at seeing them safe. "Sasha, don't do that again. Next time if you stay, we will too. I can't bear the anguish of not knowing if you are safe. If we perish, we perish together." She hugged him fiercely, grabbed Janushka in an embrace kissing her cheek and they went inside to join the rest of the family.

Bombs exploded on the train tracks near the shelter. Each explosion seemed to be closer. Sasha began to pray and others joined in. It was a time of union with God and one another.

The bombs continued to fall for what seemed an eternity, but in fact it was only for one hour. All of a sudden the planes disappeared. All became quiet...only the breathing and coughing of the people in the shelter could be heard.

"I think the raid is over," Sasha said. "I don't hear the planes." He listened again. "The sirens should go on any moment now to let us know it is time to go back to work."

"*Achtung!*" The speaker blared one afternoon. "Everyone go to the gate and wait there!" Everyone gathered by the iron gate, weary and troubled, waiting for whatever was to happen. The shouts of children, men and women were heard a short distance away. It seemed to be some sort of celebration. Someone was playing an accordion and others were singing. A group of people appeared holding sticks and branches. Some were carrying big stones. In the middle of the group was a man walking slowly, head bent, hands tied in back, being humiliated by the Nazis and the townspeople.

Anya and Sasha were standing close to the gate, watching. He was not more than twenty years old. He was tied and dragging to a big tree stump. Every few steps he would stumble and fall. The soldiers jeered at him whipping him with their belts. "He looks like Jesus at Calvary," Anya said. Blood trickled down his face from a head wound near his temple. His eyes were swollen shut, but when he came closer to the labor camp, he seemed to sense the people behind the iron gate. He stopped, tried to straighten up and looked directly at the captives from beneath a swollen eye. There was no fear in that eye, only pride, as he nodded his head toward them he smiled.

"Sasha," Anya said in a tear-choked voice, her hands were shaking, "it is the American soldier that was shot down during the raid. I can't bear this." She buried her face on his shoulder. "He is so young. He reminds me of Antos. But look, he carries himself with pride. Look, he smiled at us! He is going to his death, but he smiled at us!"

A Nazi soldier standing close by saw the American smile, with disgust on his face he walked over to him and spit in his face. Then he hit him in the stomach with the butt of his rifle. The soldier doubled over, but did not fall down. They dragged him by his arms into the woods shouting and laughing, and then a gunshot shattered the peace of the woods. Anya jumped, her body stiffened as the memory of her brother Antos flooded her mind. She started to scream.

Startled, Sasha grabbed her and covered her mouth with his hand. "Anya, please stop! They will come back and take out their revenge on us. Please, be quiet!"

The frightened children were whining and crying. "Papa, is the soldier dead? Did they kill him?" Marina sobbed.

"Marina," Sasha knelt down and looked in her eyes. "I am sure that he is dead. He was very brave, and paid with his life for freedom. Remember that word Marina, freedom. We must strive to be free at all odds. Stay strong."

The Nazis came out of the woods jubilant, dragging the dead soldier's body to a nearby tree where they tied it and left it for the animals to feed on.

"All of you! Take a look at what we do to those who try to resist us! Now go back to work!" The group of people, scared and dejected, slowly walked back to their jobs. Everyone dispersed; their hearts heavy with fear.

Anya was exhausted from trying to keep the children busy and active. She made soup for dinner with not many staples to cook with. There were some potatoes, mashed turnip and carrots. Sasha tried to sneak out of the camp many times to go to a German farmer and beg for some meat or bacon, but each time he ventured out, the soldiers caught him and sternly warned him not to do it again. But, in the middle of the night, he took chances and managed to sneak out, and by moonlight found potatoes in the fields.

It was a lovely, gentle, greening time of the year. Through the barbed wire, farm fields could be seen with young calves and lambs racing in the meadow, their mothers gently nuzzling them urging them to run faster. Willows along the path from the factory stood peeled white, the rich smell of their bark followed Sasha, Nicolaj and Marina, as they walked to their barracks after twelve hours of hard labor. Sasha glanced to his right and saw the beauty of the meadows. His heart skipped a beat and sadness filled his eyes as he remembered his father's fields, the orchards and the honeybees. It seemed a lifetime since he had brought his Anya there and watched her run through the fields. Oh, how she loved the bees and the honey.

They walked into the house as Anya was finishing the soup. She was disheveled, her hair was falling in her eyes, and she looked flushed and tired. Sasha came behind her and put his arms around her waist kissing her neck. "Anya, I missed you all day." He looked at her face, it was pale and drawn, and looked very tired. "Here, let me help you. Go and rest with the children for a little while and then I want to talk to you outside alone."

Anya looked at Sasha, alarmed. "What is wrong?" She grabbed him by his arm. "Tell me now! I won't rest until you tell me what is wrong. Tell me!"

Sasha heard the tiredness in her voice and held her tenderly. His face was very serious and quite disturbed. "Anya, come outside. I don't want the children to hear us." They stepped outside. She sat on a log with Sasha beside her. "The soldiers are gathering the men to go to another camp. I am one of them." He paused and looked directly at her. "I will have to go. I don't know for how long or even where the camp is located."

Anya gasped. "Sasha, you can't go. They can't do that! You are needed here! I can't lose you again!"

"Anya, I have no choice. They are taking many of us. The war can't go on for much longer and I will come back and find you! I always have." Anya's body was wracked with sobs. It seemed like the crying would never stop in their life. He held her helplessly his own face stained with more tears.

Nicolaj was sitting on the back steps and heard the exchange of words between his parents. His mother was crying and his father was wiping the tears from his eyes. Something was wrong. With a concerned look on his young face, he walked over to them.

Anya looked at her son with desperation. "Nicolaj, they are taking Papa to another camp. We don't know for how long or where it is. I can't bear the thought of him going away again, but he has no choice." She dabbed at tears in her eyes. "We can't stay here without him." She took her son by his shoulders and held him tight. "Nicolaj, you have to talk to the commander and ask him to let Papa stay. You know a little German now can you try to see him?" She pleaded with him.

Nicolaj nodded. "Yes, *Mamushka*, I will go and see him. He seems like he might be an understanding man." A touch of pride appeared on his face. "He seems to like me and I can talk to him freely. I will see him tomorrow." He hugged his mother and walked back to the barrack.

The following evening Anya sat at the dinner table waiting for Sasha, Nicolaj, and Marina to come home from work. Marina walked in first. She was tired and haggard. Wisps of once beautiful chestnut hair escaped from her braids unruly and matted. At ten years old, she was doing hard labor. With dull eyes, she looked at her raw hands. Her nails were dry and brittle and dry blood covered many scratches and lesions. She washed her hands carefully and wrapped them in a clean cloth, then sat down heavily on the bench with Anya and her sisters.

Shortly, Sasha walked in followed by Nicolaj. After washing the grime off their faces and hands they joined the family at the dinner table. Anya served soup made of the same staples; potatoes, turnip and onions. All were somber, wondering what Nicolaj had to tell them. "Nicolaj, have you seen the commander?" she asked.

Nicolaj did not answer for a moment. He sat quietly pensive.

Fear was in Anya's voice. "Did you see the commander?"

"Yes, Mama, I talked to the commander. He said that Papa can stay…if I go in his place." He kept his gaze steady on their faces.

Anya jumped up and cried, "No! You are only sixteen years old! I can't let you go. They can't do that. We must stay together! There must be a way to make them understand that we have to stay together!" She walked back and forth frenzied, wringing her hands, her face contorted with horror, her eyes brimming with tears.

Nicolaj came behind her and put his arms around her. "Mama, the camp is not very far. I will be able to come here once in a while and when the war is over I will find you and we will go back home together." He looked into her eyes. "I will find all of you, Mama," he assured her.

Sasha, Anya and Nicolaj stayed up late into the night talking, trying to make a decision. Finally they decided that Nicolaj would go and when the war was over, if for some reason he could not find the family, then he was to go back to Byolarussia and find them there.

Nicolaj woke up early, tired and anxious. He lay still and listened to his heart beating wildly in his chest. Quick gulps of air escaped his lips as he tried to control his anxiety. Today, he would leave his beloved family. He shut his eyes against hot, flooding uncontrollable tears. Sobbing into the pillow, he spent his last tears. Slowly on wooden legs he got out of bed and looked out the window. The clouds were heavy, dark and foreboding as was his heart. He stared blindly in deep thought. *Today, I must leave my family. Will I see them again? Will I see my dear mother's face again? I love her so. And my sister Marina…how will she manage without me? She depends on me for so much, Hospudzi, please don't let it be for too long. Please, God let the war end. I don't want to leave them but I can't let Papa go. He must stay and take care of them.*

He dressed and went to meet the rest of the family waiting anxiously for him at the kitchen table with somber faces and teary eyes. Anya was sobbing quietly in Sasha's arms. As Nicolaj walked in, Marina jumped up and ran to him embracing him with all the strength she possessed in her young body, clinging to him desperately. "Don't go, Nicolaj, I need you," Marina whispered between sobs of sorrow.

Nicolaj disengaged Marina's arms from around his neck and looked deeply into her eyes. "Marina, you must be strong and take care of your sisters. I leave you in charge. Promise me that you will do that."

Marina's face crunched up as a new flood of tears fell from her eyes. Sobbing, she nodded her head. "I...I...promise Nicolaj," she stammered.

"Good, now I will feel better knowing that you will take care of them." He leaned and kissed her wet cheek, then turned to look at his mother.

She was standing on unsteady legs holding on to the edge of the table. The pain and sorrow consumed her entire body and her eyes were ablaze with helpless resignation. "Nicolaj, my son." Choking on her tears she was barely able to whisper. She reached out to him and he flung himself into her arms. "My son...my son. How can I let you go?" She stroked his blonde hair and kissed away the tears from his eyes.

"*Mamushka,* I will be back. Papa always returned, and so will I. I promise you. Do not cry." He tried to be brave, but deep inside he was not sure of his fate.

Nicolaj turned to his father. He was seated at the table with his face in his hands. His shoulders heaved, but he made no sound. The pain and the desperation consumed him. Nicolaj walked over to him and put his hands on his shoulders. Sasha looked up at his son with eyes full of pain. "Papa, I love you. I am doing the right thing. It is time that you took care of the family while one of us is gone." He tried to make light of the grave situation by forcing a thin smile on his face. Sasha grabbed his son in an embrace hugging him desperately, feeling it was the last time he would hug him again in his entire life.

They gathered in the courtyard with twenty other men. Nicolaj was the youngest in the group. The dark clouds closed in and soft rain fell covering their loved ones with tears of sorrow.

Marina, Katrina, and Janushka stood around Nicolaj holding on to him and crying. This loving brother, who took care of them so often, was like a second father to them, and now he was going away. Marina was beside herself. This could not be happening. Her best friend was leaving her. She stood beside him in a trance refusing to believe that he was leaving. The whistle blared from the loud speaker announcing the time for departure. The trucks pulled up and the men were given orders to get in. Slowly they began to board, as the soldiers with drawn rifles stood guard.

It was Nicolaj's turn to board. Anya threw herself into her son's arms crying in protest. "I can't let you go, my son!" she wailed. "How can I let you go? Please take me…Take me." She screamed at the soldiers.

Sasha gently pulled her from Nicolaj's embrace. "Anya, you must let him go. One of the soldiers is agitated and is coming this way with his drawn bayonet. We must let him go." He held her tightly against him as her son gave her one last kiss. Sasha grabbed his hand.

"My son, take care of yourself," he said quickly. "May God guide you and keep you safe. We would not have survived without your love and help. Thank you, my son, thank you!" He squeezed his hand tightly. "We will reunite after the war. We must be together again. Remember our love. Remember that we love you and always will, regardless what happens in our lives. We love you, my son." Sasha's voice broke and he sobbed openly.

Nicolaj shook his father's hand, turned and jumped in the truck with the rest of the men. The engines started and the trucks moved. Nicolaj glanced back and waved locking his eyes with his father. His family stood in a tight little group watching their beloved son and brother disappear from their sight.

W ord was spreading quickly throughout the camp that the Americans had joined the war and were heading for Germany to fight the Nazis. Everyone was jubilant at the news and was hoping for a quick end to the war. There was no news from Nicolaj. Sasha and Anya worried that something might have happened to him. But there was no way for them to find any news of him. They missed him terribly. Gone were the teasing and the laughter. Sasha did not sing anymore and Marina was listless and lost without her sidekick. She walked to work daily, sad, depressed and crying most of the time.

"*Achtung!*" the loudspeaker blared. "Everyone must gather at the factory and wait for instructions there!" Everyone jumped out of their beds and dressed quickly, worried and frightened, wondering what was happening. The soldiers were all over the camp, running around armed and with ammunition being stacked outside the walls of the factory.

"The Americans are coming!" shouted someone.

Sasha said to Anya, "This is good news. The war may be over soon. We will find Nicolaj."

She smiled wanly. "I hope so, Sasha, I hope we will survive the fight with the Americans."

"*Achtung!* Everybody must go down to the basement of the factory and stay there until we tell you to come out!" The soldier shouted into the speaker. The captives stumbled down the stairs and found their way in the dark to the cold and damp basement with a dirt floor. The walls were wet and slimy. One small dirty window shed some light on the cobwebs, and rats could be seen scurrying across the floor and into the holes in the wall.

Sasha, Anya and the girls, carefully made their way into a corner and sat on the wet and cold ground. No one had time to take food or blankets, the clothes on their backs were all that they had. Before long, everyone was cold and shivering. They huddled together to keep warm, but the cold dampness was unrelenting. Hearing the crying of the children and women was like a litany. It seemed that the misery of their lives was never ending. Soldiers could be heard panic-stricken, shouting orders, running around preparing for the battle with the Americans.

The first earth shattering blast woke everyone with a start. Children began to scream and cry, women tried to get out of the basement falling and crawling over each other. The men held them back while they kicked and screamed. Blast after blast kept on until sundown. They sat in their corner blocking their ears to block out the noise. Finally, all was quiet.

The soldiers unlocked the door and came in with some water and dried bread. Thirstily, everyone drank and quickly ate the bread not knowing when they would eat again. The door was locked once more and the soldiers disappeared without giving any information. Everyone sat frozen and miserable. Anya was shivering uncontrollably. Sasha held her close to him while the girls clung to him and to one another. The night was never ending, and at dawn the bombs began to explode once again. This continued for another day, and then another.

On the fourth day of the bombing, suddenly all was very quiet. Everyone sat waiting for the next explosion when the door opened and a soldier shouted for all to get out.

Sunlight was blinding to light-starved eyes. They stumbled about like a blind group of miserable-looking people, being pushed toward the gate by the soldiers. They stood near the gate, not understanding why they were there. And then someone shouted, "The war is over! The war is over! The Americans are here! The Americans are here!" No one comprehended what it meant and whether it was the truth. Sasha and Anya were excited and elated. Everyone was talking all at once and smiling. Hope was taking shape on each gaunt, pale face.

As the rumbling of the American tanks came closer to the camp, the Nazi soldiers dispersed, running away like the cowards they were. The first tank appeared with numerous American soldiers sitting on top waving and throwing candy at the children. Everyone was shouting and waving their arms. It really was true; the war was really over! Anya and Sasha hugged the girls. "Now, Nicolaj will come back!" Anya said with hope in her voice.

The soldiers arriving in tanks looked like young Gods to the captives. Camp was set up and that night a makeshift kitchen was raised. Beef stew was quickly put together and the aroma of food cooking assailed everyone's senses. They brought huge kettles filled to capacity with the stew to the barracks and watched with glee as the captives ate with tears in their eyes.

Anya and Sasha filled the soup bowls for the children first and then filled their own. They sat at their small wooden kitchen table and Sasha bowed his head and said a prayer of thanks.

"*Hospudzi....* *Spasiba*, Bless this food, and the American soldiers who have sacrificed so much to free us. They are Your instruments, Your hands that guided and helped fight the Devil. Bless them and keep them safe."

Sasha looked towards heaven. "God, I need a favor from you. Please help me find my son. Please let him be alive and well. I will never ask for anything else again, if you grant me this request. Thank You, God... Amen."

The following day, the soldiers broke into the German stores. They gathered the captives and cheerfully told them to go and take whatever they needed. Everyone stocked up with food and warm clothing. People felt human again and hope of a life sprang up in their hearts.

The soldiers stayed for four weeks establishing some order. Some people chose to go back to their homes in whatever country they were from. Sasha and Anya held back from making a decision as to what to do. Nicolaj had not returned. Anya was distraught and spent her time waiting in the doorway watching the now open gate.

"Sasha, we can't go anywhere until we know where he is or if he is alive." He joined her in the doorway, his face sad and thin. His body was devoid of fat and muscle. Skin on his bones hung loosely. Anya looked deeply at him. "You are so thin. You must eat, now that we have food from the Americans. You have starved yourself to give to the children and me. My darling, Sasha, I love you."

Sasha was restless and anxious; he couldn't bear just waiting for news of Nicolaj. He decided to go and look for him himself.

"Anya, I must go and find the camp Nicolaj was in. He may still be there, maybe hurt. Or someone may know where he is. The Americans may be moving us out soon. We cannot leave without him." Anya, torn between wanting him to stay and the need to know if her beloved son could be found, agreed that he should go.

The following day, Sasha asked the American captain in charge for permission to search for his son. The captain granted him the leave. After one week Sasha returned, discouraged and dejected. Nicolaj was nowhere to be found.

Chapter Nineteen
Nicolaj, 1944

The round, smiling face of the moon looked down on the earth, illuminating the rippling water of the winding Rhine River in between dark mountains and pasture fields. The early spring night was serene and quiet; the air was cool and still with a slight frost covering the still frozen ground. The night music of the woods began playing its song with frogs and crickets calling to their mates. Silver rays of the moon shone through the branches of the majestic trees, shedding light on the birds nestling in their nests after a day of feeding and mating, while nocturnal animals stirred, getting ready for the hunt.

Suddenly, the silence was shattered like a broken piece of glass, with the thunder of running feet and voices of three young boys heading for the safety of the river.

"Ivan.... Vasily, run faster.... Come on! Jump in the river and swim.... Jump.... Do not stop for a second.... Jump," Nicolaj yelled to his friends, panic sounded in his voice.

Rifle shots and more running feet were heard in the close distance behind them. The boys stumbled through the thick brush, unaware of the scratches on their faces and arms caused by the branches. Nicolaj's vision was blinded by the little rivulets of blood mixed with perspiration seeping down his forehead and into his eyes.

They ran to the edge of the dark and foreboding river and paused, looking at the churning black water. The river was wide and appeared very deep. It would be too risky to cross it, yet they had no choice. The boys jumped in. The shock of the cold water made Nicolaj gasp, and made his body tremble and shiver. He ignored it and with powerful strokes he began to swim. Vasily and Ivan followed him.

Silver rays of the moon were like beacons shining on them, making them visible to the pursuing Nazis. There were eight Nazis, not much older than Nicolaj and his two friends. Their faces, once the innocence of youth, were now marred by the bloodthirsty chase of the kill. They gathered at the riverbank waving their rifles and firing shots toward the fleeing boys.

Nicolaj glanced back at the soldiers and saw the hate on their young faces that made him shudder. What caused this hate to be so strong and evident? The war was over. Hitler was gone, but they could not let go of the need to kill.

Nicolaj, a strong swimmer, was halfway across with Ivan not far behind him. However, Vasily, just a boy, was not as experienced. Breathless he tried to catch up to Nicolaj and Ivan but the current was too strong for him and he was making very little progress.

Bullets rained on them, hitting the water very close to the boys, causing them to swim faster. Their young arms treaded the water with strong strokes; their breathing was raspy and labored. They kept up the rhythm, nearing the other side of the dark shore.

Vasily was lagging behind; his arms were weak and his legs were tired and cramping. He was thrashing about in a circle making a good target for the bullets. One found its mark. It pierced his handsome, youthful head killing him instantly. He sank into the dark river without a goodbye to his friends.

Nicolaj and Ivan reached the other side, grabbing on to the branches and tree roots, they dragged themselves up unto the muddy grass coughing up the inhaled water. After catching a few breaths, they slowly moved their heads up looking around and realized that Vasily was not with them. Panicking, cautiously they jumped up keeping low not to be seen and staggering with fatigue, they scanned the edge of the river, calling to him softly, they strained their eyes over the black water hoping to see him, but he was nowhere in sight. Voices of the soldiers from the other side echoed laughing and yelling with victory. Nicolaj and Ivan crouched behind a tree and listened to the crazed celebration of evil.

"Ivan, I think that Vasily is gone." Nicolaj said. "The Nazis have either captured him or killed him. Our friend is lost to us."

Ivan nodded weary and dejected. "*Job twayu mac!* Son of a bitch! Those devils have no conscience! The war is over. Why do they need more blood?" Crazed by the death of his young friend, Ivan jumped up as if wanting to run back and fight them.

Nicolaj grabbed on to him pulling him back and holding him in a fierce grip he shouted into his ear, "Ivan, you will get yourself killed if you try to go back. You can't fight all of them; they will kill you before you cross the river again. There is nothing we can do!" Ivan struggled trying to get free, but Nicolaj's strong hold on him quieted him and he collapsed sobbing into his arms.

Nicolaj held his friend and felt his grief and sorrow. Thoughts of young Vasily drowning in the black forbidding water all alone brought tears to his eyes and together the two boys sobbed until they were spent of tears.

Nicolaj remembered the day he came to the camp. They were placed in the barracks with fifty other men and boys Nicolaj's age. From dawn to sunset they worked digging ditches for the soldiers and clearing debris from the bomb blasts.

One afternoon as Nicolaj was wiping the perspiration from his forehead, a young boy about thirteen years of age, came by and handed him a cup of water. "Thank you, that was very kind of you."

The boy was very shy and stood riveted to the ground.

"My name is Nicolaj. What is yours?"

The boy would not answer.

Nicolaj playfully bobbed his head to and fro trying to engage the timid boy's eye. The boy let out a small giggle. Nicolaj smiled. "See? No need to be afraid. So tell me now, what is your name?"

"Vasily."

Nicolaj smiled. "Thank you for the water, Vasily. Do you live nearby?"

"I live with my parents in that building there." He pointed to the far side of the camp, which housed some families.

"Do you have sisters and brothers?

"No, I am an only child. My mama and papa work in the fields on the farm all day. I stay home by myself, but I am not afraid!" Vasily was small in stature, but his big round brown eyes were determined to display bravery.

Nicolaj sensed that this boy was lonely. He smiled at him with compassion. "Vasily, you can come anytime and visit with me. I need someone to talk to. I am also all alone." His face clouded with sadness at the memory of his family. He missed them terribly and could not wait to get back to them.

Vasily came to see Nicolaj often, bringing him water and sometimes a piece of cheese and bread. Nicolaj thought of him as the little brother he never had.

When the fierce fighting amongst the German Nazis and invading American soldiers began Vasily brought Nicolaj to hide in the bomb shelter with him and his parents. The boys were sitting near the entrance when a bomb hit the shelter, exploding and shattering the walls causing dirt and debris to fly in all directions. The earth shattering impact threw Nicolaj and Vasily to the ground. He grabbed Vasily and crawling, dragged him into the near bushes away from the blast. Vasily struggled to get free from Nicolaj's grasp, to run back to the shelter and look for his parents. However, Nicolaj knew those unfortunate to be in that area had perished in an instant.

In a strong and forceful, yet quiet voice Nicolaj shouted. "You can't go in there. It is too dangerous. I know that your parents were there, but there is nothing left of that area. You must stay with me, Vasily. I will take care of you." Nicolaj held him in his arms like he held his sisters so many times in moments of grief. He wiped the boy's eyes gently and they walked back to the barracks.

Nicolaj and Vasily entered the compound. Chaos was everywhere; debris from the bomb blast was flying through the air. People were running in circles it seemed, frightened and grief-stricken for those they lost, yet at the same time there was an odd jubilance.

A man ran by and Nicolaj grabbed him by the arm. "*Tovarysz*, what is happening?"

The man, breathless and excited, shouted at Nicolaj. "The Americans are here! The Americans are here! Get inside a building while the fighting is still going on. The planes will be back with more bombs!" The man ran into one of the barracks and disappeared. Nicolaj's heart was pounding in his chest with excitement.

The boys entered the dim barrack. Nicolaj looked around and spotted Ivan sitting on his iron bunk bed. "Ivan! Come here quickly!" Nicolaj called out. Ivan rushed over to him. Vasily stood next to Nicolaj, crying. "What is wrong? What happened to Vasily?" Ivan asked.

"We were at the shelter's entrance watching the planes zooming around, dropping bombs like dead birds, when the bomb hit the shelter." He closed his eyes remembering the all-too-vivid moment. "The explosion was powerful, but we managed to run into the bushes across the way. Vasily is alone now."

Ivan looked at Vasily and his heart went out to him. He put his hand with compassion on his shoulder. "I am so sorry, Vasily. I am so sorry. You will stay with us. We are your family now.

"Yes," said Nicolaj. "The war will be over soon, and then we will go and search for my family. I think that I remember where the camp is. My parents will welcome you. Do not cry, Vasily. It will be all right."

The three boys, forlorn and saddened, sat for a long time into the night talking and planning. The bombing went on through the night, with explosions louder with each target hit. They made a pact between them that if something should happen to one of them, the others would go on. The fighting and bombing went on for another week. And then one morning all was quiet. In the distance the boys could hear the roaring of the American tanks. They entered the camp with arms waving in greeting and throwing cigarettes at the men who lined the street with joyous yelling and laughter.

"We are free! We are free.... Americans....Americans!" Everyone chanted to the delight of the American soldiers.

The next day Nicolaj and his two friends packed up their meager belongings and went off in search of Nicolaj's parent's camp. They slept during the day and walked during the night for fear of being seen by the retreating Nazis. Some of the German farmers they encountered were sympathetic and gave them some food. But no one gave them shelter. They slept in ravines and loose old hay in the fields on the still frozen ground.

186

Nicolaj and the boys were drenched from the relentless rain that was falling all day. Hungry and weak they stumbled through the forest onto a field and in the distance they saw a farm with a huge barn and stables. "Let us take a chance and sneak in the barn quietly so we can get dry and rest for a while," Nicolaj said.

They crept to the barn and found a loose board that Nicolaj removed and squeezed through it. They discovered inside a very well kept area that housed milk cows with udders swollen with milk. The cows moved restlessly, sensing the intrusion of strangers. "*Haraszo...Haraszo....All right...All right...*" Nicolaj said in a gentle voice, stroking them until they relaxed. "Ivan, milk this cow while I keep talking to her. Hurry; there is a bucket over in that corner."

Ivan grabbed the bucket and quickly knelt on the ground beside the cow and with expert fingers milked the cow, filling the bucket. They drank the warm milk hungrily and then rested in the dry hay until morning.

Nicolaj and the boys awoke with a start. Voices of men could be heard outside the barn. "Ivan, Vasily, be quiet. It may be German soldiers." Nicolaj quickly formulated a plan. "We will go one at a time."

First Ivan and then Vasily squeezed through the opening in the wall and ran for the open field. Nicolaj waited until the boys in the field hiding in the tall grass. Stealthily, Nicolaj made his way and joined his friends.

The soldiers were harnessing their horses and getting their trucks ready for their retreat back to Germany. One of the soldiers caught movement out of the corner of his eye. He glanced toward the fields. Three bobbing heads were visible running in the high grass. He yelled to his commander pointing out the running boys.

The commander yelled back, "Go after them, and do not let them escape!" Eight young soldiers took off on foot after Nicolaj and his friends. They caught up to them by the river.

Now Nicolaj and Ivan stood at the edge of the river straining their eyes across to the other side, hoping that Vasily had somehow escaped the bullets and perhaps swam in the wrong direction. "We must continue on away from this area," Nicolaj said. "We made a pact: if one of us does not survive; the others must go on. Vasily would want us to make it home." Nicolaj wiped a tear from his cheek. "He looked at Ivan's stricken face. "We must go on, Ivan."

The two boys moved on through the forest. Scattered deer drinking water looked up at the two intruders and, startled, ran off kicking up their heels. Dawn came with the sun peeking in through the clouds sending rays of sunshine as if giving hope to the two tired boys. Birds chirped happily, as though anticipating a bountiful day of feeding.

Nicolaj and Ivan decided that it was safe to rest now and found a tree with dry moss at the base of its trunk. The moss felt like goose feathers to them as they laid their tired and weary bodies down for a deep sleep.

The hooting owl woke the boys. It was dark and getting colder. The cast-off clothes some farmers gave them didn't offer much warmth. Their stomachs growled in protest and their weary limbs cried out from cramping pain. They began to walk through the thick, dense woods barely able to see through the thick brush. Mosquitoes feasted on them, drawn to their warm oozing blood from the scratches caused by the branches that reached out to them as if trying to keep them in the forest.

"Ivan, I think that we may be walking around in a circle. We should have reached the edge of the forest by now."

Ivan's bloodshot eyes looked at Nicolaj with disbelief. "Nicolaj, we must find our way soon or I will not be able to go on." He looked up to the sky. "I see the moon peeking out from the clouds once in a while. Let us watch it and follow the path that it illuminates."

Nicolaj followed Ivan's gaze. "Ivan, I think you may be right. There has to be an end to the forest."

Dawn came slowly and the sun soon sent its golden rays through the trees, giving warmth to the two frozen boys. Nicolaj and Ivan, weak and fatigued, stumbled through the woods. Their lips were blue from the cold wind that assaulted them.

"Look, Nicolaj," Ivan said excitedly. "I see the sun through the branches! There! Look! We are at the edge of the forest!"

Frost was visible on the still frozen ground and dry clumps of weeds and tall grass were scattered in the fields giving shelter to many animal occupants. The boys decided to stop and tumbled into the tall bush of grass and fell into exhausted sleep. The day was cold; the wind was blowing gusts of cold wind over the sleeping boys cuddled together for body warmth.

Nicolaj woke up alert and ready to flee. The sound of footsteps and dry grass rustling was coming closer. "Ivan, wake up and be quiet. I hear someone approaching."

They crouched behind the grass, peeking through the dry straw and saw a young woman walking with a little girl about three years old. She had blonde hair and dimpled cheeks. Her mother was holding her little hand as she was skipping along humming a song. Nicolaj's heart skipped a beat at the sight of the little girl. She reminded him of his sisters.

He stood up and called to the young woman. "Hello! Do not be afraid. I mean no harm."

Walking slowly with a swing in her hips, she came closer to them. She was no more than nineteen years old, slender and of medium height with long blonde braids hanging loosely. She showed no fear as she smiled at Nicolaj. "Who are you?" she asked. The dimples in her cheeks were prominent and her full lips were red and ripe to be kissed, Nicolaj thought. He stared at the lips, his heart beating rapidly in his chest.

"Where are you from?" she inquired, looking at Nicolaj with interest and amusement. His open stare made her blush. "Are you lost? Can I help you?" She was talking fast with excitement in her voice.

Nicolaj's was lost for words. It had been a long time since he was near a pretty girl. "Yes, we are lost," he answered. "My name is Nicolaj Petrosewicz. My friend, Ivan, and I are trying to find the camp where my parents were. We have been walking for days now in the woods. Can you tell me where we are?"

She looked at Nicolaj puzzled. "You are very close to Berlin."

Nicolaj's face turned ashen. "Berlin?" he gasped and put his head in his hands covering his face, trying to hide the tears that sprang to his eyes. They had been walking in the wrong direction all this time. Now they would never find the camp or their parents. *Hospudzi...God... why didn't you show us the way?* His shook with tremors as the sobs wracked his body.

"My name is Maria, and this is my daughter Ludwina." She gently put her hand on his shoulder, comforting him. "You look like you need help."

Nicolaj, ashamed of his tears, turned away from her and wiped his eyes. He found a soiled handkerchief and blew his nose.

"Please come with me to my home," she offered. "I live with my mother." A cloud passed her eyes. "My husband was killed in the war two years ago, and we live alone."

Nicolaj wasn't sure if he should accept the offer. She noticed the hesitation. "My mother will welcome you. We are not political and the war is over, so you don't have to fear us."

Nicolaj sighed with relief. "Thank you for the invitation. We do need food and rest," he said gratefully.

That night, Maria's mother cooked for them. Their hearty appetites made her smile. Seeing that the boys were in poor health and sensing they were no threat, she insisted they stay a few days and regain their strength.

Maria and Nicolaj formed a friendship quickly. Her little girl, Ludwina, brought warm memories of his sisters, though each day the loss etched a bigger gash in his heart. Each night after everyone had gone to bed they would sit and talk for hours.

After two-and-a-half weeks of relaxation and good food, it was time to go on their journey searching for Nicolaj's family. Maria and her mother packed a satchel of food for the boys and gave them some clean clothes to take with them.

"Berlin is about fifteen miles from here. If you go straight across this field, you will come out to a well-traveled road leading into Berlin," Maria instructed the two boys. "You may encounter the American soldiers, don't be afraid they will help you." Her eyes reflected the sadness in her heart. She didn't want them to leave. She had grown very fond of Nicolaj and her little daughter was crazy about him too. But she knew that they had to look for their families, so she bade them farewell and Godspeed.

The road was well traveled with many military trucks and civilian travelers. They walked on the side of it and jumped behind the bushes whenever a military truck came by. Ivan developed a very bad blister on his foot from the too tight boots given to him by Maria's mother. As they sat resting along the road's edge chewing on salt pork and bread, the faint roar of trucks could be heard in the distance. Nicolaj and Ivan looked at each and decided to hide in the bushes until the trucks passed. The tanks and trucks came into view and to Nicolaj's delight they were American soldiers.

The boys ran out to the street waving their arms. The convoy stopped with a screech of brakes. A young soldier jumped off the truck and ran over to Nicolaj and Ivan. "Who are you?"

Nicolaj didn't understand what the young soldier was saying. He shook his head at the soldier. "Rusky, Russian," Nicolaj said, pointing to himself and Ivan.

The soldier nodded and ran back to the convoy. Another young soldier came their way. He was tall and carried himself with confidence. His twinkling sky blue eyes were full of merriment and his mouth was ready to smile in a handsome face that was filled with kindness and compassion. He was a captain with many medals of valor decorating his chest.

"*Kak parzywajicie tovaryszy.*" He held out his hand in greeting. "My name is Sydney Brown. You may call me Syd."

Nicolaj was puzzled that the captain spoke Russian. "You speak Russian?"

The captain laughed and said, "Yes, I speak your language and the German language. I learned it in school before I was shipped here. Where are you heading? Are you D.P.'s?"

"We were in a labor camp and got separated from our families." Nicolaj answered sadness reflecting in his voice. "While searching for their camp we got lost and have been wondering around for days."

The captain asked, "Where are you from?"

"Byolarussia," Nicolaj said.

The captain frowned. "You are going in the wrong direction," he said.

"Can you help us, sir?" Nicolaj pleaded.

The captain smiled. "I will be glad to help you. Come to Berlin with us.

There is a Russian convoy camping there. I am sure that they will take care of you and help you find your way." Smiling at the boys, he reached into his pocket, pulled out a bar of chocolate and a pack of cigarettes and handed it to Nicolaj and Ivan. "I will take you there."

The boys grabbed the candy and the cigarettes and with hope in their hearts followed the captain to the American trucks.

After a week of rest in the American camp, as promised, Syd took the boys to the Russian camp.

Nicolaj and Ivan stood in front of the Russian commander of the convoy. With silver tipped hair and patrician Slavic features, the commander held himself with dignity and assurance. His mild manner and compassion in his grey eyes slowly dissipated the fear from Nicolaj's face and he took a deep breath.

"My name is Pietor Janoff." The commander introduced himself. He walked from behind his desk and extended his hand to the boys in greeting. "Here, sit down, boys." He pulled a couple of chairs forward and the boys sat down. Pietor stood in front of them. "I am the Commander here. The American captain tells me that you are lost and would like to find your way back home to Byolarussia. This convoy is stationed in Poland. We are on our way there now."

He walked back around the desk and sat behind it then reached across and pressed a buzzer. "Yuri, please bring some refreshments for the boys." Nicolaj and Ivan looked at the commander gratefully. Both were thirsty and hungry. The commander continued. "You are welcome to come with us. Once we get back to our base, you can decide what you would like to do. It will be easier to travel from Poland to your home."

Yuri walked in with a tray of smoked sausages, bread, coffee and tea. He placed it on the desk saluted the commander sharply and left. The aroma of sausages reached the boys nostrils and their eyes went quickly to the tray. Amused, the commander reached for the tray and offered it to the boys.

"The war is over," he continued. "And there will be many opportunities for young men like you."

For two years Nicolaj and Ivan stayed with the Russian Army. During that time Nicolaj formed a strong friendship with Pietor, and Pietor encouraged Nicolaj to study engineering to build roads and bridges.

Nicolaj took his advice and became an engineer. He loved his work. On his second year in the army, he developed serious stomach problems and was diagnosed with stomach ulcers. Surgery was recommended and after Nicolaj's recovery, Pietor called him to his office. Nicolaj saw the sadness in his friend's eyes and knew he was being discharged.

"The good news however, Nicolaj, is that I have orders to send you back to Byolarussia. Your parents may be there, and surely you must have relatives that may be able to help you."

Nicolaj shook Pietor's hand. "You have been a good friend to me."

"And you to me. I will always remember your spirit and your laughter. You could have been my brother."

With a heavy heart, Nicolaj said goodbye. Soldiers do not cry.

Chapter Twenty

The train chugged into Minsk railroad station. Black smoke plumes escaped from the huge engine reaching high into the sky. Nicolaj was sleeping on the hard bench of the train coach. The whistle blowing served as Nicolaj's alarm clock. He opened his eyes and rose with difficulty. He was stiff and his muscles ached from being cramped on this long journey. Slowly he sat up and stretched his arms and legs. With the sleep gone from his weary eyes he realized suddenly that he was home.

He pushed the old stained window shade aside and looked through the dirty window. Tears fell from his eyes as he once again saw his homeland. He eagerly watched the few people milling around and hoped to see a familiar face.

The whistle blew again. Nicolaj saw the conductor walking along the train calling for everyone to disembark. Nicolaj grabbed his few belongings and stepped onto his home soil. It was 1947 and Nicolaj had not been home in three years.

He saw that there were no trains going to Sorojevsko. He walked over to the ticket counter. "*Zdrastwijcia Tovarysz.* I am looking for a way to get to Sorojevsko. Do you know of anyone going that way?"

The sour-looking man pushed his glasses back on the bridge of his nose and said wearily, "There is a man going that way soon. He is over there." He pointed in the direction of a very sturdy wagon harnessed to a well-fed workhorse. A man dressed in work clothes with hard muscles on his arms and a strong muscular body was loading the wagon.

Nicolaj approached him with a friendly smile. "*Tovarysz,* my name is Nicolaj Petrosewicz. I have been on a very long journey home and am looking for a ride to Sorojevsko. I am hoping to find my family there."

The man stopped loading and looked at Nicolaj suspiciously. He saw the weariness and sadness in Nicolaj's eyes and his heart went out to him.

"I am Fedor Fedorovich." He shook Nicolaj's extended hand. "I live in Vasilivna. It is about ten miles from Sorojevsko. You are welcome to join me. I need some company."

The door slowly opened creaking as if in protest. A middle-aged man of medium height with graying hair and deep-set eyes that registered much sorrow and resignation greeted Nicolaj. The old man's face was familiar to Nicolaj. He could hardly contain himself. Nicolaj trembled inside and his knees went weak. He held onto the doorframe with one hand as he reached out to the old man with the other. But the old man moved out of Nicolaj's reach.

"Who are you?" the old man asked.

"*Dziadzia* Adolka, it is I, Nicolaj, your nephew. Don't recognize me?"

Adolka peered at Nicolaj uncertain as to what to do. If he acknowledged him and took him in, they all could perish in Siberia. The government was not forgiving and was prosecuting all those who left. He did not want to jeopardize his family, yet how could he reject his brother's first born?

Adolka held onto the door with hands too weak to support him. His decision tore at this heart. "I am sorry, Nicolaj, but you can't come in. Please know it breaks my heart. When your family left for Germany, the Communists came and deported many people for being friendly with them."

"*Dziadzia,* but do you know where my family is?" Nicolaj's anguish was deep, yet he understood.

"Your parents did not return. Everyone thought that all of you perished in the camps." The old man touched his nephew's cheek. "Perhaps it is better that you go to your Aunt Juzia. She lives with your grandmother. They may be able to take you in." The creaking door slowly closed, shutting from sight the grief-stricken face of the man who was Nicolaj's uncle.

Nicolaj stood on the doorstep of his boyhood home bewildered and rejected by his own kin. Bitter tears welled in his eyes and sobs of desperation and sorrow came from deep within. He doubled over with pain and slowly walked over to the nearest tree and retched until there was nothing left. He straightened up and wiped his mouth with his sleeve. The surgery on his stomach had left him weak and fragile. His knees buckled under him and he sat on the ground and closed his weary eyes. He was eighteen years old and all alone.

Slivers of sunshine shining through the branches of the lipa tree woke Nicolaj. He was too tired last night to walk all the way to his aunt's house, so he found a comfortable spot under the lipa tree with branches reaching wide and high. He brushed the dry leaves and grass off his clothes and with a quick step walked the remaining distance to the house where he had known so much happiness. In the distance he could see the log buildings and the road leading to the village. Nicolaj's heart pounded with anticipation at seeing his grandmother and aunt.

Not much had changed physically in the town, except now numerous houses were empty and desolate. Not long ago life and laughter filled these homes. Now the former occupants were in Siberia where most had undoubtedly perished. A few old people were sitting on the benches minding their grandchildren and paying no attention to the stranger walking by. It was not an uncommon sight; many have passed this way before. They glanced up curiously at Nicolaj, but no one stopped him. He was walking casually, keeping his head down and eyes downcast not wanting anyone to recognize him.

At the sight of his house he quickened his step. He could hardly contain himself from running. He stopped abruptly, shocked. It was not as he had remembered. The house was in need of repair. The roof had rotted in several places and broken windowpanes were boarded up with plywood. The once well-manicured garden and frontage was full of weeds.

A Russian wolfhound bounded toward him wagging its tail happily in recognition. Nicolaj fell to his knees and embraced the mighty head of Layka. She licked his face with a wet tongue making him laugh. "Layka, *Ty istos krasiwaya. Haraszo Layka...Haraszo...*Layka you are beautiful...all right Layka...all right."

Juzia was inside preparing breakfast when she heard Layka yapping and barking. Wondering who it may be, she came out to see a young man petting the dog lovingly.

Nicolaj looked up and his heart seemed to stop for a moment. It was his *Mamushka*...standing there outside his childhood home, wiping her hands on her apron. He wanted to run into her arms, lay his head against her breast and feel safe and protected once again. And then the vision seemed to dissolve into another.

Juzia walked slowly to the boy. She saw the familiar blue eyes and blonde hair so much like his father's falling on his forehead. She grabbed at her heart. It was Nicolaj! She threw her arms around him and held this nephew of her heart whom she thought was dead. Sobbing, they held onto each other in an embrace filled with joy and sorrow.

"Is *Babushka* here? Do you have any news of Mama and Papa?" Juzia put her finger to her lips silencing him and motioned for him to follow her inside.

"*Babushka* is gone to deliver a neighbor's baby. She is the only midwife around now. She will be so happy to see you. Her heart was broken when all of you left. Your return will bring a smile to her sad face."

Juzia quickly prepared a meal for her nephew. A shot of vodka, some soup, and dark bread with sweet butter on it revived Nicolaj. He sat in a familiar chair at the kitchen table looking around at this room where he spent so much time with his family. Layka was sitting beside him licking his hand. The comfort of homemade Nicolaj drowsy and soon his eyes were slowly closing.

Juzia watched her nephew fall asleep at the table and tears clouded her eyes. He had suffered so. Much tragedy had happened in his life. She thought of her dear sister. *Anya, where are you? Are you still alive? Your son is here, how handsome he is. You would be so proud of him. I will take care of him for you. I promise you, my dear sister!*

To protect his family, Nicolaj found work on farms in other villages where no one knew him. Each day he'd ride his white stallion, Fikus, miles from home in order to help support his aunt and grandmother.

Tired from the long day's work in the fields, Nicolaj stopped to rest beside a brook with cool, clear water running briskly over pebbles and cobblestones. Nicolaj watched his horse nibbling on the plentiful green grass. He stretched out, leaning his head on the tree trunk and then he dozed. Layka, who often made the journey with him, was resting her head on his stomach, dozing quietly with her master. All of a sudden Fikus whinnied, shaking its great head and stomping its hooves. Layka, alarmed, growled deeply, her ears standing alert, as she listened to the approaching horses. Nicolaj knew instinctively that he was in trouble.

He ran to Fikus and jumped into the saddle, urging him into a fast gallop. But it was too late. The riders were behind him approaching at a fast pace, and ahead of him were more riders blocking his escape. He slowed his horse to a stop and with resignation waited for the riders.

He noticed the Communist uniforms and knew immediately that they were after him. He sat still while one of the soldiers approached. "Petrosewicz! You are a traitor!" He shouted at Nicolaj, and with the butt of the rifle hit him on his ear knocking him off the horse.

Nicolaj fell to the ground, blood oozed from the gash in his head. Layka sprang into action attacking the soldier on his horse. She had him by his leg with teeth biting in to the bone. The soldier screamed in pain and grabbed his rifle to shoot. Nicolaj was clearing his head from the blow and saw Layka attack the soldier. He saw the rifle being aimed at his beloved Layka and yelled an order to her.

"Layka! No! Let go! Go home, Layka. Now! Go home!" Layka reluctantly let go of the soldier's leg and scampered into the woods. The soldier fired a shot in her direction, missing her. Nicolaj gave thanks.

"Who are you? What do you want?" Nicolaj asked.

The soldier jumped down from his horse. He winced as his leg hit the ground. He grabbed Nicolaj by the collar and slapped his face.

"We are the future of Mother Russia and you are a traitor. You will come with us."

Hands tied in back of him, Nicolaj stood in front of the commander, a short, stocky man with eyes of steel and slits for lips. "Petrosewicz, we have been looking for you, and finally we have found you. Your parents did not return to Mother Russia after the war and so you must pay for their defection. I sentence you to hard labor in Ural Mountains in Siberia for the rest of your life."

Nicolaj sucked in his breath. The words of the commander hammered his brain. He closed his eyes. *Papa, am I to following in your footsteps?* Nicolaj held his head high and with tearless eyes glanced toward the woods. Layka was gone. She would return home without him. *Babushka* and his aunt would know that something had happened to him.

Chapter Twenty-One

"It's called a Displaced Persons Camp. The American Red Cross is organizing camps for people who don't have homes to go back to," Sasha explained to Anya. "I think that we should go with them. If we go back to Byolarussia, they may send us to Siberia for life." He walked back and forth, agitated and distraught. "Anya, we have no home to go to. And Nicolaj may be in one of the camps. We have to find him." He wiped his face as if warding off a vision. "What we had belongs to the Communists now."

Anya was sitting by a window looking at the wonder of nature at its finest. This year, the fall was beautiful, burned orange leaves, with splashes of red in between, adorned the trees. Beneath them, the ground was covered with color. Squirrels were darting in and out, gathering their catch for the winter months. It was a glorious sight and she did not want to lose this magic moment. But the anguish on Sasha's face frightened her. Sasha needed her support in this decision. She placed her head against the windowpane feeling its coolness, thought for a moment and nodded her head. "You are right Sasha we will go with the D.P.'S. We have to find Nicolaj."

The American Red Cross building loomed in front of Sasha. It was nothing more than one of the several barracks built for the American troops occupying them. Sasha cautiously entered the building. He was perspiring and shaking inside.

What if they don't take us? What shall we do? God please listen to me one more time. Sasha knocked on the office door. A voice inside called out, "Enter." Sasha turned the door handle and opened it slowly. He walked in to a sunny room with a huge desk and loads of papers scattered on top of it. Behind the desk was the American Red Cross counselor. He looked up at Sasha from under black eyebrows. His eyes went directly to Sasha's face.

200

"Can I help you?" he asked, motioning for Sasha to come closer.

Sasha hesitated, unsure if this was the best thing to do.

"Come in, come in. Don't be afraid. We are here to help you, not harm you."

Sasha relaxed and walked closer to the desk and stood in front of the counselor.

"What is your name?" the counselor asked.

"Sasha Petrosewicz," Sasha replied his voice shaking.

Extending his hand to Sasha the counselor introduced himself. "My name is Jesse Moreno. Relax, Sasha, and tell me what you are here for." Sasha took a deep breath.

"Sir, my family and I would like to go to the D.P. camps." Jesse's eyebrows went up in curiosity. Sasha quickly continued. "Sir, we can't go back to Byolarussia for fear of being deported to Siberia. And we have no other place to go to. My son was taken away from us before the war ended, and I think that he may be in one of the camps. I would like to look for him." Sasha bowed his head in resignation and clasped his hands tightly together. Compassion filled the counselor's eyes.

"Sasha, I have seen many people who came to me with similar requests. I will do what I can. I know that there is a group of people being shipped to the camp in a couple of weeks. I will do my best to find out if there is room for you and your family." Jesse stood up and walked around the desk. He clasped Sasha's hand. "Goodbye and good luck in finding your son."

True to his word, the counselor found room on the trucks for the Petrosewicz family and they were on their way to their first D.P. camp

The Displaced Persons Camp or D.P. camp as it was called was in the German town Menden. Sasha, Anya and the girls with much anticipation and hope boarded the trucks that were to take them there. They were not going home to their country, but they would have shelter and a chance for a better life. And maybe they would find Nicolaj.

The trucks rolled in on a wide dirt street with willow trees on each side

201

guarding the houses behind them. Long tree branches hung low, slightly swaying in the wind, creating an arch as if to welcome the strangers. Scattered along the street were red brick houses, most were two stories high. Windows were decorated gaily with snow-white lace curtains and underneath each window flower boxes displayed a profusion of colorful flowers.

Anya watched the bees darting in and out of the flowers and her heart ached for another time in her life when she walked with her father-in-law through the beehives. Those were happy times with family and neighbors, times filled with laughter, music, singing, and hard work. Oh, how she missed her dear *Mamushka* and sisters. She wondered where they were and if they were alive. Sasha, sensing her sadness, took her hand in his and held it tightly.

As the trucks moved along, Sasha and his family sitting atop their meager belongings were awed at the sight that greeted them. Menden was a lovely town. The May sun high in the cloudless sky seemed to smile, sending down rays of golden sunshine to warm the upturned faces of young and old seated in the trucks. It was very quiet. Only the chirping of the birds and humming of the bees could be heard. A song only nature can create.

"Sasha, the houses are so beautiful," Anya said. "But where are the people that live here? I don't see anyone on the streets." She leaned in close and whispered, "I am scared. Do you think it may be a trap? I know that we are with the American soldiers, but maybe some of the Germans are still holding a grudge."

Sasha looked around cautiously. Anya was right. There was no one on the streets. He was puzzled. To quiet her fears he said, "I don't think it is a trap. Don't be scared. The soldiers would not bring us into a town that is not safe. However, I don't understand why there are no people here. But, we will see soon enough. The trucks are stopping."

The convoy rolled to a stop in front of a long, wooden building. Red Cross personnel came out, waving and greeting everyone, helping the children off the trucks. In front a long table was set up with milk and cookies, bread, butter, cold cuts, and coffee for the grownups. The

202

children's eyes were big as saucers with wonder at seeing such treasure. They couldn't wait to bite into those delicious-looking cookies!

Marina carried Alexandria in her arms with Katrina and Janushka behind her they stood in line and finally got their share. "Oh...how good this tastes!" Janushka squealed. "Try it." She broke off a piece and handed it to her mother.

Anya's heart was filled with joy at seeing her beloved children happy, yet her eyes welled. Sasha noticed the cloud of sadness pass her beautiful face and took her hand lovingly in his. "Anya, I think I know why you are sad, my love. God willing, we will find him. We will find our son."

After everyone ate hungrily the food, they were told to form a line so they can be assigned their lodgings. Anya and Sasha were surprised to learn that each family would be assigned a room in one of the houses.

The room on the first floor of the two-family house had four iron beds, a kitchen, a table and a wooden stove. Anya was thrilled. "Oh, Sasha, look! We have a stove!" She inspected the top, the inside. "Please get me some wood," she begged. "I want to make dinner! Oh... what a luxury it is to have a stove and some privacy!"

She grabbed a giggling Janushka and pulling her with her, they danced around the room. Seeing his Anya dance, Sasha slowly began to sing...something he had not done for a very long time.

Marina and Katrina glanced happily at each other. "Mama is happy. Look at her dance!" Marina said to Katrina. Tapping her foot to the rhythm of the song, she joined her father in the singing.

Sasha put his arm around his beautiful daughter and together they harmonized in unison as Anya and Janushka collapsed on the bed exhausted and laughing. The happiness of his girls filled his heart. He stopped singing, and looked at his Anya on the bed with Janushka. "I think that we will survive now. Things will be better. And we will find Nicolaj."

Order was established. Polish teachers organized schools and the children finally attended school. Sasha and a Polish priest, Father Pietrowski, looked for a suitable building to set up a church. They found an empty hall and with much excitement, Sasha and Wladek, one of the men with whom he made friends, built an altar. Anya found a beautiful linen tablecloth in the home they occupied and lovingly draped the altar. Sasha watched her smooth out the folds and thought back to the circus hall and the scarf Kasia so lovingly had placed on the altar. It seemed like ages ago.

The priest produced a real chalice and a crucifix, which he had hid on his body when taken by the Germans. Now, he set it on the altar and with tears of thanks to his God, he knelt in prayer.

Sunday services began with good attendance of people who were starved to practice their faith. Sasha attended the priest as an altar boy and Marina, Katrina, and Janushka joined the choir conducted by one of the teachers.

Anya was pregnant again and in February of the following year she gave birth to a baby boy. Sasha was ecstatic to have another son. They named him Kazimierz. After one week in the hospital, Anya and Sasha brought the baby home. The girls squealed with happiness at having a little brother. They loved his chubby little cheeks, his fair hair and deep-set blue eyes.

Yet, the arrival home of their new son made the unknown whereabouts of their first-born son all the more distressing. Sasha stopped to talk with every stranger that came through the camp hoping to perhaps get information about a young boy looking for his parents.

One day, a man came to the camp. He stopped at the Red Cross office, begging for some food and shelter for the night. He looked weary and tired, and, obviously, had been on the road for some time.

Sasha happened to be in the office getting some powdered milk for the children and overheard the stranger talking about the camp he was from. He went over to him. "Excuse me, my friend," Sasha said. "Are you coming from one of the camps?"

The stranger eyed Sasha with suspicion. Times were still dangerous; one never knew who was a spy for the Germans and the Russians.

"I am searching for my son," Sasha explained.

"I, too, am searching for my child...for my daughter who was taken away from us before the war ended. I have been to numerous camps, but have not been able to find her."

Sasha looked sadly at the stranger, feeling his pain. "My son is seventeen years of age with blonde hair and my height. He resembles me in facial structure. He would be alone and looking for his family. Did you encounter anyone like that in your travels?"

The stranger thought for a moment, then said, "There was a boy in Munchen. He was alone. He was blonde. And I heard talk that he was looking for his family. But there are so many looking for their loved ones that no one really pays attention to it anymore. The camp is not too far from here. You should try and go there. He may be your son."

Sasha, excited and elated, ran home and told Anya the news. "I would like to go to the camp, Anya. It is not far from here. I can hop one of the trains that will take me there. I should be back in a few days."

Anya worried about him leaving the safety of this town, but in her heart she hoped that he might find Nicolaj. "Sasha, I am so scared that something may happen to you again. I can't bear the thought of losing you again." She paused, fighting her fear. "But, you are right. Without Nicolaj, our family is not complete. Go, my darling, and God guide you."

It was early April. Sasha had been gone now for almost a month. Anxious and worried, Anya waited for her beloved Sasha. The melting of snow and ice revealed young shoots of grass finding its way through the patches of soft ground, reaching for the warmth of the sun. Low clouds hung in the horizon and the air was cool, with the breeze blowing through the still bare trees.

Anya was walking home from the distribution building where she got her ration of food. She entered the house with the heavy satchels in her arms and placed them on the kitchen table, letting out a sigh of relief. "Kalina," Anya whispered, "How is Kaz? Was he a good boy?" Kalina was a good neighbor who had lost her husband and her children in a bomb blast in one of the camps. She was alone now, and enjoyed sitting for little Kaz.

"Yes, he was a good boy," she said. "He cried a little when you left, however, I sang to him and he quieted down." Kalina smiled. "I guess he misses his father's singing."

Anya nodded sadly. She stoked the fire in the stove, warmed her hands and took little Kaz from Kalina's arms and felt the softness of his chubby little body. Nuzzling him, she stroked his fair brow. *How sweet he is.*

"Thank you, Kalina, for being so good to me. There is some bread and butter in one of the satchels. You are welcome to take some."

"Thank you." Kalina took a slice of bread and some butter. She looked at her worried neighbor. "He will be home soon," she said gently.

Sitting by the window waiting for the children to come home from school, Anya hummed a song to Kaz, who was happily pulling on her heavy dark braided hair. He was gurgling, making baby talk while Anya played with his chubby little hands. Before long, his eyes grew heavy with sleep. Anya placed him on the bed securing the side of it with a pillow. Wearily, she sat back at the window and stared at the gloomy afternoon.

My heart is gloomy like the world outside. I am tired of grimness and tired of fear. Hospudzi, I am tired.

Tears of loneliness filled her eyes clouding her vision. Straining her eyes in the direction of the street, she thought she saw movement. A shadow of a man appeared. She blinked and wiped her eyes with her fingers and stared. Yes. A man *was* walking toward the house. She stood up, placed her hands on the windowpane and took a deep breath. She stared again... hard... his walk was familiar. It was him...her Sasha.

Anya stumbled out of the house and ran down the rocky street to him like a young girl. "Sasha.... it is you! Oh... my darling it is you."

He opened his arms and she fell into them. His arms, his beloved arms were tight around her. His hands stroked her hair, saying her name over and over as she began to cry. Her Sasha was here...alone. Nicolaj was not with him.

He held her tenderly and looked deep into her eyes, shining like sapphires from her tears. "I didn't find him," he said, holding back the tears. "I spent all my time talking to people hoping that someone knew of a young boy by himself looking for his parents. But, he seems to have disappeared."

He leaned into her in dejection. "Maybe he went back to Byolarussia. If he did go back, I know the family will help him."

"But they do not know where we are, if we are even still alive," Anya cried. "Nicolaj will not know what has happened to us. How will he know we are here?"

Sasha could not answer her questions. He held on to her with sorrow and pain in his heart until both of them were spent and had no tears left.

They resumed their lives and made the best of their survival. The girls were blooming like flowers. Marina was a beauty. Her lightly slant blue eyes, light brown hair with golden highlights streaked through it and braided into heavy braids, made her the envy of many girls. She was slender with a slender body that held a promise of a beautiful young woman. The boys gave her more than one glance when she appeared walking, with a slight swing to her hips that suggested budding femininity. Marina was very active in school plays and loved singing in the choir.

Katrina was a pretty, quiet child with blonde hair and deep set blue eyes, very much like her mother. She joined Marina in many activities, but she was not as outgoing and kept to herself and studied hard.

Janushka was a complete opposite. She was a tomboy—a free spirit, adventurous, and curious—always getting into scraps with boys, skipping school whenever possible. Her hazel eyes were sparkling with mischief and her very fine blonde hair hung limply in all directions. Her facial features were a combination of both parents.

Alexandria, blonde and pretty with a sunny smile, was a happy little girl who tagged along with Marina or played with her little Kaz.

 Sasha got a position as a food distributor. Once a month he played "Santa Claus," handing out powdered milk and other food staples. Children from all over the D.P. camp waited on the doorstep for Sasha to come out and give them their share of the beautifully wrapped treasure. Once in a while there was candy in the packages. American candy was a big treat and Sasha enjoyed this part of his job most. To see the children smile with joy lifted his spirits and he always thanked God for their good fortune.

He loved children and whenever he walked down the street there was always a trail of them following him. Many evenings, a large group gathered on the doorstep of Sasha's house, while he sat amongst them, telling them stories and singing his favorite songs. Sometimes if a little girl got too close to her father, Janushka showed a little jealousy and would wriggle herself into his lap letting everyone know that 'this was her father.'

The one room they lived in was adequate enough to give them comfort. However, the longing to find Nicolaj was a never-ending, burning desire. Now and then Sasha went to search for him whenever he heard of a young boy looking for his family. He always returned alone.

After one year in Menden, they were moved to another D.P. camp. And for the next seven years they moved from camp to camp by way of military trucks and trains. Sasha and his family lived in a total of eleven camps. Each camp was very different from the last. Some were military barracks, and some were warehouses with big halls where everyone was herded together and separated by hanging blankets for privacy. And the Red Cross was always there to provide food and clothing.

Reckenfeld was a camp similar to Menden. The streets were lined with trees, well-kept front lawns and gardens in the back of mostly two-story houses. Sasha and Anya were assigned two rooms on a second floor in a house with fruit trees growing in the back garden. Janushka and Alexandria were delighted, and immediately ran to pick cherries hanging low on the branches.

"Look, Sasha, we can plant some vegetables here. Oh! I can't wait to feel this rich soil in my hands." Sasha hugged her and smiled. It was rare to see his Anya happy. Her sadness over Nicolaj was like a growing thorn.

They walked up the one story of steps to the second floor. Sasha opened the door to the two rooms; Anya gasped with pleasure. Each room had four iron beds with sagging mattresses on top of iron springs. Clean sheets and blankets were scattered on the beds with pillows that looked like they may be filled with goose down. Anya sat on the bed and felt the pillow. It was soft and smelled fresh. She grabbed Sasha by his hand and pulled him on the bed with her. "Feel this pillow, Sasha. Feel how soft it is!" She flung her arms around her husband's neck and cried with happiness.

Anya set out to explore the house. To her dismay there was no kitchen, only a sink with running water. All the meals, they would later learn, would be prepared and served by the Red Cross in a separate building. In the hallway was a door she assumed was a closet. When she opened it, she was shocked and surprised.

She ran to the bedroom and called to Sasha. "Come! Come here and see what we have in our hallway!" Excited she pulled him with her. "Look!" She opened the door. "Look! It is a toilet! We don't have to go outside anymore! How does this work?" she asked, bewildered by this contraption.

Sasha spotted a rope hanging from what looked like a basin by the ceiling. Curiously, he pulled on the rope. Water came down from the basin into the toilet flushing into the drain.

Anya jumped back, afraid of getting splashed. "Oh, Sasha. This is wonderful!" Sasha nodded and hugged his Anya. *Thank you, God, for giving my Anya some happiness,* he prayed to himself.

Polish teachers organized schools in the large barrack that also served as headquarters for American soldiers. Five rooms separated the different grades, from kindergarten to seventh grade. All subjects were taught in the same class and despite the limited education, the children hungry for knowledge absorbed everything taught to them with glee.

Marina, now sixteen years old, was sent to a sewing school at another camp. After completing her three-month tenure, she returned to her family as a confident young woman. She met her first beau and fell in love. He was tall with dark curly hair, a very handsome face, and a very charismatic personality. He also came from a nice family. The romance was blooming. Sasha and Anya were pleased to see Marina pick such a fine, young man and approved of their courtship.

Life was going on for Sasha and Anya with the family growing. But there was no direction or future. They couldn't remain in the D.P. camps for the rest of their lives. Sasha wanted more for his family.

The Red Cross was organizing immigration to different countries. Farmers and factories needed workers and they were willing to sponsor the

D.P.'s. Sasha heard about it and it sparked his interest. Hope of finding Nicolaj had faded through the years and the children needed a permanent home in their lives. They were tired of moving to different camps every few months. The children's schooling was constantly interrupted and their stability was non-existent. This new opportunity was very exciting to Sasha.

"Anya, we have to move on with our lives. We can't continue to move around any longer. The girls are getting older and will need to find husbands. Nicolaj is gone. If he were in the camps, we would have found him by now. But, he is gone. We have to think of the girls and little Kaz."

Anya was distraught at having to make another move and this time to another country. Thoughts swirled through her mind. *I will never see my mother or my dear sisters again. I will never see my son's beautiful face or his happy smile. I will never hold him again.* Yet, Sasha was right. Her family needed stability. "Go and inquire." Anya said. "But, keep in mind that I would like to go to a farm. I don't care what country, as long as it is on a farm. I want to run in the fields again."

Sasha was elated and immediately sought out the counselor. After looking at a dozen different countries, he decided on Australia.

"There is a farmer there with much land and milk cows," he told Anya. "He needs workers and will provide housing, food and pay us wages. Maybe we could make it our home."

They passed the examinations and were to leave for Australia in a month's time. Excited and looking forward to having a stable home, Sasha and Anya began packing their meager belongings. However, Marina was not happy. She didn't want to leave her sweetheart behind. Sad and despondent, she tried to talk her parents out of going.

Two weeks before their departure date, Anya confronted Sasha with unexpected news. She was pregnant. "Sasha, what will happen now? I won't be able to travel such a distance." She was agitated and upset.

Sasha patted Anya's hand. "I will go and talk to the counselor. Maybe it will be all right for you to travel."

He went to the office and explained the situation. "Petrosewicz," the counselor said, "unfortunately, your wife will not be able to make that journey. There is no adequate medical facility on the ship that could help her if needed. You will have to wait until she gives birth." Sasha was devastated. He hoped to give his family a permanent home, but now the future was again uncertain.

Seven months later, Anya gave birth to a chubby baby girl. They named her Zofia. The girls loved having another sister, but Kaz felt a little jealousy toward her. After all, he was the prince of the family.

Anya and Sasha asked their good friend, Wladek, to be Zofia's godfather. He accepted without hesitation. Shortly after the baptism, Wladek and his family were selected to go to America. As Wladek prepared to leave he stopped to visit his dear friend and hold his godchild. "Sasha, when I get to America, I will find you sponsors. I promise you that."

Several months later, Wladek kept his promise. A letter came in the mail informing Sasha that he had found sponsors who guaranteed a job and housing for them. A Polish organization in New York agreed to pay for the passage. All Sasha had to do was go to the American counselor and give him the enclosed paperwork.

Sasha took deep breaths of air to calm his racing heart. He couldn't believe the good news. He grabbed Anya in a bear hug, lifted her off her feet and twirled her around, laughing with happiness.

"Put me down, Sasha," she laughed with him. "You will frighten the children. What is in the letter you are holding?"

Sasha let her down gently, but still held on to her. He handed the letter to her. Anya's eyes widened as she read it. She clasped her breast. "Oh, Sasha!" Anya grabbed Sasha's hands and began to dance around the room. "America! America! We are going to America!"

It was a dream come true.

Chapter Twenty-Two
1951

The day was hot and humid. The few scattered clouds floating in the sky offered little protection from the burning rays of the sun. Seated on their belongings in the military truck, the Petrosewicz family was uncomfortable in the stifling heat. The journey they were about to embark on made them nervous and apprehensive, yet at the same time, elated. They were leaving the D.P. camps behind. A life of stability and opportunity awaited them.

The busy port was crowded with huge, dark looming ships, tug boats, and pleasure yachts. Sailors in their neatly pressed and crisp uniforms were everywhere, waiting to board or stretching their legs in between ports. Ships ready to depart were pulled away from the dock by huge tugboats that sputtered huge plumes of smoke into the air. Colorfully dressed passengers waved their goodbyes to loved ones on shore.

Music could be heard from a luxury yacht slowly making its way out of the port. On deck of the yacht beautifully dressed ladies with wide-brimmed hats leaned leisurely against the railing, holding iced drinks with their manicured fingers. Sasha and Anya looked around in awe at the contrast of old and new, beautiful and ugly.

Marina and Katrina noticing the ladies dressed in their finery, glanced at their own worn clothes and became aware of their circumstances.

"Katrina," Marina said. "Did you notice that everyone that passed us gave us curious looks? Pity was in their eyes."

Katrina nodded. "I did wonder why they were looking at us so strangely. I guess we stand out as D.P.'s."

Their truck pulled up at pier number five. They got off and stretched their legs. An American Red Cross worker approached them. "Are you the Petrosewicz family?" he asked.

Sasha nodded. "Yes, I am Petrosewicz."

The man glanced over them and said hurriedly, "You will board the General Taylor military ship. It is located to the far right of you. Over there," he pointed. "You can see it from here. Go there now and another Red Cross worker will direct you on board." He quickly walked away and toward another waiting truck.

Sasha and his family walked the short distance to the ship. The dark and foreboding gray shape looming in front of them looked like a monster to the children, frightening them.

"Mama, I don't want to go on that ship. It is scary!" Janushka said to her mother in a whisper.

Anya agreed that it looked scary and tried to reassure her. "Janushka, it will be alright, you will see. It will be a lot of fun to be on the ocean. Don't worry."

Although Janushka was not totally convinced, she did sense possible adventure. At fourteen years of age she was pretty. Her hair was still very fine and stringy, and she still wished to have thick braids like her sisters, but she was always so busy discovering new things that she preferred to stay a tomboy.

They slowly made their way aboard. The enormous deck was damp and smelled of fish. Sailors were organizing the people into groups; Sasha and Anya kept their little group close together for fear of being separated. The Red Cross worker was waiting for them and directed them to the cabins below in the bowels of the ship.

They walked unsteadily down the narrow stairs holding onto the railing along the wall. Down, down, down they went into the stifling, still heat, barely able to breathe the stale, musty air. Anya started coughing and began feeling faint. "Sasha, I cannot bear this heat. And the stench! Do we have to go below? Maybe we can stay on the deck." Her legs were wobbly, threatening to collapse under her.

Sasha supported her with an arm around her waist. He kissed her damp brow. "We are almost there, Anya. You will be able to lie down in the bunk and I will get you some water." She nodded weakly and continued struggling down the stairs.

As they reached the cabins people were arguing and yelling about their space on the bunks. Children were crying from hunger and thirst. The oppressive heat was making everyone on edge. Sasha and Anya entered their cabin. Marina, Katrina, Janushka and Alexandria assigned bunks in the cabin across the hall. "Marina, look after your sisters. Get them settled. I will be in shortly."

Sasha's cabin was big and filled with bunk beds, some already occupied. He pushed his way to the back of the room and found an empty stack of beds. He quickly threw his belongings on them and settled Anya on the bottom bunk. She was very faint and nauseous.

He looked for some water; there was none to be found. He checked on Anya. She was still pale and breathing rapidly. He was alarmed, concerned as to whether she should be traveling in this condition. He kissed her forehead and tried to soothe her. "I will go look in on the children. I will be right back. Try to close your eyes and rest a bit. I will take Kaz and Zofia with me.

He checked on Marina and the girls. They were settled in their bunks and were talking quietly. "Take care of your sisters, Marina. I have to stay with your mother. She is not feeling well." He hugged them and went back to his cabin.

The engines of the ship started with a deafening whir. Not knowing what was happening, everyone jumped nervously. They felt a slight movement, then a tug...and then movement. The tugboats pulled the ship out of the port and out to the open sea. Sasha stayed next to Anya, holding her hand and wiping her damp forehead. As he felt the movement of the ship he prayed, *Hospudzi...guide this ship and keep my family well. And if you know where my son is, please take care of him for me. Amen.*

The ship labored through heavy waves, heading for the open sea with the horizon getting darker, the shores of Düsseldorf, Germany were barely visible, slowly disappearing from sight. Anya was violently seasick. She could barely lift her head to sip water.

Sasha, increasingly worried about her condition, went in search of the American Red Cross worker. Stumbling and falling numerous times while trying to make it to the deck, he opened the door. The fresh sea air hit his lungs with force. He inhaled deeply savoring, every breath. He looked around and stopped a passing sailor. "Excuse me, sir I am looking for the American Red Cross worker. Can you direct me to his quarters?"

The sailor pointed to a cabin marked "Red Cross Office." Sasha, unsteady on his feet, walked over and entered. The Red Cross worker was seated at his desk talking to another man. Sasha stood inside the door quietly waiting for him to finish. Finally, the man left and Sasha was alone.

"Sir, my wife is very sick. I am worried about her. Is there a doctor on board?" Sasha was nervous and scared, his voice shaking and cracking. "Can you help me?"

The man got up and extended his hand. "I am Joseph Dion. Come with me. I will take you to the ship's doctor." Noticing how weak and scared Sasha was, he took him by the arm to steady him as he guided him to another office. "If you need anything else, please do not hesitate to come and see me."

Sasha smiled broadly. "Thank you, Joe. I am very grateful to you. And should we talk again, I am Sasha Petrosewicz. And, please, call me Sasha."

Anya was moved to the sickbay with baby Zofia. Kaz stayed with Sasha. The storm dragged on for two agonizing days, almost overturning the ship. Everyone on board was violently sick. No one was able to hold any food or water. Those on the lower bunks got sprayed with vomit from those in upper bunks. The stench was unbearable and there was no one to come and clean the waste.

On the third day the sea became calm. Sasha went on deck with Kaz and the girls to get some fresh air and feel the warmth of the sun. He tried to see Anya in the sick bay, however the doctor would not allow anyone in there. Later that afternoon Sasha tried again to see Anya. This time he was permitted to visit for a short time.

Hearing the sound of his familiar footsteps, Anya lifted her head and smiled at her Sasha. Pale and weak, her eyes came alive when she saw him. Sasha held back a sob as he knelt by the bed.

"Anya, I was so worried." He kissed her dry lips.

215

"I will be fine Sasha," she whispered. "How are the children? Are any of them sick?"

Sasha held her pale hand. "The children are fine. They were sick for a day, but now they are up on the deck enjoying the fresh air. I wish I could get you up there also." Sasha glanced at the untouched food on the tray. "You must eat and get well. We need you with us," he urged her.

Anya smiled and nodded weakly. "I will try to eat more. I miss all of you."

A few weeks later on a beautiful early morning in August, the ship inched its way to the American dock. Everyone felt the ship slow down and stop. The tugboats met the ship, pulling it into the harbor and the sailors secured the lines and threw the anchor down. With much excitement and chatter Sasha and his family gathered their belongings and waited for orders to go up on the deck. Sasha urged the girls to get ready. He couldn't wait to go up and get Anya from the sickbay. She was feeling better, but was still very weak.

The announcement for the passengers to go on deck blared on the loud speaker. They ran for the stairs pushing and shoving each other, trying to be first, anxious to see America. Sasha and the girls with Kaz in tow made their way and found a spot near the ship's railing. Their eyes were wide in wonderment at such tall buildings. And then their eyes came upon a vision in the distance. All was quiet as the Statue of Liberty came into view. She stood tall and majestic, reaching out to those in need, to those who were weary, to Kings and Queens, to rich and poor. She welcomed all.

Sasha anxiously ran to the sickbay to get his Anya and Zofia. Her once glorious hair was stringy and matted; her thin body was slightly bent, but she was determined to walk on her own. The sight of her children brightened her eyes and she wanted to run to them. But she needed her energy to get off the ship and start her new life in America. Slowly she made her way to the girls and hugged each one in a warm embrace. Then she looked at her only son and tears of happiness flowed down her cheeks. "Kaz, you have grown in the past ten days." She held on to him not wanting

216

to ever let him go. She smiled weakly as she stood near the railing, inhaling the fresh sea air.

Marina put her arm around her shoulders. "Mama, we were so worried about you. They wouldn't let us come see you." She kissed her thin cheek.

Another announcement blared through the speaker. "Welcome to Ellis Island. Everyone, please get in line and wait to be processed."

The human line moved at a snail's pace. Weary, hungry and frustrated people were losing patience, arguing and yelling at each other. After four hours, Sasha and Anya made it to the immigration officer.

"Petrosewicz Sasha, welcome to America. This process won't take too long. I know that all of you are very anxious to get to your new homes. Please sign all these papers, and here is fifteen dollars for you start your new life." He shook Sasha's hand and waited for him to finish with the paperwork. "Go through that door into the lobby. Your friends are probably waiting for you there."

Sasha and his family moved through a massive door into the lobby. They were startled to see so many people. "How are we to find Wladek in this mass of people? Help me look for him, Anya."

While Sasha was looking around for Wladek he spotted a store. "Anya, keep looking, I will be right back. Don't move, I don't want to lose you." Several minutes went by before he appeared flushed and happy and holding a paper bag. Anya took the bag from him and looked inside. It was filled with candy for the children. Anya laughed and the girls giggled. Sasha reached in and gave a candy to each of them, as if he was giving the most precious gift he had.

"Sasha! Sasha!" Someone was yelling at the top of his lungs. Sasha turned toward the voice and saw Wladek running to him. He grabbed Sasha in a bear hug and lifted him off the floor. "Sasha, I am so glad that you made it! I was so worried that something may have gone wrong. Thank God you are here!" He put Sasha down and turned to greet Anya. He noticed how thin she was and gently placed his hands on both her cheeks and kissed her brow. "Anya, you are still beautiful. You will love your new home." Then he looked at the girls and greeted them with as much enthusiasm.

217

"Wladek, how are we getting to our home? Do you have a truck?" Sasha asked.

Wladek laughed and slapped Sasha on his back. "No, I don't have a truck, but I do have a very good friend here with his automobile waiting outside for us, and I have an automobile also."

Sasha was astonished, "Wladek, you have an automobile? Do you think that I will be able to get one?"

Wladek laughed again. "Anything is possible in America!"

They arrived late that night in Chicopee, Massachusetts. The car stopped in front of an apartment building five stories high. The night was hot and humid, with dark clouds covering the sky. Everyone got out of the automobile, stretched their legs and looked around at their surroundings. In the dark it was hard to distinguish the shape and form of the apartment building, but they could see that it was made of red brick. A dim, naked light bulb visible through the door glass window illuminated the stairs leading to the second floor.

They gathered their belongings and on wobbly legs followed Wladek up the five stories to their apartment. Wladek had the keys and opened the door to a very spacious kitchen. There was a stove, a table with six chairs, a kitchen sink with a faucet and running water. Anya walked around with excitement. Wladek pointed out a door and then another door and another.

"Sasha, we have five rooms!" Anya hugged Wladek and kissed his cheek. "Wladek, how were you able to do all this? We will be forever grateful to you."

For the first time in years, the Petrosewicz family slept in real beds with no one else sharing their space. The bedroom doors were closed, and all was quiet.

The following day Sasha and Anya went to the paper mill and filled out applications for employment. Sasha was hired to sweep floors. He didn't mind doing that. He was thankful for his freedom. He could be heard laughing and singing while the broom was making *whooshing* sounds, back and forth, the dust flying all over. He was happy. He was free. For the first time in many years, Sasha had a choice.

Anya's job was to sort and tear the rags that were used to make paper. It was hard work for her, but she didn't mind it. And at the end of the week when Sasha collected his pay, he counted the dollar bills with disbelief. He had actually earned ten dollars! He went shopping and purchased bacon, white bread, real butter, milk and sugar. He carried the parcels up the five stories to the apartment and proudly displayed the food to his Anya.

"Look at this! Bacon! And this white bread... how soft it is! Anya, we will never be hungry again!" They couldn't get enough of white bread and ate it with butter, strawberry jam, butter and sugar, or plain. Once in a while they bought a steak. That was a real treat and everyone celebrated.

The girls now went by more American-sounding names: Mary, Kathy, Jane, Alexia, and Sophie. The older girls Mary, Kathy and Jane signed up to work in the tobacco fields. Each morning at five o'clock a tobacco truck picked them up with several other girls. Tired and hungry, they returned at six in the evening. When the summer was over and the tobacco field was closed, Mary and Kathy went to work in the factory. Jane and the younger siblings attended the Polish Catholic School.

However, Mary missed her sweetheart who was still in Germany. He wrote to her regularly and in one of the letters he asked if Sasha could find sponsors for him and his family. Mary begged her father to find someone who would be kind enough to do that. Sasha liked the young man Mary was pining for and asked his friend Wladek if he could help. Wladek approached the same people who sponsored Sasha. They kindly agreed and six months later, Mary's sweetheart arrived. The following year, they married.

The Petrosewicz clan began a normal way of life with stability and security. The fear of being taken away by some authority diminished, and Sasha walked the streets as a free man, always laughing with the people he met, always humming or singing.

After two years of living on the fifth floor, the first floor apartment became available. Sasha immediately applied to move there. The landlord agreed and the Petrosewicz family moved their belongings, which now included furniture and a television. The apartment was much nicer and had its own bathroom.

219

Yet, despite the comfort of this New World, there was emptiness in Sasha and Anya's heart. They longed to know what had happened to their first-born son. "Anya, I heard that some people were able to find their lost family members through the Red Cross," Sasha said one day as they were preparing to go to work.

"I have been thinking the same thing, Sasha. But we must be very careful and not bring any attention to our family in Byolarussia. They may still be in danger. But, yes, go and talk to the Red Cross. They will know how to approach the situation there."

Sasha contacted the Red Cross and after an extensive search through their files they found nothing. Sasha and Anya once again lost hope of ever finding their beloved son.

Then, one day in 1964, Sasha received a phone call from a former priest from their parish. "Mr. Petrosewicz, this is Father John. I am at a Red Cross office in Watertown, Connecticut. They have information about your son, Nicolaj. He is looking for you from Siberia."

Sasha was rooted to the floor unable to move. There was a roaring in his ears. "Father John," he could barely speak, "please repeat what you said. I don't think that I heard you."

"It is true, Sasha. Your son is looking for you. His name is Nicolaj, yes?"

Sasha nodded into the phone. "Yes, his name is Nicolaj. And you are sure it is him?" Sasha's hopes were very fragile. Too many times he had the same hope and it was for naught.

Father John confirmed the name. Sasha's breath caught in his throat, his knees gave way and he collapsed in a nearby chair, sobbing. "Father John," he cleared his throat, for his voice sounded small and squeaky from nerves, even to his own ears. "God answered my prayers after all. Thank you for calling me. Anya will be home soon. I can't wait to tell her. Father John, I can't tell you what it means to us. God bless you!"

The clock hands on the wall were not moving fast enough for Sasha. He stared at it, willing it to move faster, but the hands continued to move in its own pace. He sat in the chair watching...watching...memories flooding his mind. His son was alive! Nicolaj, who had sacrificed so much, was alive. Sasha sat as if paralyzed, waiting excitedly for Anya to come home from work. The news of Nicolaj being alive was too much to comprehend alone. He needed his Anya. He checked the clock again. Anya would be walking in at any moment now. After what seemed like an eternity, he heard the door open in the hallway. He ran out of the apartment as Anya was walking down the hallway.

"Anya!"

Alarmed, she ran to him. "What is wrong? What has happened?"

He grabbed her in a bear hug. "Anya," he stuttered, "Father John called..." he choked on his words, unable to go on.

"Sasha, what are you trying to tell me?" Anya's heart pounded with excitement and apprehension at the same time. "Tell me, what is it?"

Sasha hugged her again. "The Red Cross had information about Nicolaj. He is looking for us. He is alive and living in Siberia." He felt Anya exhale. She blinked her eyes once, with disbelief and shock and then went limp in his arms.

Anya wrote to her mother in Byolarussia. She was very careful in wording the letter, fearing interception from the Communist government and possible retaliation against her family. Several months went by before a very well-traveled envelope arrived. With trembling hands she opened the precious letter and thirstily read the words her beloved mother wrote to her.

My dearest daughter of my heart,

What a blessing it was to hear from you after so many years. I rejoice at the news that you and your family are alive and well. I am happy to learn that I have two other grandchildren. I would love to meet them. Life has so many different twists...and who knows...maybe someday I will see them. My other grandchild was here. But, he chose to go to Siberia where he is living now. I am enclosing his address, but he is very busy, so, take your time in writing to him.

We are well, and your sister Juzia sends her love.

221

I love you, my dearest daughter. Hug and kiss all my grandchildren and give my love to Sasha.

Your loving *Mamushka*

Anya held the letter in her cold hands. Her fingers felt its texture, tracing it, as if hoping to feel her mother's fingerprints on it. Slowly, she brought it to her lips and kissed the writing on it. She held it to her nose and exhaled deeply, hoping to catch the remaining scent of her *Mamushka*. Her eyes filled with tears and deep sobs broke the silence.

My Mamushka held this letter...I can see her tear stains on it. Oh...my Mamushka... how I miss you...how I long to see your face... you saw my Nicolaj...they captured him and sent him to Siberia...but, my son is alive!

Every now and then they received a letter from Rozalia. In one of the letters she enclosed a small photo of Nicolaj wrapped in tissue to hide it. Sasha and Anya sat on the bed and stared at it, registering every little detail of his face.

"Sasha, look how handsome he is. He looks so much like you, except for his eyes." Sasha's eyes were misty, blurring the photo. He wiped a tear away and stared at the son whom he hadn't seen in so long.

"Anya, he is a very handsome man. His eyes are very much like yours, the same twinkle in them. But look at that devilish smile..." Sasha grinned and shook his head. "That smile is still the same. He appears to be as much of a charmer as when he was a boy." They smiled. "I bet there are many girls with broken hearts!"

"We have so much that we could share with him." Anya said to Sasha.

"Your mother is very careful not to disclose any details," Sasha said as he was reading. "She must fear that the Communists will retaliate and send the rest of the family to Siberia or, make it very difficult for Nicolaj." He patted Anya's hand. "At least we know that he is alive."

Chapter Twenty-Three
1959

"Anya, there is a house for sale in Fairhaven. It is a small house, but it has a piece of land where we could make a garden. The price is reasonable and I think that we may be able to afford it. I will have to work more overtime. What do you think?"

Anya was seated at the kitchen table of their first floor apartment in the same building they originally came to live. She liked this kitchen. It was big and sunny in the morning. She loved their new gas stove and the refrigerator. She was comfortable. The girls were married, only Kaz and Sophie remained at home. But it would be a dream come true to own a home.

"Sasha, can we really afford it? Can we go and look at it?" She jumped up from the chair and danced around the kitchen, making Sasha laugh. He grabbed her by the waist and singing they danced a polka to their bedroom. Exhausted, they collapsed on the bed, excited and happy. "We may have our own home! Can you imagine?"

Sasha and Anya Petrosewicz made their final move to their little house in Fairview. It was located on a dead-end street with woods in the back and an adjoining lot for a garden. It was a small house with five rooms—a large kitchen, a bathroom with a bathtub and a sink, dining room, living room, and two bedrooms. The front of the house had a big porch where Sasha and Anya kept their many houseplants and Anya's sewing machine.

It was a happy little house. Sasha's joy was to see his girls come to dinner each Sunday with their husbands and the brood of grandchildren running in their garden picking berries and cherries off the cherry tree. Anya bustled around cooking, while Sasha prepared the bottles of distilled vodka in his cellar. Then he would say a prayer of "Thanks" and with much laughter and singing, everyone enjoyed the family unity.

223

Christmas holidays were the happiest and full of festivities. Every year, Sasha along with several of his grandchildren, decorated a real Christmas tree with bright lights and many colorful bulbs. He was like a kid himself, reveling in the joy of happy little voices around him. The grandchildren loved their *Dziadek*. Sasha was the happiest when the house was full.

On Christmas Eve the entire Petrosewicz clan gathered to celebrate the birth of Jesus. The aroma of baked cookies and breads assaulted everyone's senses the moment they came near the house. Anya always waited for them at the kitchen door, a kitchen towel on her shoulder and her hands full of candy for the children. Food was plentiful and the house resounded with the happy singing of Christmas carols.

Sasha managed to obtain a driver's license and bought a small car. He now was working for Fisk Tire Company. It was hard work and he worked many hours. Each night he came home smelling of burned rubber, his hands stained black from the rubber, yet he always came home laughing and singing. His grandchildren teased him often. "*Dziadek*, why do you wear gloves all the time?"

Sasha was happy. He brought home a good paycheck which paid the mortgage and car payments. Every morning he drove Anya to her job at a hat factory where she was a seamstress, and every night he picked her up when she was finished for the day.

They applied for American citizenship papers four times, but were denied because neither one could read or write English. It was their dream to be American citizens; they needed to have a country to belong to. They applied one more time.

The immigration officer seated behind the desk reviewing their application papers was a young man in his thirties. His brown hair was combed neatly to the side and his piercing green eyes were observant and kind. Sasha and Anya stood meekly in front of him, desperation showing in their face. He glanced at them thoughtfully, sensing they were honest people, the kind of people our country needed. How could he deny them their dream?

He shuffled the papers on his desk trying to hide the smile spreading on his face. He pursed his lips and softening his expression, smiled. They stood confused and worried. Anya held on to Sasha's hand with shaking fingers.

"Mr. and Mrs. Petrosewicz, my name is Joseph Mark. I am very proud to tell you that you have passed the test. I congratulate you. You are now, American citizens." He came around the desk and shook Sasha's hand, then Anya's. Sasha and Anya stood transfixed, not understanding fully what had just transpired. The immigration officer smiled at them and repeated. "You are American citizens now. You can go home and tell your children." His face beamed. *These two people deserved to belong to this country,* he thought to himself. "You will receive a letter notifying you when the swearing in ceremony will take place. Good luck."

Finally, the realization of what he said came upon them. Sasha grabbed the immigration officer's hand and shook it gratefully. "Sir, I can't tell you what this means to my wife and me. We are very proud to be American. We love this country and we will always remember your kindness. Thank you! Thank you!" Anya with tears in her eyes hugged the young man and kissed his forehead. *He reminds me of Nicolaj.*

They walked out of the immigration building holding hands as they did when they were young. Sasha stopped his wife in the middle of the sidewalk and pulled her to him. Surprised at such a show of affection, Anya blushed as he kissed her fully on her mouth in front of several people passing by, glancing at them and smiling. "Sasha, what are you doing in front of all these people?" Anya protested.

Sasha picked her up and twirled her around as he did so many years ago. "Anya, now we really are a part of a country where we have freedom. Our children and grandchildren will have freedom and education."

Anya laughed gaily with visions of her grandchildren enjoying the fruits of this wonderful country. Then, sadness filled her eyes momentarily. "Sasha, if only Nicolaj was here to celebrate with us." She brushed at her eyes to dispel the dark cloud, and turned to her husband. "Sasha, we must celebrate tonight."

"Yes, let us go home and have a toast to our new country."

Sasha retired at age sixty-five. He spent his days working in his garden and driving Anya to work. Every morning he got in his car and drove to each daughter's house to say good morning. The girls laughed at this ritual, yet looked forward to the door opening revealing the man who was their beloved father. On the days he didn't make it to their house, he called each of them to make sure they were well and happy.

As was his habit, Sasha waited for the mailman each day. As he sifted through the day's delivery a letter with a very different postage caught his eye. His heart began to race and his hands shook as he reached for the odd-looking envelope. He placed his hand on his wildly beating heart and took a deep breath. "Where are my glasses?" he asked himself. His hands fumbled through his pockets. Then, he realized that he was wearing them. He shook his head and looked at the address the letter came from. His knees turned to water. The letter was postmarked from Siberia. It was from Nicolaj. His hands shook violently, his vision blurred as he crumbled to the floor and cried. His crying spent; he got up from the floor and sat at the kitchen table. He wiped his eyes and tore the envelope open with shaking hands.

> *Darahaja Mamushka i Papa,*
> I hope and pray that you and my sisters are well and happy. I am living in Siberia, Ural Mountains. I have a wife and four children, three sons and one daughter. We all work for the *Kolhozy*, and have a good life. Are my sisters married? Do they have children? There are millions of things I would like to know... maybe someday we will see each other again. I pray for that day. So many years have passed...I will try to write again.
> *Ja was miluju Mamushka and Papa.* Give my love to my sisters.
> Your son, Nicolaj

The letter was short and carefully written, revealing very little. Sasha's tears rolled down his cheeks. *My son Nicolaj, he gave so much to me and to the family.* How he longed to hold him and tell him how grateful and thankful he was to him. Sasha held the letter to his lips, talking to it softly.

226

"You have suffered so, my son...all alone." Sasha raised his eyes towards the heavens. "*Hospudzi*, I thank you."

As always after work, Anya waited for Sasha to pick her up in front of the factory. She glanced at her watch. He was ten minutes late. She frowned, worried. It was unusual for him to be late. Normally, he was early, waiting for her at the curb. Cars passed by her as she stood on tired feet. When he finally appeared and pulled up by the curb she got in the car, a little irritated. Glancing at him she knew immediately that something was bothering him. He was sitting very still, staring at her. She noticed his red-rimmed eyes.

"What is it, Sasha? Are you ill?" Her voice trembled with worry.

He shook his head, unable to speak, still overcome with emotion. Sasha held up the envelope to her. A new flood of tears began to flow.

Alarmed, Anya asked, "Sasha, what is in this envelope? Is it bad news from someone?"

He continued to hold the letter. In a hoarse voice he whispered, "Anya, it is from Nicolaj. Our son wrote to us." He choked on the words, barely able to finish the sentence.

"It is from Nicolaj?" Anya whispered the words. She touched her fingertips to the envelope. "Sasha, tell me what he said. I can't read the letter right now. All I want to do is hold it and touch it. Nicolaj's hands held this, Sasha. I can feel his touch." She lifted it to her face and traced the lettering with her lips. "Is he well?" Tears were flowing freely from her eyes; she did not hide them.

"He is well," said Sasha smiling. "He is married and has four children, our grandchildren whom we will never know." He turned to Anya. She was still as a statue, frozen in time. "Anya?" Sasha's voice sounded with concern.

Anya's eyes flickered nervously; she slowly took a breath then turned toward Sasha like a sleepwalker. Her body began to tremble and big heavy sobs escaped from deep inside her. Sasha pulled her into his arms. Together they cried, holding the letter until it was soaked with their tears.

They corresponded regularly with Nicolaj. The letters took a very long time to get to and from Siberia, sometimes as long as six months. They lived for news from him.

Over the next few years Anya noticed a change in Sasha. He was slowing down. When he turned seventy years old, he began to have health problems. Sasha suffered two minor strokes that were not noticed by Anya or anyone else in the family. Everyone assumed the changes in his mental and physical behavior were due to his age. In Sasha's seventy-fourth year he suffered a major stroke. Anya retired from her job of twenty-four years to take care of him at home. She nursed him lovingly, refusing any help offered by her daughters. "He is my Sasha and I will take care of him until the end."

Sasha lay in the hospital bed very still and peaceful. She reached out and touched his beloved face. "I loved you so." She held his hand against her breast as grief welled in her, grief that was dark, bottomless, opening like a dark hole ready to swallow her. She stared at his face, wanting to talk to him, wanting to hear him sing, wanting to run to him as she did as a young girl.

How tired I am, she thought, *Sasha, take me with you. You have left me behind so many times...don't leave me again.*

In her heart she heard a voice from within, caressing and soothing.

My Anya, you must stay and take care of the family. It is too soon for you to go. I will wait for you.... I will come for you.... when the time is right.... maja darahaja, my darling.

She closed her eyes and touched her heart.

Kaz took her arm, steadying her, letting her lean against him. Her daughters and all the grandchildren gathered around her, their love reaching out to caress her in her time of sorrow.

Anya buried her beloved Sasha in the midst of summer. His garden was full of flowers that he loved so much. It seemed like they were more beautiful than ever, as if to honor him. She gathered a bouquet of his favorite tiger lilies and one-by-one his family placed the lilies on his coffin as they said goodbye to this remarkable man who had battled the

228

Bolsheviks, the Partisans, the Communists and the Nazis in order to bring his family to a better life.

Anya continued to live in the little house that her beloved Sasha bought for her. She busied herself with her garden in the summer, planting every variety of vegetables, flowers, and berries. She arose with the sunrise and tended the new life springing up from the ground. Her greatest joy was to share the fruits of her labor. The garden was magnificent and people from all over came to see it. Anya proudly walked around showing off her precious treasures. In the fall, she lovingly covered the berries and other winter plants. When snow covered the garden, she stayed indoors crocheting blankets for all her children and grandchildren. She lived for her family.

At age seventy, Anya decided that it was time to do other things. She began to travel. She took her first airplane ride all the way to Hawaii where Jane lived. For six weeks, Anya enjoyed the sun and the ocean and time with her daughter and her family.

She also traveled to Poland and Switzerland to see Pope Paul IV. He resembled her Sasha a great deal, she thought. Anya lived a full life, with her children and grandchildren visiting her every Sunday for the traditional dinner. Yet, she was lonely. Her Sasha and her Nicolaj were not with her.

Chapter Twenty-Four
Glasnost

The brutality of the Stalin regime was acknowledged and the corruption of the Brezhnev era came under sharp criticism. Soviet leaders were more receptive and a new period of détente opened between East and West. Mikhail Gorbachev began to promote a policy of openness known as *Glasnost*. Glasnost gave new freedoms to the Russian people. Russian citizens were now allowed to travel to other countries.

In 1988, a letter from Nicolaj informed Anya that if she sent him an invitation, he and his daughter, Ania, would come to America. They could visit for three months. Joy and jubilation enveloped the family. The sisters couldn't wait for their brother to come to America. The phone rang constantly between their houses, each one crying and laughing and making plans for their brother's visit. Mary made arrangements to send a letter of invitation in November of 1988.

In May of 1989, Nicolaj wrote saying he was ready to make plans to arrive in America in August. He and Ania would travel first to Moscow where they would stay with friends and leave from Moscow airport. He included a phone number where he could be reached.

Anya wished Sasha were still alive. She went to the grave and talked to him as she often did. "Sasha, we will have a visitor. Nicolaj is coming to America with his daughter Ania. How am I to meet him without you? What am I to say to him? Oh... my Sasha... if only you had lived long enough to see him again..." She talked to him for a long time, spilling her heart out, telling him of her happiness and sorrow. "Why is it, Sasha, that happiness and sorrow, go hand in hand? We have experienced this so many times, my love. It is as if sorrow is jealous of happiness and must strike fast at the happiest times in people's lives."

On August fifth, Jane arrived from Hawaii for Nicolaj's upcoming visit. Anya was excited at the prospect of having all her children together for the first time. Her house, the home she had made with her Sasha, was filled with happiness and joy.

Two days later at five in the morning, the phone rang waking Janushka from a deep sleep. Fearing bad news from Hawaii, she jumped out of bed and ran to the kitchen to answer it.

"Hello," she said quickly into the receiver. There was silence on the other side. Then she heard a choking sound, as if someone was crying and unable to speak. "Hello!" she repeated anxiously.

"Jane? It is I, Alexia. I am at Sophie's house. Something awful has happened. Cindy was killed in a car crash last night."

Jane stifled a scream. Her niece was only fifteen years old. "Alexia, how did that happen? Was Rosemary with her?"

Alexia's daughter, Rosemary, and Cindy were very close. They were always together. "Rosemary was not with her. Cindy was with her friends. The boy driving had been drinking and lost control of the car. It overturned, killing Cindy. The driver and the other girl survived.

"Oh, Jane, how are we to tell Mama? Nicolaj is coming from Siberia in two weeks, and now we have to bury one of our own."

Stunned by the news Jane struggled to comprehend what had happened. "I will tell Mama as soon as she wakes up." Her voice broke and deep sobs wrecked her body. "We will come to Sophie's house soon. Stay with Sophie."

Having heard the telephone ring, Anya got out of bed. She stood in the doorway of her bedroom listening to the conversation. A knife slashed through her heart and she collapsed onto a nearby chair.

Jane heard a moan and ran to her mother. She staring was into space her eyes were dry and unblinking. She kept staring as if not seeing, as if not wanting to see any more. Janushka knelt at her feet and held her mother in an embrace, soothing her with words that seemed empty.

Cindy was buried with the Petrosewicz family gathered by the graveside, each face held a look of bewilderment and shock. Anya stood amongst her daughters and son, watching one of her grandchildren being lowered into the ground. Dry sobs escaped her lips. There were no more tears to shed.

The Petrosewicz family went home grieving, yet anticipating the arrival of Nicolaj. Guilt from feeling happy at the prospect of the reunion assaulted all of them. But life has a way of healing wounds quickly and Nicolaj's pending arrival was the balm the family needed.

On a Tuesday morning a week before the date of Nicolaj's arrival, Mary, Jane, and Alexia met at Kathy's house for coffee. Alexia was last to arrive. While they were sipping coffee and sampling Kathy's sweet bread with butter, Mary said, "I wonder if Nicolaj is in Moscow now? He said that they would be arriving there about now."

"Mary, do you have the phone number in Moscow? Let's try and call there. Maybe we can talk to him." Kathy asked.

"Yes, I have it here in my purse. Let me get it."

Jane clapped her hands. "I wonder what he sounds like. I don't remember him at all. Do you, Kathy?"

Kathy was thoughtful for a moment. "I remember very little. Mary is the one who was old enough to have spent time with him."

Jane glanced at Mary. "What were his ways and what did he look like?"

Mary smiled with memory. "Well, his hair was very fine and blonde and it kept falling on his forehead all the time. He always pushed it back with his hand, just like Papa. I would say to him, 'Nicolaj why don't you cut it shorter so it doesn't do that?' but he would just laugh and say, 'It doesn't bother me, and the girls like my hair this way.' Then he would wink at me. He was a lot of fun, always upbeat, regardless how bad things were. Let's call him right now."

"Yes, Mary, you call him, since you are the only one who can still speak Russian," Jane said.

Mary dialed the phone. The excitement was mounting; the phone was ringing in Moscow. "*Zdrastwijca,* this is Mary calling from America. Can you please tell me, is my brother Nicolaj there?" Pause. "Yes? Can I talk to him please?"

232

Mary looked at her sisters. "Girls, he is there! She is calling him!" The wait seemed interminable.

"Nicolaj? This is Marina..." She couldn't talk. Tears choked her voice hearing his voice, his dear voice, after so many years. She cleared her throat. "Nicolaj...." She couldn't say more and handed the phone to Kathy.

"Nicolaj?" after hearing his sobbing voice she handed the phone to Jane. She, too, could only sob into the phone. Jane handed the phone back to Alexia. No one could talk. Only tears of happiness could be heard flowing.

Finally, Mary took the phone again and controlled herself. "Nicolaj, we will go to Mama's house now and we'll call you from there. We won't tell her that it is you on the phone. Stay where you are. We love you!"

The girls drove down the five miles to Anya's house. "Mama," Mary said, "can I use the phone? I want to call a friend."

Anya gave Mary a curious look. "Go ahead, Mary. Why are you asking? You always use the phone." Mary grinned and dialed the phone.

"Mama, somebody wants to talk to you."

Anya frowned, but took the phone. "Hello?"

From the other side of the world she heard a familiar voice...*"Mamushka...Maya Mamushka..."* Anya swayed slightly, her hand holding the phone trembled and tears welled up in her blue eyes. She glanced at the girls with a look of utter disbelief.

"Nicolaj?" Her shaking voice was barely a whisper.

"Mamushka," he whispered back, "it has been so long since I have heard your voice. I am longing to see you." He choked back tears. "Ania, your granddaughter, and I will arrive in New York next Tuesday."

Anya was laughing and crying, trying to hold a conversation with her Nicolaj. "Nicolaj, my son, I will all be there to greet you. Take care of yourself my son. *Ja cibie miluju,"*

Plans were made to meet Nicolaj in New York. They rented a big van and Anya, the girls and their husbands set out on the journey, which would put the past forty-five years behind. Nicolaj was sixteen years old, a boy, when he left...and now the family was about to meet a sixty-year-old man.

Chapter Twenty-Five
Reunion with Nicolaj
August 1989

The morning sunlight caressed Anya's eyelids. She blinked and then quickly opened them. Today was the day she has waited for such a long time. Today, she will be reunited with her beloved son Nicolaj. "Forty-five years have passed...." she whispered to herself. Forty-five years..." She repeated over and over. She hardly slept last night, how could she? Forty-five years of waiting and hoping, and now the day was here. She was as nervous as a bride.

Anya got out of bed slowly, ignoring her aching bones from arthritis. Today she didn't mind it at all. "What shall I wear?" She rushed around her bedroom talking to herself. Sipping on her morning coffee, she looked in the closet and chose a floral pattern dress. "Nicolaj likes flowers. Now, what shall I do with my hair?" Passing the mirror she looked closely at the gray surrounding her temples. Her hair was not as long as Nicolaj would remember it to be. She laughed to herself. "Nor will Nicolaj remember my face so wrinkled!"

She bathed and dressed and had Jane combed her hair to hide some of the gray.

"Mama, you look beautiful. Just as beautiful as when he last saw you. Don't worry so much. He will know you."

Anya held a bouquet of flowers in her arms, her family surrounding her. Everyone was quiet, pensive, and nervous, each one with their own thoughts. They had been at the airport for over an hour now, and the plane had just landed. The excitement and anxiety was like a thick fog enveloping them.

Mary's thoughts went back to when she and Nicolaj were children.

Now he is a man. Will I recognize him? Will he recognize the sister who depended on him so much? He was the one who held me and wiped away my tears. He was the one I ran to, when I fell and bruised my knee. He was always there when I needed him. In her mind, she saw him walking away, a handsome young boy who was waving goodbye to them, with that charming grin on his face, trying to be brave. That was forty-five years ago. Mary's hands were damp with perspiration and her eyes welled with unshed tears.

Anya's deep blue eyes were riveted to the gate door that had just opened. Spilling out were weary travelers from Russia. She felt almost faint from standing so long and her knees were giving way. She leaned on Kaz for support. The anxiety and anticipation was overwhelming. Her whole body trembled; her mind was spinning around with thoughts.

"My beloved son Nicolaj should be passing through these doors soon. Forty-five years have passed since I've him. He was just a boy of sixteen then. And now he is sixty years old. Will I know him? Will he know me? I am old and wrinkled now. What will he think of me? Oh, my son.... After all these years I will hold you again. If only you're Papa was here to see you.... How he longed for you. On his deathbed he said that he saw you standing in the corner of the room bidding him goodbye. Were you there for him? Oh, Nicolaj, how we looked for you in the D.P. camps. And now you will be here in a few minutes with your daughter, my granddaughter Ania. I have lived to see you again. So many years have passed; so many things have happened. But my love for you has not wavered. My longing to see you has not diminished.

The lifetime of waiting was over.

Her children stood beside their mother: Marina/Mary, Katrina/Kathy, Janushka/Jane, Alexandra/Alexia, Kasimir/Kaz, and Zofia/Sophie. Impatience to see him was visible on their faces. Eagerly, they examined each face that went past them.

And then....

A blonde man came through the door with a beautiful young girl beside him. He was bending down to pick up a suitcase and when he straightened up, he pushed his hair off his forehead. Jane saw the gesture. "Could he be Nicolaj?" She strained her eyes to see his face. "It is Nicolaj! Nicolaj! It is Nicolaj!" Jane called out to him, pointing to the man and the young girl.

Nicolaj heard his name and turned toward them.

Anya stood rooted to the floor. *My son is home.* Commanding her legs to move and with a gentle push and prod from Kaz, she headed towards the gate.

Nicolaj was looking around, searching the many faces. And then he saw her, his *Mamushka* walking toward him, his sisters behind her, with tears of happiness streaming down their faces. All were in their middle ages, but to him they were the young girls that he remembered fondly and loved dearly.

Filled with emotion, he opened his arms to his mother. Anya stared at him, drinking in the vision of him as if afraid that it may disappear. He looked deep into her blue eyes so much like his own.

"*Mamushka, Maya Mamushka*...." He enfolded his beloved mother in his arms and held her, melted away forty-five years of loneliness.

The hustle and bustle of many different nationalities at the airport lobby was astounding to Nicolaj and his daughter. They glanced around with wonder in their eyes. Groups of people passed each other showing no fear or hesitation. Nicolaj shook his head in disbelief. "This is America," he said out loud.

They boarded the van and Nicolaj sat next to his mother unable to take his eyes off of her. "*Mamushka*, I can't believe that I am really sitting with you next to me." He put his arm around her shoulders hugging her close to him. "I wish Papa was here," he said squeezing his mother's hand.

Anya nodded her head and closed her eyes tightly forcing the tears away from her eyes. "Nicolaj," she said to him. "Papa's last wish was to see you again. Before he passed on he said that he saw you in the corner of the room waving to him. I believe that he truly did." Anya looked up to see her son's eyes brimming with tears.

"There is so much I would like to tell him," Nicolaj said sadly. *"Mamushka*, I would like to go to the cemetery as soon as we arrive. I brought some soil from Byolarussia to put on his grave. I think that he would like that."

Anya nodded. "Yes, Nicolaj, Papa would like that very much."

"Kalinka.... Kalinka..... Kalinka, maya,"

The sisters' voices rose from the back of the van as they sang their father's favorite song. Mother and son wiped their tears and turned to look at the girls singing. Nicolaj's heart swelled with love for his family; he smiled and in a strong voice like his father's, joined his sisters in song.

Nicolaj visited twice more, the last time in 1997. Anya corresponded with him and sent him packages regularly. She was getting on in age and slowing down. She now had several great-great grandchildren. The family was expanding and everyone came to see their *Babcia* on Sundays.

Although Anya was ninety-three years old, she insisted on living alone. Her daughters and son visited her daily, seeing to all her needs. When Jane visited, Anya sat by the window and recalled her life. Jane listened attentively, committing every detail of her family's journey to memory.

"I have lived so many years, gave birth to so many children, and now I sit here alone. However, I am in my own house. Look, Jane, how beautiful my garden is." The garden that her beloved Sasha had planted and lovingly tended to bloomed every year as bountiful as ever. It was to be the last year that she enjoyed her beloved garden.

On New Year's Eve 2001, Anya was taken to the hospital with heart failure. Not much could be done for her and so the family decided to bring her home. Hospice arranged for a hospital bed to be set up in the living room and provided all the other essentials for the girls to take care of her. Kaz carried his mother into the house with his sisters behind him and placed her in the hospital bed securing the sides. Jane stayed with her through the night, and the sisters took turns caring for her during the day.

By the third night, Anya had slipped into a coma. Mary and Kathy said goodnight to their mother and Jane. Alexia stayed a while longer, then left shortly afterwards. Jane made sure her mother was comfortable, tucking her blankets in. She shut the lights off and went to bed.

At five in the morning, Jane awoke from a sound sleep, startled. Alarmed, she jumped out of bed and ran into the living room. She put the light on to check on her mother. The hospital bed was exactly as she left it. However, she didn't see her mother in it. Bewildered, she looked again; her mother was not in the bed. She thought for a moment that perhaps she was still asleep and dreaming. She walked closer to the bed. It *was* empty. The covers were neat and undisturbed.

"How can this be?" Jane said aloud. She looked on the other side of the bed to see if perhaps her mother had slid through the rails and fallen to the floor. But she was not there. Jane panicked. *How could I lose my unconscious mother?*

She ran into the kitchen. There was no one there. She went next to her mother's bedroom and switched on the light on. Jane gasped. Anya was lying in her own bed in her own room, her covers neatly pulled up around her.

"Mama, can you hear me?" Anya did not stir. Jane sat on the bed beside her beloved mother and took her hand. It was cold. She felt the pulse; it was very weak.

Jane called Mary first and then the rest of her sisters and her brother Kaz. To each one she told the story and urged them to hurry to the house. Sophie arrived first. She sat on the bed beside her mother and Jane. Anya seemed to have some color and was restless. "Mama, can you hear me? It is me...Jane. Sophie is here also." Anya moved her head from side to side moaning. "Mama, if you can hear me tell me how you managed to get into your own bed."

She tossed her head restlessly, moaned several times and then whispered, "Sasha carried me to the bed."

Jane glanced at Sophie. "Did you hear that?" Sophie nodded with amazement. "Mama, who did you say carried you?" Jane asked. But there was no response. Anya slipped back into a coma never to return.

"Sophie, did you hear what Mama said?"

Sophie nodded, her eyes filled with tears. "I heard it. She always said that our father would come for her. I guess he did, and placed her in the bed where the two of them slept all those years. They truly loved each other."

Two days later on the sixth of January 2002, Sasha came for his Anya. As she took her last breath, the snow fell with heavy flakes covering their garden in winter whiteness. The two lovers, Sasha and his Anya, walked hand-in-hand through their garden. They stopped for a moment and glanced back at their little house and their loving family gathered together, grieving. Sasha looked at his Anya, took her in his arms and twirled her around in the snow...and singing, he walked her out of this world.

Epilogue

The journey into the past has been an emotionally wearing venture. I have felt my parents' pain, struggle, and triumph, and I've relived my own. I've traveled on the trains to the camps again...I was hungry and cold again...I was happy and excited to come to America. But in the end, even the darkest of memories were worth reliving.

I began this book because I wanted to convey to the reader the importance of family unity. Love truly does conquer all. Love defeats evil, regardless of circumstances and how long it takes.

Sasha and Anya, like my parents, conquered all the trials and tribulations of the worst that life had to offer. They succeeded in keeping their family together against the most horrific of odds; they nurtured children and made them strong through example.

I thank God every day for giving me such loving and wonderful parents. This book is a tribute to them.

About The Author

Janina Stankiewicz Chung was born in Belarus in 1938, and came to the United States with her family through the Displaced Persons Resettlement Program in 1951.

Far East Of The Sun, her first novel, explores another side of World War II, that of the displaced person. Janina and her family endured thirteen years of life under Communist oppression in Russia, forced relocation to Hitler's Germany and its hellish concentration camps, and the confusion of postwar displaced persons camps.

As a mother of four, with four grandchildren and six great-grandchildren, Janina thanks "God everyday for my mother and father. They had the vision and endurance to bring us to freedom and opportunity that my family and my sibling's families now enjoy."